IF I LOST YOU

SHEILA NORTON

Boldwood

First published in Great Britain in 2025 by Boldwood Books Ltd.

Copyright © Sheila Norton, 2025

Cover Design by Colin Thomas

Cover Images: Colin Thomas

The moral right of Sheila Norton to be identified as the author of this work has been asserted in accordance with the Copyright, Designs and Patents Act 1988.

All rights reserved. No part of this book may be reproduced in any form or by any electronic or mechanical means, including information storage and retrieval systems, without written permission from the author, except for the use of brief quotations in a book review. This book is a work of fiction and, except in the case of historical fact, any resemblance to actual persons, living or dead, is purely coincidental.

Every effort has been made to obtain the necessary permissions with reference to copyright material, both illustrative and quoted. We apologise for any omissions in this respect and will be pleased to make the appropriate acknowledgements in any future edition.

A CIP catalogue record for this book is available from the British Library.

Paperback ISBN 978-1-78513-679-5

Large Print ISBN 978-1-78513-680-1

Hardback ISBN 978-1-78513-678-8

Ebook ISBN 978-1-78513-681-8

Kindle ISBN 978-1-78513-682-5

Audio CD ISBN 978-1-78513-673-3

MP3 CD ISBN 978-1-78513-674-0

Digital audio download ISBN 978-1-78513-677-1

This book is printed on certified sustainable paper. Boldwood Books is dedicated to putting sustainability at the heart of our business. For more information please visit https://www. boldwoodbooks.com/about-us/sustainability/

Boldwood Books Ltd, 23 Bowerdean Street, London, SW6 3TN

www.boldwoodbooks.com

1

The day I start to really worry about my son is the day the doctor looks at me across his desk, his eyes full of concern, his voice low and serious – too serious for my liking – and says, glancing at George, who's sitting next to me and beginning to fidget:

'I think it would be a good idea for me to send a referral.'

'A referral? Who to?'

I need to stay calm. A referral is a good thing, right? It means he'll see someone who knows more. A specialist, someone who deals with kids with asthma every day, who knows the best treatment, who – unlike Dr Jackson here with his worried expression that's putting fear into my heart – will be used to this kind of situation. They'll have seen this all before: the worsening of the asthma to the point where poor George is having repeated serious attacks that don't respond well to the usual medication, where he's coughing himself sick, wheezing whenever he tries to run, and Dr Jackson's prescriptions don't seem to be having much impact. The specialist will know what drugs George needs, everything will settle down and we'll get some respite. *We* being George himself, and perhaps even the rest of our family, although that might be asking too much.

'A paediatrician,' Dr Jackson says. 'There's a consultant who specialises in childhood asthma. I'll get an urgent referral sent to him.'

'Urgent?' I repeat, another stab of fear passing through my heart.

'Yes.' He sighs and looks down at his computer, beginning to tap on the keyboard as he's talking. 'Unfortunately, sending something as *urgent* these days doesn't always guarantee the kind of speed we'd like. Let me know if you don't hear anything within a couple of weeks, and I'll chase it up.'

'A couple of weeks?' I sit back in my chair. I need to ask this question, and I don't want to. I don't want George to ask me, afterwards, what it means. At five years old, he shouldn't have to know. But he's looking down at the toy car he's got on his lap; he might not be listening, or be interested, and I have to know. I whisper it. 'You don't think it's... something... *life-threatening*, do you, doctor?'

He looks back up. 'I hope not, obviously. But as you know, asthma itself can be life-threatening if it's out of control. I'm not sure any more, though, whether this is normal childhood asthma or not. There are some other indications here. Dr Taylor will be able to get to the bottom of it. Try not to worry.'

He gives me a smile, but it doesn't reassure me. I thank him and we head out to the car park, George walking slowly beside me, still fiddling with the toy car.

'OK, back to school, then, Georgie,' I tell him, with forced cheerfulness.

'Can't we go home?'

'No. It's not even lunchtime yet. And I've got to go back to work.'

My heart sinks at the thought. My boss, Trevor, is a hateful, misogynistic little man who makes unpleasant comments whenever any of us – usually me – needs to take time off. I gave him plenty of notice about this appointment, but unfortunately because of George's asthma, there have been a lot of times when I've had to rush him to hospital or stay at home with him with no prior warning. I take the time off without pay, and I always try my best to make up the work in my own time. To be frank, the only reason I work in such a low-paid, unrewarding job in the first place is that I've got two little kids, one of whom repeatedly gets ill. I'm a qualified yoga and fitness instructor but I can't run classes any more because I'd have to keep ducking out at the last minute and cancelling, so I sit all day at a computer inputting data that makes no sense to me, for a man who's a

If I Lost You 3

bully and pays peanuts. I know he'll be sarcastic when I turn up this morning, despite the fact that I'm going back earlier than I said I would.

'How did you get on at the doctor's?' Nadia asks me when I get back to the office and log in to my computer.

'He seems worried,' I admit, sighing. 'He wants to refer George to a paediatrician – urgently.'

'Well, that's good, isn't it?' she asks gently. 'Hopefully the paediatrician will have a better idea of how to treat his asthma.'

'Dr Jackson isn't even sure it's normal asthma now. I don't know what to think. The attacks are definitely getting more frequent; he seems to have a cough nearly all the time and gets exhausted when he tries to run or do anything physical.'

'And the trouble is,' Nadia says sympathetically, '*you're* getting exhausted too, aren't you.'

'Oh, I'm all right. It's just such a worry, having to keep taking time off.'

'Trevor's an arse. Ignore him, he's just bad-tempered.'

'That's all very well, but I know I'm getting behind.' I drop my voice, glancing across the office. 'And it's giving you and those two over there extra work, so we're having to all play catch-up all the time.'

The work is so mundane that we can easily chat while we're working, but we both fall silent for a moment now as we're aware that our two older colleagues, May and Pauline, who aren't as sympathetic as Nadia, always have their ears flapping.

'And it wouldn't be so bad,' I go on after a few minutes, 'if things weren't so awful at home at the moment.'

'Still no better between you and Ben?' she asks quietly.

I shake my head. 'No. I know we're both anxious about George – and Molly too – and we're both tired. But it's more than that. We just don't seem to be able to talk to each other without arguing, these days.'

'Poor you. So many worries,' she says, touching my arm briefly – and this simple touch, these simple words, actually bring tears to my eyes for a moment. I shake my head, finding it hard to respond.

'Better get on,' I say more brusquely than I intend, and turn back to my keyboard.

SHEILA NORTON

* * *

Molly comes out of school looking cheerful enough this afternoon, but as soon as she remembers George didn't go into school this morning, her expression changes.

'Did he have the *whole morning* off school?' she demands. 'Again?'

'No. We just went to the doctor's and he was back before lunch,' I tell her.

'Did he get a treat?'

'No, Molly. There's nothing to be jealous about.'

George smirks. 'But the doctor was nice to me. I showed him my car, and he said—'

'Who cares?' she retorts. 'Can we go home now, Mummy?'

Molly's seven, and normally a placid, easy-going child. Well, she was until fairly recently. She was also, until fairly recently, very fond of her little brother; but since his asthma became so much worse, taking up so much of my, and his father's, time and concern, she's started to resent him. Talking to her, explaining George's problems, used to help; it used to make her sympathetic and caring. I still see that side of her sometimes. I think some of George's attacks actually frighten her, and when that happens, I can see that she really does still love him and care about him. But, inevitably, she feels left out; she complains about him getting time off school and being allowed to stay at home, lying on the sofa. And, of course, she doesn't like the way Ben and I are snapping at each other these days, however hard we try to restrain ourselves in front of the children. I tell her we're both just tired. I give her lots of cuddles and reassurances about how much we love her. But I can understand her resentment, especially as George often plays up to it.

'I had nearly the whole morning off,' he gloats now, and I give him a warning look.

'All right, George, we all know that now. How was your day, Mollipop? How did you get on in the spelling test?'

'I got nine out of ten,' she says, instantly more cheerful. 'I only got *shell* wrong cos I forgot it was two *Ls*, but I got all the others right and only one person got ten out of ten.'

If I Lost You

'Wow, well done,' I say, giving her a high five and a hug. 'Clever girl.' And everyone's happy again – for now.

* * *

Ben's in a tense mood when he comes home, muttering about having a lot of marking to do and asking the kids to be quiet. He's forgotten to ask about George's appointment, but I tell him about it, briefly, while he's in the kitchen with me, making himself a cup of tea.

'A paediatrician?' he repeats, looking up from pouring the milk into his mug. 'That's good news, isn't it? They might be able to prescribe stronger drugs.'

'Dr Jackson seems to be having doubts about whether it's even just asthma,' I say quietly.

'It must be asthma, surely,' he retorts. 'He's never seen George actually having an attack, has he.'

'No, that's true. But he seemed worried, Ben. He's referring George urgently.'

'Well, of course he's worried, because he's out of his depth. George should have been seeing a consultant months ago. That was what I said all along, but the speed at which things work these days in the NHS is pathetic. It's just not good enough, when it's a five-year-old child.'

'All right, keep your voice down,' I snap.

'Well, you stand there telling me Dr Jackson's worried – what about how worried *we* are? Why haven't you pushed for this urgent referral before, Jo? I've been saying for ages—'

'Well, perhaps you should have taken him to the doctor's once or twice, instead of it always being me having to take time off and getting into trouble at work.'

'My job pays *slightly* more than yours does, if you really need me to tell you.'

And here we are again, fighting about the children, fighting about our jobs, fighting about who does the most in the house and even who earns the most money. It's miserable, it's horrible, it's not like us... or it never used to be. We'll have been married for nine years this year, living together for

6   SHEILA NORTON

two before that, and we hardly ever used to argue until the last year or so. Now it's so bad that we've even talked about splitting up, but we don't want to hurt the children.

Ben goes off upstairs, grumpily, and I turn back to preparing dinner with a sigh. There was something else I wanted to talk to him about this evening, something important, but I don't think he's in the right frame of mind now. It had better wait.

I tuck the letter I'd intended to show him – the letter from my birth mother that had brought me so much excitement until the anxiety of today's appointment spoilt the mood – back into my pocket for another day.

2

'All I'm saying is...'

It's a few days later, and Ben's using the tone that irritates and exasperates me the most: his tone of strained tolerance, pretending to be understanding when, in fact, I know perfectly well that he doesn't understand at all and probably, within minutes, he'll lose his patience and start showing how he really feels.

'All I'm saying is that you need to be honest with yourself.'

Of course, this isn't *all he's saying* at all. He's had so much to say since I finally brought up the subject of my birth mother that we've been sitting here at the kitchen table for at least fifteen minutes while he's made his points. A whole list of points, ending with this gem about me being honest with myself.

'I *am* being honest,' I protest. 'It's honestly what I'd like.'

'You know what I mean: be honest about *why* you want this. Why you want to do it. And, more to the point, why *she* wants to do it. Why, all of a sudden, after all these years, you're happy for her to get in touch with you. She's never bothered before, Jo.'

'She wouldn't have been allowed, until I was over eighteen.'

'But you're thirty-six now,' he says, sighing with exasperation. 'And she's never bothered until now.'

I look away, down at the table. I'm feeling rattled. He asked me what I wanted to do about this, didn't he? And now I've told him, he doesn't like it; he's sounding exasperated, almost angry, and I sense it's going to build up into yet another argument.

'I know it's a bit sudden, but it's what I've always wanted – you know that,' I begin, but he cuts me short.

'You don't know who she is, what she's like. And how do you know whether this woman is really even your mother?'

'Her letter's come via the adoption agency. They'll have checked all her details; they wouldn't send it on to me without doing that. Look, I've finally got the chance to meet my real mother, and obviously I want to. Anyone would.' We've been through all this already. I sigh again and shake my head. 'I thought you'd be pleased for me, pleased that I've got the chance to meet someone actually related to me, for the first time in my life. Can you not see why that excites me? Why it's going to make me happy?'

'You've got no idea whether or not it'll make you happy. Just because she's got in touch now, it doesn't change the fact that she gave you up over thirty years ago. She didn't want you then, did she? So why now?' He stops, looks away and adds, half under his breath, 'Anyway – *I'm* related to you. The kids are related to you. I thought *we* were supposed to be your family.'

I want to be sarcastic, to reply that, yes, he's related to me, he's my husband, but these days it often feels like we're almost strangers – strangers who don't understand each other any more. But what's the point? It'd only provoke yet another row.

'I know. I didn't mean it like that, obviously. You're twisting my words.'

He sighs again and for a moment I think he's going to give up the argument – until he suddenly adds, like an afterthought, 'And how about your mum and dad? They're your family too.'

'They're my *adoptive* mum and dad.'

'Oh, come on. You've never called Liz and Harry that. They're your *parents*, Jo; you're their daughter, and they brought you up from the age of two. They love you, and they love the children – their grandkids. They'd be so hurt if they heard you relegating them to *adoptive* parents.'

'I'm not relegating them, of course I'm not. Yes, I love them, I always

If I Lost You 9

have done. I was just making the point: they adopted me. I'm glad they did, I'm eternally grateful, I had a wonderful childhood.'

'And yet...?'

'Now my birth mother's got in touch, I want to find out what she's like, and find out more about her life. Did she go on to have any more children, for instance? I might have brothers and sisters, Ben. I want to find the missing pieces of... of me. My *origins*. Can't you understand that? It's how I've always felt. I'm rootless. I don't know where I came from, and even now, all I know is her name.'

'You could exchange a few more letters to find out all of that.'

'We could, but why waste time? This letter the agency forwarded says all I need to know: that she'd like to meet me. That's all. If it's a disaster, I don't have to meet her again, do I?'

Ben closes his eyes for a moment. 'It's not that I don't understand. I do – or at least, I'm trying to. OK, you're going to meet up with her, whatever I say. But don't get carried away by this fantasy of a mother–daughter relationship until you've got to know her properly. I just hope you don't end up being disillusioned. Disappointed.'

'It's only one meeting – for now – and no, I'm not getting carried away. All right?' I get to my feet, fed up with the whole conversation now. I'm sure, at one time, I might have expected my husband to be pleased for me, pleased the one thing I've always longed for might actually be coming true. But no, not any longer. Our relationship isn't like that now. Perhaps he's right that my parents might be hurt, but I hope not. They did give me a good childhood, but the fact is that I've always dreamed of meeting my birth mother, I've just never found the time to do anything about it. But since the agency got in touch to tell me she was asking to forward me a letter, with a view to possibly meeting me, I've thought about it constantly. The very idea of having someone, anyone, who knew me when I was born, is so tantalising that it's what I think about every night while I'm lying there, trying to sleep. I'm grateful to have something to take my mind off all my worries. And whatever Ben says, I'm going to do it: I'm going to reply to her letter, and I'm going to meet her.

* * *

My parents – it's true, that's all I've ever called them – have always been open with me about my adoption. I don't remember any of my life prior to being their child. All they've ever said about Barbara, my natural mother, is that she was a single mum, who gave me up for adoption so that I'd have a better life than she could give me on her own.

'So why couldn't she give me a better life herself?' I started asking as soon as I was old enough to think this through.

'Sometimes that's easier said than done,' Mum told me. 'She was probably very hard-up and perhaps she had nowhere decent to live. I'm sure she loved you, JoJo, but it was a selfless thing to do: to give you up so that you could have a happier life.'

JoJo. Her pet name for me, that nobody else has ever used. Like I call Molly, my own daughter, *Mollipop*. I never felt the need for any other mother. But needing is one thing – *knowing* is another. I try to explain this to her, the day after the conversation with Ben, when she and Dad come for Sunday dinner.

'Nobody will ever replace you,' I tell her gently while she's helping me with the washing-up. 'I'd just like to see what she's like. My birth mother.'

She nods, calmly wiping a plate without looking at me.

'Of course. We always thought you might decide to try to find her one day. I'm surprised it's taken this long, to be honest.'

'I'm not sure I ever would have, if she hadn't made the first move. All that business with DNA and research seems so complicated, and I've just never had the time to get into it – with the kids and everything...' I leave this hanging in the air for a moment, both of us knowing what I mean. The worries about our children, the problems with my job, the things she and I disagree about. 'Although,' I go on, 'I've often looked at Molly and George, seeing their different traits develop, and wondered which they've inherited from me, which from Ben or his family, and—'

'And which from your family,' she finishes for me. 'I do understand, JoJo.'

'You're not hurt?'

She looks up at me and smiles. 'No. I'm not hurt and I'm sure Dad won't be, either. It's natural for you to be curious. As long as *you* don't get hurt.'

I shake my head. 'I won't. I haven't got any preconceptions. Anyway, she might only want one meeting, out of curiosity, and I might never hear from her again. But at least I'll know I've tried.'

She puts down the plate, reaches out and gives me a hug. The tea towel in her hand is hanging down the back of my neck, tickling me, and we break apart, both laughing.

'You're sure you're OK about it?' I repeat, looking into her eyes. Those warm, loving eyes that have followed me and watched over me all the years of my life – apart from the first two. We may sometimes have our differences these days, but I do know she still loves me.

'I'm sure. Good luck with it, and keep us posted,' she says.

'I will. And thank you – for being so understanding.' I pause, then add quietly, because I don't say it often enough now, 'As well as for everything else.'

3

'What was it like being adopted, Mummy?' Molly asks me, twirling her fingers around a length of her long dark hair as I sit on her bed, reading her a bedtime story. The children both take after Ben – beautiful dark hair and big brown eyes. Molly's at such a lovely age, still so innocent but growing more curious, more enquiring every day. And although we've been having a few issues with her recently, she's still basically a sweet, bright, thoughtful little girl.

'Well, actually, it didn't feel very different at all,' I tell her. 'Your grandma and grandpa felt just the same as if they'd been my birth parents. I had a perfectly nice, ordinary childhood.'

'But you never even met your own real mummy,' she says, shaking her head sorrowfully. 'That must have been *so* sad. I would hate it if I didn't know you.'

'Well, it's hard for you to understand, but if you'd never met me, and had grown up with a different mummy, who loved you, you *wouldn't* feel sad.'

'I would,' she asserts fiercely, and I laugh as she puts her arms around my neck and pulls me close, hugging me desperately, as if she's afraid I'm going to disappear.

'Don't worry, you've got me as your mummy for always,' I reassure her.

'You wouldn't ever give me or George away, like your real mummy gave you away, would you?'

I knew this was where she was leading. I didn't tell the children about my adoption until I felt they were old enough to understand, but whenever the subject comes up, especially with Molly, who's more able than her little brother to think things through, I sense there's a frisson of fear as they automatically turn this around to imagine it happening to themselves.

'Give you away?' I retort. 'After all the money I spent on your Christmas presents? No way.'

'Not even if we were really, *really* naughty?' She looks down as she says this. I've never had to tell Molly off very much until the recent bouts of spite aimed at her brother, and I imagine this plays on her mind.

'Not even if you burnt the house down and crashed my car,' I say, smiling at her.

'Crash your car?' she squawks. 'I can't even drive yet, Mummy.'

'I know. But you might do, one day. And I still wouldn't give you away.' I pretend to think for a minute before adding, tickling her at the same time to show I'm still joking, 'But don't try it, will you?'

'No, I won't,' she says vehemently after she's stopped giggling. 'We wouldn't be able to go to see Grandma and Grandpa if your car got crashed.'

'Well, there you go, then. Now, come on, off to sleep. School tomorrow. Night-night, Mollipop. Love you lots.'

'Love you too, Mummy. Night-night.'

It's been about a week since I got my birth mother's letter, and almost as long since Dr Jackson said he'd refer George to a paediatrician. He did say to give it two weeks, so there's nothing I can do for now, apart from worrying myself sick. But I've responded to Barbara's letter now, suggesting we meet up this coming weekend if she's free and giving her my phone number to make it easier to reply. I feel jittery and nervous whenever I think about it, but I've been trying not to let the children notice. Molly tends to pick up on everything, whereas George isn't quite as emotionally perceptive as his sister; even if he has heard us talking, he still falls asleep every night without voicing any concerns. That's when he's even well enough to fall straight asleep.

To be honest, I've barely got over the excitement of my mother getting in touch with me, let alone the fact that I've agreed to meet her. I suppose I should ask myself whether I'm excited *only* because meeting my birth mother has always been such a dream of mine, or whether almost anything out of the ordinary, anything to take my mind off the pressure and anxiety of my life at the moment, would excite me. Am I just focusing on my birth mother to take my mind off everything else?

But I really do want to meet her, this *Barbara King* who gave birth to me and then gave me away. Not that I blame her, but I *came* from her. My DNA is half hers. I want to find out if I'm like her, if I've inherited things from her. So it's mostly just curiosity, I suppose. It's clear Ben doesn't really want me to go ahead with this. But if I don't try, I know I'll always regret it.

* * *

For another three days, life goes on as usual. I take the kids to school, I go to work, I return to the school, take the kids back home, prepare meals, feed the cat, supervise reading and spelling sessions, put washing in the machine and take it out again, read bedtime stories. On the third day, Trevor is even more grumpy than usual, George's teacher tells me he was too breathless to do PE, despite having his inhaler, and I'm worried and in a tetchy mood when my phone pings with a text message. I'm too busy to read it when we first get home, checking that George's breathing's OK now, listening to Molly telling me about what she did in her lessons and how one of the boys in her class fell over and cut his knee so badly 'there was blood all over the playground'. So it's not until they're both in bed and Ben and I are clearing up the dinner things that I remember to check it.

'It's from her,' I say breathlessly, staring at my phone. 'My birth mother.'

He turns to look at me. 'What does she say?'

'She's suggested we meet in the Teapot café, at three o'clock on Saturday.' I swallow back the lump in my throat. I'm not sure whether to smile or cry. 'She only lives on the other side of town, Ben.'

If I Lost You

'OK,' he says, flatly.

'It's just curiosity, all right?' I say, irritated that he can't even try to look pleased for me. 'I realise she's a stranger and that we might not get on together. I realise all of that. I'm prepared for it. But I want to find out.'

'Yes.' He shrugs. 'OK, I get it. Whatever.'

'If I get bad vibes from her I won't meet her a second time.'

I don't understand why he's so against this. It's almost as if he's jealous, despite the fact that things have got so bad between us now.

I get straight back onto my phone to respond to Barbara's message, and within minutes it's all agreed. I can't believe how quickly this has happened. Or how long it's been since I've looked forward to something so much.

* * *

Sometime after midnight, I wake up with a start, instinct kicking in before I've even understood what woke me. It's the sound of coughing and wheezing coming from George's room. The sound I always dread. He's trying to call out for me but struggling to force his voice through the constriction of his airway. I jump out of bed, shivering in the cold and almost tripping over my slippers.

'All right, sweetie, I'm here,' I call as I rush into his room.

He's sitting up in bed, gasping, clutching his chest. I pick up his reliever inhaler, fit the spacer and put it into his hand.

'Don't panic,' I remind him – as if it were that easy. 'Take a puff, that's it. OK, now another one. Slowly, Georgie, try to breathe it in deeply. OK, another puff now. Any better?'

He shakes his head, his eyes wide with anxiety, his breath coming in short gasps, the wheeze whistling up from his windpipe.

'Lean forward a little bit.' I take hold of his shoulders – hunched from the effort of breathing – and sit him up more comfortably. 'Right, try another puff. Slowly, OK? That sounds better. And again. Good boy.'

It's easing a little. His shoulders relax, his breathing slows down and quietens but he's racked with another spasm of coughing. He takes another puff of the medication without me prompting him, then puts the inhaler down, closing his eyes. He's exhausted.

'Do you want a drink of water?'

He shakes his head. 'I want to go to sleep, Mummy.'

'Want to come into my bed?'

'OK.'

This is as much for my benefit as his. I can't relax, can't go back to sleep after he's had an attack. There have been several times when we've had to rush him to hospital. This time I think he's going to be OK, but still, I'm anxious, however much I pretend not to be. He slides wearily out of bed and pads across the landing in front of me. Ben's awake, of course, and is sitting on the side of our bed, waiting for us. He knows the routine.

'You all right now, Georgie?' he says, ruffling our son's hair as he crawls onto the bed. 'Come on, snuggle down next to Mummy. I'm going to go and keep your bed warm.'

George could actually squeeze in between us easily. These days, Ben and I usually sleep about as far apart as it's possible to get in a standard double bed, and George is small for his age anyway. But there's no point all three of us sleeping badly for the rest of the night. I know I'll probably lie awake, listening to George's every breath, listening to him tossing and turning, his dreams interrupted by the anxiety of the night.

'Do you think you should take him back to the doctor again?' Ben asks me in the morning. 'Get him to chase up the referral? Or,' he gives me a meaningful look, 'do we have to think again about the cat?'

Ebony is nine years old; we adopted him as a kitten, before we had either of the children. They both adore him, and the feeling is mutual; he lay next to them on rugs when they were babies, sat gently on their laps when they were toddlers and patiently put up with being dressed in hats and knickers, pulled around the room in toy trucks, chased by robots and barked at by toy dogs. When George was first diagnosed with asthma we were asked about animals. *He's a short-haired cat*, I said. *He hardly sheds any fur.* As the asthma got worse, we banned Ebony from George's bedroom, discouraged him from getting his face too close to the cat, or from brushing him. It was hard. I'd often catch him nuzzling against Ebony and tell him to stop, but it felt like banning him from hugging one of us, one of the family.

Eventually our doctor arranged allergy testing for him, and we were relieved to be told that no, pet dander didn't seem to be a trigger. So Ebony got a reprieve, but nevertheless Ben still brings the subject up almost every time George has an attack.

'It's not Ebony,' I remind him again. 'George isn't allergic.'

'Well, whatever, the poor kid's exhausted,' he says, crossly. I know it's just his own anxiety, but I'm exhausted too and he's not helping. 'Will you keep him off school today?'

'This morning, at least.' It means calling Trevor, taking another morning off myself. 'Can you drop Molly at school?'

'Yes. I'll go and get her up now.'

He trudges up the stairs and I sit down to sip a cup of tea, sighing to myself. Why do we mothers always feel as if everything's our fault?

* * *

Trevor sounds even more bad-tempered than usual when I call him to apologise for having to take the morning off.

'Again?' he snaps. 'What is it this time?'

'The same as last time, I'm afraid. George's asthma.'

'It's becoming a regular thing, isn't it. Can't you take him to a doctor?'

For God's sake! I want to say that not only does George see the doctor – as Trevor knows quite well – but he also sees an asthma nurse and a physiotherapist, and all these appointments add to the number of occasions when I have to take time off. I want to remind him that I take these odd hours or mornings off without pay. *This is how life rewards parents*, I'd like to tell him. But, of course, I don't say any of this because, like it or not, I need the job. Nadia sympathises and will try to cover for me, but I'm always conscious of the fact that the other two women resent the amount of time I take off. The work does get behind, however hard I try to catch up, and I apologise, every time. All I seem to do is apologise, but Pauline and May just give me black looks and probably wish Trevor would replace me with someone more reliable.

Luckily, George doesn't have any further problems this morning. He's still tired and he's still coughing, as always, but I drop him back at school just before lunchtime again so that he can eat his sandwich with his friends. The drama of his asthma attack has slightly dampened my excitement about my birth mother, but while we're working I tell Nadia about meeting her tomorrow.

'Oh my God, how exciting!' she exclaims. 'Has she had any other children? Have you got any brothers or sisters?'

'I don't know. I haven't asked her anything yet. All we've done is arrange to meet up.'

'Have you told your mum – I mean, your adoptive mum – that you're actually *meeting* her?'

'I told her I was going to, but I'll tell her tonight that it's actually happening now.' I fall silent. However I try to rationalise it, I still feel a bit like a traitor, and I still suspect that Mum's secretly hurt. 'She does understand,' I add, almost to reassure myself. 'She gets why I want to see what my birth mother's like.'

'Of course she does. She'll be fine,' says Nadia, who's got two loving natural parents, a whole host of sisters, cousins, aunts and uncles and no idea how it feels to have virtually no family.

But she's right. Mum *is* fine when I call her to tell her about meeting Barbara.

'You must let me know how it goes,' she says.

'I will, I promise. I'm not getting my hopes up,' I add, although it's a lie.

'Good. Just take it one step at a time. I'll be thinking of you.'

'Thanks, Mum. I love you.' I don't often tell her this, these days; we've had so many disagreements since George was born, or, more specifically, since his asthma symptoms started, that it's not always been easy to say. But it feels like I need to, now, to reassure her – and myself. Despite everything, she's my mum, and nothing's going to change that.

4

Saturday morning, I'm up early to do some shopping and housework while Ben keeps Molly and George occupied.

'I'm going out for a little while this afternoon,' I tell the children as we're having lunch. 'Meeting a friend for a cup of tea.'

Ben and I have already agreed that we won't tell them I'm meeting my birth mother until we know whether or not she's going to become part of our lives.

'What friend?' Molly asks.

'A friend from work.'

'What's her name?'

I smile. 'Barbara,' I say. At least that part isn't a lie.

'But *we*,' Ben says, giving both children a look of fake excitement, 'are going to play Pop Up Pirate, and *I* am going to win.'

'No you're not, Daddy,' George shouts. '*I* am!'

'You never win, George. I bet I win this time,' Molly says, and within minutes there's a full-scale argument going on about who cheats at games, who sulks if they don't win, and Ben's beginning to sound like he wishes he'd never suggested it.

'I'll leave you to it, then,' I say, putting my coat on and grabbing my car keys.

'See you later,' Ben says without looking at me, and I can't help wishing he sounded even half as excited for me as he sounds about playing Pop Up Pirate with the children.

* * *

The café where we're meeting is right in the centre of town; Barbara said in her message that she doesn't drive and would be coming in by bus. We told each other what colour we'd be wearing, and I spot her straight away, sitting in a quiet corner by a window, in a dark blue coat, a black scarf thrown over the back of her chair. My heart feels like it's thudding in my chest as I cross the café to join her. She looks older than I expected – but why didn't I expect that? She's probably in her sixties, after all. Her hair's light brown with grey roots showing, her skin looks pale, as if she's never been outside, and she's getting slowly to her feet, watching me approach through steel-rimmed glasses. Suddenly, I feel horribly like I'm going to cry.

'Joanne?' she says.

I nod. 'Barbara.' We look at each other for a minute. 'What should I call you?' I add, my voice sounding husky. 'I mean...'

'*Mum*,' she says – and she holds out her arms to me. 'I'm your mum, Joanne.'

'Well – hello, um, *Mum*.' I try to smile, but using the word *mum* feels like a betrayal; I'm not sure I can ever do it again. She pulls me into her arms and I notice the thinness of her body through her coat. 'It's good to meet you,' I add, then I shake my head, laughing at the ineptitude of the phrase. I don't know what else to say. I don't think either of us do. We sit down opposite each other and smile across the table.

'So, tell me about yourself,' she says. 'You said in your message that you're married.'

'Yes – to Ben. We've been married for nearly nine years now.'

'Is he good to you? Got a good job, has he?'

I laugh. 'Well, he's a teacher. He teaches biology and chemistry at the high school.'

'Oh, very nice. Have you got any children?'

'Two. A girl, Molly – she's seven – and a boy, George, he's five.'

'That's nice.' She takes a deep breath and adds, 'My grandchildren.'

I feel a pang; just for a moment I find myself wanting to say that they're not her grandchildren, they're my mum and dad's, Liz and Harry's. But I swallow and nod.

'Have you got any others?' I ask her. 'I mean, did you have any other children?'

'No,' she says abruptly. 'You were the only one.'

'What was I like as a baby?' I smile at her. 'I don't suppose you've got any photos of me?'

She looks surprised. 'I might have. I'd have to have a look. I did keep a few things but they'll be in a box somewhere at the back of the wardrobe, if anywhere.'

The waitress comes for our orders, and it takes a moment, afterwards, for either of us to think what to say next. I'm feeling overwhelmed. Barbara's a stranger. I don't know anything about her, except for the fact that she gave me up. Was this a crazy idea after all? I decide to grasp the bull by the horns.

'So... my mum – my, er, adoptive mum – she was told you gave me up because you were on your own?'

'Yes, I was – once I'd walked out on your father. He was violent. Pushed me down the stairs once. Used to hit me when I was pregnant with you. After you were born, he used to threaten to drown you in the bath because you kept crying.'

I flinch. She's telling me all this without a flicker of emotion. I guess she hardened herself to the details over the years.

'Oh, I'm so sorry, I didn't know that. Couldn't social services have helped you to keep me with you after you left him?' I ask, gently.

'I gave you up for your own protection,' she says. 'He might have come after me. I was always looking over my shoulder.'

'How awful for you. And I'm grateful, honestly. I've never blamed you for giving me up. I had a brilliant childhood; my parents – I mean, well, sorry, but they *are* my parents – were wonderful. I'm just curious, that's all.'

'*A brilliant childhood*,' she repeats, looking at me wistfully. 'I couldn't have given you that. I had no money. Nowhere nice to live. It was always a struggle. I lived in one room, with no heating. Mould on the walls, paint peeling off everywhere, cockroaches. It was disgusting.'

'I understand.' I reach out and touch her hand. 'That must have been so tough.'

'Well, I'm glad you had a happy childhood,' she says. 'That was what I wanted for you.'

Our tea and scones arrive. Barbara reaches for a scone, cuts it in half and begins to smother it in jam and cream before biting into it hungrily.

I don't feel like I can eat at all. I want to know more about my childhood – or, rather, my babyhood.

'Was I a big baby? Did I cry a lot? Was I difficult as a toddler?'

She smiles. 'You were seven and a half pounds at birth, born on your due date. You never slept through the night, though. I was always having to get up and sit with you. And yes, you cried a lot. I think you were probably frightened to death of your father, and I couldn't blame you. He made me cry, too.'

'Oh.' This has taken the smile off my face again. 'Oh, it must have been awful for you.'

'Well, I don't dwell on that any more. No point. What were your kids like as babies?'

'Terrible – especially Molly. I didn't really know what I was doing with her and I think she picked up on it. She was really fussy, fed badly and slept badly.'

'At least you had a good husband to help you.'

'Yes.' I try not to sigh as I remember how good Ben and I used to be together, during those early years. What went wrong? It can't just be the strain of George's condition, can it? We've lost each other somewhere along the way. I give myself a little shake and change the subject.

'Where do you live now?' I ask Barbara.

'On the East Ford estate,' she says. 'On the edge of town, up where the gas works used to be.'

'Yes. I know it.'

'Got a council flat. One bedroom. I'd like something bigger, nicer – it gets damp, and the neighbours are a pain in the neck: noisy, playing music

If I Lost You   23

all times of night, shouting and yelling outside. But it's all they'd give me, on my own.'

'What do you do?' I ask.

'Do?'

'For work.' I study her face again. Perhaps she's even older than I thought. Old enough to be retired?

'Oh, I was a nurse. But I retired at fifty-five, when I could take my NHS pension early. It's not enough, mind – I need my state pension, really, but I've got to wait for that. I had to give up work because my arthritis got bad. Doctor keeps giving me pills, not that they do any good. I need knee replacements, but the doctors say I'm not old enough and my joints aren't bad enough yet.' She laughs. 'Easy for them to say; they don't have to walk on them.'

'Sorry to hear that.' I take a bite of my scone. 'It must be horrible, living with that kind of pain.'

'Ah, well, I just get on with it,' she says. 'I don't suppose you need to work, with your husband being a teacher.'

I laugh. 'Actually I do need to. Teachers don't earn a fortune, and our mortgage is astronomical. But it's difficult, with the children. Especially as George quite often has to have time off school. He's got really bad asthma.' I think, again, about the serious expression on Dr Jackson's face when he told me George needed to see a specialist, and I feel a cold shiver run down my spine.

'Poor kid, that's a bugger, isn't it. I did paediatric nursing for a while. We often had kids with asthma on the ward.'

'Did you?' I sit forward, immediately interested. 'You must understand what we're going through with George, then.'

'Yes.' She nods. 'Sometimes those inhalers don't work. They're not always enough.'

'I know. He's on tablets too. But he still seems to be getting worse. I've had to take him to A&E quite a few times.'

'Really?' She frowns. 'Take him back to the doctor's, love. They might be able to change his medication.'

'I'm waiting to hear about an appointment with a specialist. My GP thinks it might be something else – not even asthma.'

'Well, they'll sort him out at the hospital.' She reaches for another scone. 'These are lovely. I was hungry.'

By the time we've drunk our tea, Barbara's eaten three scones. I offered her my second one as I struggled even to eat one. The conversation has flitted from past to present and back again, and my head is in a complete whirl. I can't decide if I feel sorry for her – well, yes, I do, because it sounds as if she's hard-up, hungry and living with pain – but she also seems down-trodden and hopeless, living a sad life in a flat she doesn't like.

'It's been lovely to meet you,' she says finally when the last crumbs have been eaten and I'm looking at my watch. 'Can we stay in touch? Can I come and meet the children?'

'Oh.' I'd been planning to suggest another meeting, of course. There was so much more I wanted to ask her about. But I hadn't expected her to want to come to the house, meet the children. Not yet, anyway. 'Well, I don't know.'

'Sorry, of course, it's a bit soon, isn't it,' she says, pulling her scarf round her neck and looking hurt for a moment before forcing a smile and nodding. 'Let's leave that for a while.'

'No, it's fine,' I say, suddenly making up my mind. This is what I want to do, regardless of whether Ben agrees. For one thing, she used to be a paediatric nurse. She can meet George – she might have some good advice. 'It's only that I haven't told the children about meeting you yet. They're still only little, and they might find it confusing. But...' I take a deep breath. I don't actually think they'll find it confusing at all. They know I was adopted. Kids are more adaptable than we think: they'll probably take it in their stride. 'It's fine. I'll tell them.'

'Lovely.' She smiles. 'So shall we make it the same time next week?'

Next week? I try to imagine Ben's face when I tell him Barbara's coming to the house in a week's time. Yes, she's my mother, yes, I want to try to build a relationship with her, and yes, I'd like her to meet Ben and the children, but... already? She's still virtually a stranger. I know almost nothing about her. But I look at her face – so different from the face of my other mum, who must be a very similar age. Barbara looks ten years older. She's thin, gaunt, sallow-looking; her eyes look sad, even while she's smiling. She must have had a horrible life, and it sounds like she still doesn't get much pleasure from it. But she *is* smiling now, anticipating something different and exciting, for once. To be honest, I just haven't quite got the heart to say no.

'I'll look forward to it,' I say.

'Lovely,' she says again. 'Would you be able to pick me up, though? The bus doesn't go out to *Budleigh Heath*.' She says *Budleigh Heath* in an exaggerated posh accent, as if it's an exclusive area full of huge gated properties, rather than the modest estate of new semi-detached houses it is in reality.

'OK, that's no trouble.' I look at her and realise what she's expecting. 'So would you like me to run you home now? Then I'll know exactly where to pick you up from, next week.'

'Good idea,' she says, giving me a smile. 'Thank you, dear.'

* * *

'So how did it go?'

Ben's been waiting patiently until the kids were in bed to ask me about Barbara, but I just sit here, staring back at him, not knowing where to start. All I said when I came home was that my *friend* and I had a really nice tea and scone, and a good chat. What else could I say? I still don't know how to tell the children that I've met her, that she's coming to our house soon.

'It went well,' I say now. 'We were obviously both a bit emotional. It sounds like she's had a hell of a life, Ben. She got away from my father because he was violent. But she's living in a pretty rough area, in a tiny flat, by the look of it.'

'The look of it?'

'I took her home. Well, it was the least I could do; she doesn't have a car, so she came on the bus. She doesn't work—'

'How come?'

'She's got really bad arthritis, and she used to be a nurse, so she was able to take her nurse's pension early.' I pause, remembering the pain on her face as she walked out to the car, using a stick, wincing with each step. 'She doesn't look well, to be honest. When she left my father, she lived in one room with no heating, and even now, she says her flat's damp and the neighbours are noisy but the council won't give her anything better. She seems *browbeaten*. Like life hasn't given her much.'

'I guess that came from living with a bully. Your father,' he adds unnecessarily.

'I suppose so. No wonder she gave me up for adoption. I'm even more grateful for that, now. I told her I had a wonderful childhood.'

'Hopefully she'll have been pleased about that, then.'

'And guess what? She nursed children with asthma.'

'OK. So you're glad you went? Glad you've met her, at least?'

'Of course.'

'Are you thinking of seeing her again?'

'Yes.' I pause, then go on quickly, 'In fact, I've invited her to come and meet you and the children. Next Saturday.'

He blinks. 'She's coming here?'

'Yes.' I straighten my shoulders, preparing for an argument. I know I let Barbara invite herself, gave in to her. So I'm being defensive now, challenging him unnecessarily. 'I take it that's OK with you?'

He's staring at me in disbelief. 'Is that really what you want – so soon? You'll have to tell the kids. You can't keep on telling them she's a friend.'

'I know. Of course I'll tell them. She's keen to meet them; they're her grandkids.'

He frowns, but doesn't bother to dispute this.

'Well,' he says, 'it's nothing to do with me, obviously. I suppose my opinion is irrelevant.'

'Ben, I don't see how you can even have an opinion until you've met her. She seems really nice; you'll like her, and she's keen to meet you as well as the children.' I pause, and then add, more quietly, 'I'm wondering if it'll be helpful, too – having a nurse in the family. She might be able to help with our worries about George.'

'She's in the family already, is she?' he says sarcastically. Then he shrugs and agrees reluctantly, 'I suppose that's a point, though. If she knows about asthma, perhaps she can help.'

I know he's as worried about George as I am. Otherwise, I'm pretty sure he wouldn't have agreed so quickly.

5

'I've got something to tell you both,' I say to the children over breakfast the next morning.

'Is it about a holiday?' George says, looking up, his eyes brightening.

'No, but it *is* exciting. You've got another grandma.' I take a deep breath. 'And guess what? She's coming to meet you next week. Next Saturday.'

'Another grandma?' Molly says, frowning. 'But we've already got Grandma Liz, *and* Grandma Sally that we hardly ever see cos she lives in Spain.'

'I know. But you know how I've told you Grandma Liz and Grandpa Harry adopted me when I was very little? Well, my *real* mummy, who had to give me away to be adopted, is your other grandma. And she'd like to meet you both.'

'I don't know if I want to meet her.' Molly's eyes are round with anxiety. 'If she gave you away when you were little, Mummy, she probably isn't very nice.'

'And she might give *us* away,' George joins in.

'Don't be stupid, George,' his sister scoffs, even though she herself looks worried at the idea. 'She can't give us away when we're not her children. We're Mummy's and Daddy's children and they're never going to give us away, are you, Mummy?'

I flinch at the anxiety in her tone. I know I've been snapping at her more than I normally would, recently, but surely she doesn't really worry that I'm going to give her away?

'Never, ever, ever,' I say firmly, smiling at them both. 'Look, it's nothing for you to worry about. I just wanted you to know, and understand.'

'But I *don't* understand,' Molly says. 'Why does she want to meet us, if she doesn't like children?'

'Nobody's said she doesn't like children. She couldn't have me living with her when I was little, because she had a very tiny house that was very cold and damp. It would have been really bad for me and it might have made me very ill. So she gave me to your Grandma Liz and Grandpa Harry, who had a nice warm house and loved me just like any other parents would do.'

Ben gets up from the table, taking his plate to the sink, as if he can't sit and listen to this heavily edited version of my early childhood for a moment longer. What does he expect me to tell them? I'm hardly going to say that their grandfather beat their grandmother, pushed her down the stairs and threatened to drown me in the bath, am I?

'So I had a lovely, safe, warm life, like you're having,' I remind them. I've told them most of this before, and they've always enjoyed the Happy Ever After aspect of it. But this time, there's an added dimension: they can probably imagine the *wicked stepmother*-type figure they remember from fairy stories coming back – *boo, hiss* – and they're frightened there'll be an unhappy ending. 'So you see, my birth mother wasn't being nasty,' I go on, 'when she gave me away; she was actually being kind. She's a perfectly nice lady who just wanted me to have a better life. OK?'

'Is she old now?' George asks.

'Probably about the same age as Grandma Liz.'

'Very old, then,' he says, nodding to himself.

'I think I'm going to like her,' Molly says. 'Because it was nice of her to give you to Grandma and Grandpa and let you live in a nice warm house.'

'Exactly, Molly.' I smile at them both.

'What do we have to call her?' George says, looking anxious. 'She can't be another *grandma*, can she?'

'No,' Molly says. 'It'd be confusing.'

If I Lost You   29

'Well, she's coming on Saturday, so let's ask her,' I suggest, and they both agree, looking satisfied.

'Phew,' I say to Ben as we're washing up the breakfast things later, and the kids have gone upstairs – probably to talk it over between themselves. I'm trying my best to talk civilly – pleasantly – to him, even though he's barely spoken to me since I told him about Barbara coming next week. 'I was worried about how they'd take it.'

'You don't give them enough credit. They're bright kids, they'll judge for themselves. If she's nice, they'll react accordingly. If she's not, they'll see through her – probably quicker than you will.'

I ignore the implied criticism, the suggestion that I'm being naïve, because I suppose I probably am. Perhaps I'm being a bit too trusting, a bit too prepared to go along with this without being absolutely sure it's the right thing to do. The truth is, I'm *not* absolutely sure. It's true that I wanted to get on with things quickly – at least, have the first meeting quickly. But this – coming to the house, meeting Ben and the children – if I'm honest, it feels too soon. I don't feel ready. I wasn't going to admit it to Ben, but I feel like I've been pushed into it, and I almost wish I'd said no. I probably would have done, would have asked to leave it until we'd met up on our own a couple more times, if Barbara hadn't looked so hurt. Now I find myself wondering why she's in such a rush. All these years without a word, and now, suddenly, she's kind of full-on. I haven't even had a chance yet to process how I feel about the first meeting. Was Barbara what I expected? But what *did* I expect? I had no idea. After all, I hadn't known the first thing about her. I admit I was shocked to see how thin and gaunt she looked, and to see the poor state and neglected, miserable air of the flats where she lives. Perhaps I'd imagined she'd have somehow prospered and got a good life for herself since she left my father; I'd pictured her being more like my mum, Liz: bright, happy, confident, with a good marriage, a good job, a good home. But, of course, abuse can affect people for their whole lives. If she seems downtrodden, that's surely because she's *been* downtrodden, perhaps not just by my father but perhaps by teachers or other kids at school, by the council, by everyone, getting more downtrodden every year, enduring life instead of having any enjoyment from it.

So, more than anything else, I feel sorry for her. But it's still, somehow, quite hard to believe that she's my mother – and I suppose that's going to take time.

* * *

Mum and Dad come for Sunday dinner, and Mum engineers a couple of minutes with me on our own in the kitchen to ask me how it went with Barbara.

'Yes, it went well, I think,' I say. 'Apparently, she used to be a nurse, looking after kids with asthma, so she knows quite a bit about it.'

Mum looks at me, frowning slightly, and I realise she's probably wondering if that's all I can think of to say.

'Anyway, she seems nice,' I rush on. 'I think she's had a tough life, though. Apparently, when I was a baby, she was living in one room, with no heating, and mould on the walls.'

Mum frowns. 'Sounds grim. No wonder she felt she had to give you up. Was it emotional, meeting her?'

'Yes. I felt a bit teary for a moment – and she hugged me and then I don't think either of us knew what to say, where to start.'

'Ah, it must have felt strange, but it'll get easier, I'm sure. I mean, sorry, I presume you're going to meet her again?' She pauses and looks at me, her head on one side, because I'm hesitating. 'Or are you going to leave it at that?'

'No. We're meeting up again. In fact, she's coming here. On Saturday.'

'Oh.'

I'm dishing up roast potatoes, but I can feel Mum's eyes on me. I don't look up.

'She said she'd really like to meet the children,' I say in a rush. 'So I thought, OK, why not.'

'Have you told them? How have they taken it?'

'Very well, really. They're sensible kids, and they understand the situation.' Finally I look up at her, putting the serving spoon down with a clatter. 'They know you and Dad are always going to be their *proper* grandparents, Mum. That's never going to change – biology's got nothing to do with it.'

She doesn't say anything, just reaches out a hand and squeezes mine.

If I Lost You 31

* * *

However true it might be that Molly and George are *sensible kids*, they are still kids, subject to all the normal fears and flights of fantasy of childhood. As the week goes by, they veer from excitement about meeting their new grandma to worrying about whether she might not be nice, might not like children (the act of *giving Mummy away* still playing heavily on their minds) and might, in fact, be a big bad witch. To be fair, this is mostly George enjoying scaring himself a bit and trying to scare his sister in the process – but Molly gets tired of the game eventually.

'You're just being silly, George,' she tells him scathingly a couple of days before Barbara's visit is due. 'There's no such thing as witches, and anyway, Mummy says she's nice, so stop being horrible about her.'

'All right, Bossy Boots,' George says with a shrug. 'But if she does turn out to be a witch—'

'That's enough, both of you,' Ben tells them.

'Your new grandma is definitely not a witch,' I add, 'and we don't make judgements about people, OK? Especially when we haven't even met them yet.'

It feels like a long week, and I'm quite relieved when Saturday's finally here. I've made a chocolate cake, with Molly's help, and after it's cooled I leave Ben to supervise her and George icing it while I go to pick Barbara up. I feel far more nervous than I did when we met in the café. I tell myself it's ridiculous: what am I worried about? The house being untidy? The kids playing up or, at the very least, George asking Barbara if she's a witch? I give myself a shake. This is my family, my home, and Barbara has invited herself into it. I'll make her welcome, of course – but I don't have to worry about whether she likes it or not. It's up to her, now.

* * *

When I arrive at Barbara's place, I can see straight away that she's made an effort. She's done her hair, put on a nice blue shirt and cardigan, and a bit of lipstick, and this makes me warm to her, wondering if she feels as anxious about meeting my family as I feel about it.

'The children are excited to meet you,' I tell her.

'How old did you say they are, again?' she says.

'Molly's seven, George is five.'

'That's what I thought. I've bought them a bar of chocolate each.'

'Oh, you didn't have to do that.'

'I wanted to.'

We fall into silence. I'm still finding it hard to make conversation with her; I don't know why – there's a lot I want to know, questions I'd like to ask about my first two years, for instance, but I feel awkward about it.

'Nice houses down here,' she says as we turn into my street.

'Yes, it's OK.' Again, I feel uncomfortable, almost guilty, for living in a three-bedroomed house while she's in a tiny damp flat. 'Well, this is us.' I pull onto our driveway, behind Ben's car.

'Two cars!' she exclaims.

'Well, we have to, really. We both need to drive to work, and I have to take the kids to school and back.'

Even as I'm saying this, I'm annoyed with myself. Why am I apologising for our lifestyle? We work hard for it, and can still barely afford it. But to be fair, Barbara doesn't sound resentful, or even envious. If anything, I suddenly realise, she sounds pleased. Almost as if she's proud of me. I turn off the ignition and look at her. She's smiling.

'It looks a lovely house,' she says. 'Good for you.'

I smile back at her. 'Thank you. Come on in, then – I'll introduce you to my family.' I hesitate, then add softly, touching her hand, 'The *rest* of my family.'

6

The children have gone shy, hiding behind the lounge door as Barbara and I walk into the house, but Ben comes out of the kitchen to meet us, holding out his hands to clasp Barbara's.

'Hi, I'm Ben. Really pleased to meet you, Barbara,' he says with a warm smile, and I feel a burst of gratitude to him, for making an effort now, despite all the arguments.

I take her through to the lounge, where the kids are now sitting together on the sofa, looking up at Barbara apprehensively.

'This is Molly, and this is George,' I tell her. 'Say hello to your new grandma, children.'

'Hello,' Molly says shyly.

But George is frowning. 'We can't call you Grandma,' he says. 'Because we've already got two grandmas. So Mummy said we have to ask you what to call you.'

Barbara goes to sit down next to George, smiling at them both.

'Well, that's a good point, George. It really would be confusing to have *three* grandmas, wouldn't it. How about calling me *Granny*?'

George and Molly look at each other, considering this.

'Yes,' Molly says. 'I think that would be OK. If you don't mind,' she adds politely.

'I'd be very happy to be your granny,' Barbara says. 'Now then, we've got an awful lot to catch up on, haven't we, as this is the first time we've met? I've got you a bar of chocolate each. Keep it for later, eh? And perhaps you can tell me what you like doing, where you go to school, and what your favourite toys are? Molly, you go first.'

Barbara seems to be surprisingly at ease talking to the kids, and they're responding, immediately competing to tell her everything about themselves, as fast as possible.

'I'll go and get the kettle on,' I say, but when I get to the kitchen, Ben's already made the tea and is putting the freshly iced cake onto a plate in slices.

'They seem to be bonding in there,' he says. He sounds, again, like he's determined to make an effort.

'Yes, I think it's going well,' I agree.

We carry the tea and cake into the lounge, and I ask Molly to hand a slice to her *granny*.

'This looks lovely, thank you,' Barbara enthuses.

'I helped make it,' Molly says.

'And I helped ice it. It wasn't *just* you, Molly,' George says, pulling a face at her.

'All right, so what, don't be such a baby,' his sister retorts.

'That's enough, both of you,' Ben warns them before it can escalate into a full-blown fight; George is already having another coughing fit and the more they bicker and the more upset he gets, the worse it always becomes. He turns to Barbara. 'So, Jo tells me you live alone, and you didn't have any other children. Do you manage OK on your own? I mean, as you don't drive, it must be quite difficult for you.'

'I can get the bus into town when I need to,' she says with a shrug. 'I manage all right. It can be difficult sometimes if I have appointments – you know, dentist, doctor, hospital appointments. Sometimes I have to ask a neighbour for a lift, but my neighbours aren't very nice.'

'Hospital appointments can be difficult even if you drive,' I comment. 'The parking is dreadful. We have to take George there sometimes, unfortunately.'

If I Lost You 35

'I get asthma,' George says with a shrug, going into another bout of coughing.

'Poor you. It's not very nice, is it.'

I think again about the conversation with Dr Jackson. Every time I do, my heart starts to beat too fast and I have to take a deep breath to calm myself down. What is it, if it's not asthma? And why did Dr Jackson look so worried? It's been longer than two weeks already since he said he was sending the urgent referral. I need to chase it up if the appointment doesn't arrive on Monday.

'So you've been living on your own ever since you split up with Jo's father?' Ben asks Barbara after a few minutes.

'Yes. Once bitten, twice shy,' she says with a grimace. 'Put me off men for life.'

'I can imagine,' I sympathise.

Molly's watching her thoughtfully as she finishes off the last few crumbs of her cake.

'Why did you give my mummy away?' she says. She sounds genuinely interested, rather than accusatory, but even so, I give her a warning look, shaking my head at her.

But Barbara's looking back at her thoughtfully. 'It wasn't an easy thing to do, Molly. But I had no money, you see, and nowhere to live – just a cold, smelly room with water running down the walls.'

'Yuck,' George says. 'That sounds horrible.'

'It was. And your mummy was very little, much younger than you are now, so she would have got very ill if she'd had to keep living there.'

'Do you *still* live in the horrid place with the water running down the walls?' Molly asks.

'No. Luckily not. But I do still live in a very small flat. Not a lovely house like this.'

'But why didn't you ask to have Mummy back again, when you moved to your new flat?' Molly says.

'Because she had a better life by then. She belonged to your grandma and grandpa. When children get adopted, those people are their real parents. They can't just be taken back again. That would be horrible for them, being given back and forth like a parcel.'

'I'm going to adopt a baby when I'm grown up,' Molly decides. 'I like that idea better than what happens if you have one the other way.'

Ben and I exchange alarmed looks. I wasn't aware that Molly had been told the full facts about conception yet; perhaps some of the kids at school had been talking. I was going to have to have a chat with her this evening.

'Like, finding out there's a baby growing in your tummy, just because you've got married – that must be really scary,' she goes on, and I smile at Ben, breathing easier as he smiles back. The talk with Molly could wait for a while yet.

Fortunately, before any of us are forced to discuss any further the scenario of finding ourselves pregnant, Barbara is looking towards the door and saying, 'Well, hello. Who's this?' as the cat slinks into the room and heads straight for George's lap.

'He's Ebony,' Molly says. 'Mummy and Daddy called him that because it means black. George, you know Daddy says you mustn't let him get near your face. Let him come to me.'

'No, Molly. You always have him. I want him.'

'George,' Ben warns him gently. 'You don't want your asthma to get worse, do you?'

'Is that what the doctor says?' Barbara asks. 'No, he needs to get used to a bit of animal fur; it won't do him any harm. Let him cuddle the cat, build up his resistance. I lived in a tenement in the East End when I was a kid; we had rats running in and out of the building, and we needed cats to keep them down. It never did me any harm.' She turns to George. 'Do you get out in the fresh air, George? That's what you need: running around outside; that's good for your lungs.'

'I can't,' George says sadly. 'I get a really, really bad cough if I run around, don't I, Mummy?'

'Yes, sometimes.'

I don't want to talk about my worries about George, in front of him. He's holding Ebony as close to his face as he can, grinning cheekily at his father, while Molly tuts and mutters, 'Tell him, Mum. Make him give Ebony to me.'

'I'm sorry to hear about your bad cough,' Barbara says to George. 'Let's

If I Lost You

hope the doctor can find a better medicine for you and make you all better.'

George beams at her. 'You're not like a witch at all,' he says. 'I think you're a nice granny.'

* * *

'Well,' I say to Ben when, an hour or so later, I've delivered Barbara back to her flat and we've sat down to dinner. 'I think that was a success? She was a lot chattier today than when we met last week.'

'Yes,' he says. 'She seemed to get on well with the children.'

'What did you think of her?'

'She seems nice enough, but let's be honest, Jo, we hardly know her.'

'I think she's *very* nice,' George says enthusiastically.

'So do I,' Molly agrees. 'She gave us chocolate.'

'She probably wanted to be extra nice to you,' I say, 'because it was her first time meeting you.'

'So maybe when she meets us again she won't be so nice,' Molly says.

'Maybe she'll turn back into a witch,' George suggests, looking quite excited about it.

'OK, no more about witches, thank you,' Ben says. 'Eat up your dinner, please. And we're going to Grandma and Grandpa's for Sunday dinner tomorrow.'

Molly grins as she sits down. 'Our *old* grandma and grandpa, you mean.'

'Oh, they're not old, Molly,' I protest.

'I mean, like, not the *new* granny.'

Ben glances at me, eyebrows raised, but I don't say anything. My feelings are all over the place; one minute I'm still feeling excited about finally having met my real mother, but the next minute, worried about Mum and Dad and how hurt they'd be to hear Molly referring to them as the *old* grandparents. How hurt they'd be if they knew I've already – without even mentioning it to Ben yet – agreed that Barbara can come to the kids' end-of-term concert.

'Why do you call Granny *Barbara*, and not *Mum*?' Molly's asking, and I just shake my head because, quite honestly, I can't answer her. But I suppose it's because I feel, out of loyalty, that I've got to hold on to that special name for Liz. After all, the kids can have more than one grandma, but I can't have more than one mum, can I?

7

It's the school concert this Wednesday; I've booked the afternoon off work for it. I don't tell the children their granny is coming, until we're on our way to school this morning.

'Oh!' Molly says, looking pleased, and then, suddenly, her smile drops.

'But won't Grandma and Grandpa be upset? Or are they coming too?'

'No, they only come to weekend things, don't they, because they live a bit further away and they're both working.' Both are due to retire soon, in fact, and looking forward to it desperately.

'So it'll just be you and Granny?'

'Yes. Is that OK?'

Molly's going to be reciting a poem, with just one other child, as well as singing a song with her class. George's class only have a short song to sing, but he's not particularly looking forward to it.

'Will Granny think I'm stupid?' he says.

'Why would she think that?'

'Because we've all got to wear these paper hats we made that make us look like chickens, and we have to do like chickens with our arms. That's what the song's about.'

'Chickens, because it's Easter, that's fun,' I say, laughing. 'Nobody's going to think you're stupid, George.'

'I do,' Molly says, and then, 'Ouch! Stop it,' as George has retaliated, probably with a shove or a pinch – I'm too busy finding a parking space to look round at them.

'Right, that's enough.' I get out to open the rear door for them and walk them across the playground, George coughing again as they go. 'Have a good morning and I'll see you later.'

* * *

'You're off again this afternoon, then, are you?' Trevor says, irritably, almost as soon as I've got to my desk.

'A half day, out of my annual leave. I gave you plenty of notice.'

'Yes. It's happening a bit too often, though, isn't it. Well, get on with it, then. Do a full morning's work at least, while you're here.'

Nadia pulls a face at his back as he walks away.

'Miserable old git,' she says. 'Anyone would think we do anything other than *get on with it*. Like we sit around all day reading the paper, or playing games on the computer, like I've seen him doing.'

'One rule for him, another for us, unfortunately,' I say, quickly logging on and making a start on my work.

'It's the school concert this afternoon, isn't it?' she says. 'Is Ben going too?'

'No, he can't take time off from his school. But I've asked Barbara to come.'

'*Barbara*? Your birth mum?'

'Yes. I haven't even told Ben, yet. He already thinks I'm rushing things with her, but she got on so well with the children, so I don't see what harm it can do. She's really excited to come and see them do their singing and stuff.' I pause. 'I think she's got a pretty miserable life. She seems lonely. It'll be nice for her.'

'Ah, I'm so glad you're getting on well with her.'

'I know. I'm still having to pinch myself. It's all happened so suddenly.'

* * *

If I Lost You 41

I'm still thinking about this, hours later, when I drive out to East Ford to pick Barbara up. It's a nice day, warmer, and it's finally beginning to feel properly like spring, but she's wearing the same blue coat, and the same thick beige trousers she's worn on both the previous occasions we've been together. I'm guessing she can't afford many clothes – I don't suppose her pension stretches to it. I feel sad, realising how little I know or understand about her life. I complain about my job all the time, but at least I'm employed, at least I'm earning something, however little, and however much of a struggle it still is to pay for everything the children need, to say nothing of the mortgage and all the bills. I can't often afford new clothes myself, but I manage; Ben and I manage OK, really.

'I've been looking forward to this,' Barbara says as she gets in the car. She's beaming with obvious excitement – it transforms her face.

'Well, I hope it doesn't disappoint. George was nervous this morning. He's got to wear a chicken head and flap his arms, and he's worried everyone will think he looks stupid.'

She laughs. 'Poor George.'

I smile back. She seems on good form today; it feels like we've come a long way already from that stilted first conversation in the café. Like we're warming up to each other now.

'Do you think I take after you?' I ask, suddenly overcome with curiosity. Ben's already said he didn't see much resemblance between us.

She turns and looks at me. 'Well, in looks, you're much more like your father,' she says. 'He was a handsome devil – tall, with blond hair and blue eyes, like you. But, thank God, I can't see anything of his character in you. So, I don't know, perhaps you take after me in that respect.'

'Well, we don't know each other too well yet, but from what you've said, I'm sure I'd rather take after you than him,' I say, as tactfully as I can.

Fortunately I find a parking spot near the school fairly quickly and we manage to get good seats in the hall, only a couple of rows from the front. I sneak a look at Barbara from time to time as the youngest children – the reception class – perform their little song. She looks absolutely entranced, and claps like mad as the kids are led off stage, some of them waving to their parents.

'It's George's class next,' I whisper to her – and here they are, coming onto the stage, a crowd of chickens, jostling each other to form their three rows. George, because he's not very tall, to his noticeable chagrin has to be in the front row.

The teacher playing the piano counts them in, and their little voices sing the words of the silly song about being a chicken that poor George has found so mortifying to have to learn. I can see his little face, red with either nerves or embarrassment, not meeting our eyes as he performs his chicken dance. He looks as if the effort is tiring him, or making him wheeze, and I wonder if the teacher has noticed. But fortunately the song ends just then, and he finally looks our way and gives us a thumbs-up and a big smile, probably of relief.

'Oh, I *did* enjoy that,' Barbara says, and to my surprise, I see her wiping a tear from her eye. Perhaps she's crying with laughter.

There's one more class, and then it's the turn of year three, Molly's year. In contrast to her brother, Molly comes on stage confidently, looking around the audience and smiling happily at us. The children sing their song, before Molly and her friend Sophie step out to the front of the stage to recite their poem, 'Spring is Coming'. There are three short verses: Molly speaks the first, Sophie the second, then they both join in to recite the third. I'm really impressed by how confident Molly sounds.

'She was brilliant,' Barbara whispers as the girls go back to their places amid thunderous applause, and the class begins to march off the stage. 'What a clever girl, learning all those words off by heart.'

'She's got so much confidence,' I agree. 'I think she gets that from Ben.'

'Well, it's a wonderful gift. She'll go far.'

We fall silent again as the next class of kids troop onto the stage, and for the next half hour or so we're entertained by the older children of the school. Afterwards, we wait outside the school gate for Molly and George, who both look flushed with success. They start to ask whether Barbara enjoyed their performances, but she's already hugging them both and telling them they were wonderful.

'Are you coming back to our house for dinner, Granny?' Molly asks her.

'Oh, no,' she begins, and I stop her, suggesting that she could at least have a cup of tea with us. But I haven't thought it through properly, because of course, by the time we've all had tea and biscuits, and another chat, and the children have persuaded Barbara to go upstairs to look at their bedrooms, it's already time for Ben to come home. I'm just trying to decide whether I've got time to get her and the kids into the car and run her home before he arrives when I hear his key in the door.

'Hi,' he calls out. 'How did the concert go? How were the funky chickens?'

I go out into the hallway to meet him just as the children run down the stairs, followed more slowly by Barbara, who's telling them how lucky they are to have a bedroom each.

'Oh, hello,' Ben says. He's at least trying to be polite, but I can hear the strain in his voice. 'How nice to see you again.'

He looks from her to me, raising his eyebrows slightly.

'Barbara came to the concert with me,' I say, dropping my eyes.

'Lovely,' he says evenly. 'And are you staying for dinner, Barbara?'

'Well, I really should get back,' she begins, but she's interrupted by both children, begging her to stay, asking her to play a game with them. 'Are you sure?' she finishes.

'Of course,' I say. I head into the kitchen, avoiding Ben's eyes and going to the fridge to see what I can rustle up to feed an extra one.

He's behind me within seconds, pulling the door closed after him.

'I thought we agreed to take it slowly?'

We didn't actually agree, he just told me what he thought I should do, as usual. But now isn't the time to argue about it.

'Sorry. I just had this, um, last-minute idea that she'd enjoy the kids' concert. And she came back for a cuppa. I wasn't going to invite her for dinner,' I add.

'It felt kind of difficult not to, as she's here now.'

'OK.' I shrug. 'Well, I've got to make the shepherd's pie go a bit further now, unless one of us has fish fingers instead.'

'I suspect George will be happy with that.' He watches me as I turn the oven on to cook the shepherd's pie I prepared last night. 'Did she enjoy the concert?'

'We both loved it. Molly was brilliant, and George's class were so funny. I'll let them tell you all about it.' I pause, then go on quietly, 'I'm glad I took

Barbara with me, Ben. I don't think she gets out much, and it was lovely to see her looking so happy.'

'Fair enough. But we *did* say we'd take it slowly.'

I sigh. 'OK, well, it was just an impulse, all right?'

Over dinner, after the children have regaled their dad with every detail of the school concert, I tell Barbara a bit more about my job, explaining how difficult Trevor makes it for me to take time off when one of the kids is ill.

'It's particularly difficult when George has an asthma attack, because obviously I never know when that might happen, or whether we might need to dash to A&E.'

'I can imagine,' she says. She goes quiet for a moment, then adds, 'But, well, if George wouldn't mind, I'd always be happy to come and sit with him. Not if he needed to go to hospital, obviously, but if he just needs company while he's getting over an attack?'

'We couldn't ask you to do that,' Ben says immediately.

'I could! I could ask!' George says. 'I would like it if Granny came to look after me.'

'Don't interrupt, George.' Ben gives him a warning look, and George scowls, putting down his fork.

'Nobody cares what I want, and it's me what's got the asthma.'

'Let's talk about this later,' I say.

George gets on with his dinner, sulkily, while Molly pulls a face at him across the table, obviously feeling left out of the conversation.

'I'd like it too if—' she begins.

I silence her with a warning look.

'Well, that was lovely, thank you,' Barbara says, putting her knife and fork down. I'm not sure whether she's changing the subject because she's aware of the atmosphere, or whether she honestly hasn't noticed.

I take Barbara home after we've all finished, and by the time I get home again, Ben's washed up and the children are in their pyjamas.

'That suggestion about looking after George if he has an attack,' Ben says after they've gone upstairs. 'I think it's far too soon; we hardly know her yet.'

'I know. But it was nice of her to offer.'

If I Lost You

'You don't usually even ask your parents to help out with him when he's ill,' he points out.

'I can't, Ben. They're both still working; it wouldn't be fair.'

'I bet Liz would come like a shot if you asked her. She's only part-time, and she says she's winding down to retirement now.'

'I know, but I don't think it'd be right to ask her,' I insist. 'Apart from anything else, you know Mum and Dad live nearly an hour's drive away. If it's an emergency, we have to take George to hospital straight away. It's OK, I've managed so far. I just have to put up with Trevor moaning at me.'

'Well, it's the school holiday now. I can take over; you won't have to worry for two weeks, at least.'

I somehow manage to restrain myself from saying that he knows nothing whatsoever of how it feels to worry about the domestic arrangements, childcare, doctor's appointments. He has a wife to organise all of it for him.

8

It's true that the school holidays are easier. Ben looks after the children, so at least over the Easter break, I can put in two full weeks of attendance at work. I don't, of course, expect this to bring a resounding cheer of appreciation from Trevor, but I could do without his constant sarcastic comments whenever he passes my desk.

'You're still here then?' he says on the first Monday of the holiday. 'It must be at least a week since you've taken any time off.'

'Don't rise to it,' Nadia whispers, but I wasn't going to anyway. He's not worth it.

When I get home the same evening, Ben tells me George has had another attack.

'He's OK now,' he reassures me. 'There was no point calling and worrying you. He's resting on the sofa. I've shut the cat out of the room.'

'It's not...' I start to protest, but what's the point? Ben seems determined to go on blaming poor Ebony for George's symptoms, despite evidence to the contrary.

Instead I go into the lounge to comfort George, who's propped up under a blanket, watching a kids' film on TV, with Molly sitting next to him.

'Daddy said George could watch TV for the rest of the day, so I said I'd watch it too,' she says. 'Otherwise it's not fair.'

If I Lost You   47

She seems to be so focused at the moment on what is, or isn't, fair. I know it's understandable; I know George often seems to get extra attention, but when I point out that it isn't very fair that George has these horrible attacks, she sulks. *It isn't my fault he's got asthma,* she said recently, stomping upstairs to her room after being told off for calling him a baby. Because Ben and I are both only children, I always thought it would be lovely to have a brother or sister, but these days the reality doesn't always seem quite as lovely as I imagined.

I crouch down next to George to give him a quick hug.

'How are you feeling now, sweetie? Not wheezing any more?'

'No. I'm just tired, Mummy.'

But he's started coughing with just those few words. I feel another frisson of alarm. It doesn't feel right. I've already called Dr Jackson's surgery asking for the paediatric appointment to be chased up, but I've still heard nothing from the hospital. I'm going to have to chase it again.

I stroke the hair off his forehead. 'Just stay here and rest till dinner time. Do you want a drink of water or anything?'

'No. I want Ebony.'

'Daddy won't let him in,' says Molly. 'He says Ebony's moulding a lot.'

'*Moulting,*' I correct her with a smile. 'It means shedding fur.'

'Daddy says because he's moulting, George might breathe his fur in. He says because it's spring, he moults more.'

'Well, that's true. I'll brush some more of his loose fur off, outside in the garden where it'll blow away. Then maybe when you're feeling completely better again, George, you can give him a cuddle.'

'Daddy says if I keep having more and more asthma,' George says, tears suddenly coming to his eyes, 'Ebony might have to go and live somewhere else.'

'Oh, I'm sure that won't happen,' I say. 'Come on, don't cry, Daddy was just worried about you, and he didn't want Ebony to make you any worse. You can cuddle him later.'

I go back out to Ben, who's preparing dinner in the kitchen, and close the door behind us.

'I thought you were supposed to be a scientist,' I challenge him, my annoyance making it difficult to keep my voice down.

He swings round, potato peeler in his hand, looking at me in surprise. 'What's that supposed to mean?'

'Well, I'm *not* a scientist, I'm just a mum, but I've read just about everything there is to read about childhood asthma – have you?'

He sighs. 'I take it this is about the cat.'

'I don't know what to remind you first. But OK, one: George has been tested and found *not* to have an allergy to cats; two: the allergy isn't usually to fur anyway, it can be to cats' saliva, or to *dander*, which I'd have thought, as a scientist, you'd know is—'

'Dead skin cells,' he says, raising his eyebrows at me. 'And what's all this sarcasm about me being a scientist? I'm also a father, who hates seeing his son gasping for breath.'

'You think I *don't*? It's usually me who has to look after him, Ben. Usually me who has to rush him to A&E and sit with him while he's put on a nebuliser and monitors.'

'That's not fair,' he says quietly. 'You know I'm aware of the fact that it mostly falls on you to deal with these things. I'm sorry, Jo, but that's just the way it is. I do as much as I can.'

I capitulate. 'I know.'

This is pointless, anyway. Ben seems determined to ignore medical science. Why do men always seem to need someone to blame? In this case it's poor Ebony, even though he's been proved innocent.

'Anyway,' Ben goes on, 'from what you've said about your appointment with Dr Jackson, we don't even know for sure if it is asthma now, do we?'

'It has to be.' I don't meet his eyes. I don't want him to know how scared I already am – don't want him to make me feel even worse.

'But the inhalers and the tablets aren't always working. And it's getting worse; he's coughing and wheezing even when he's not having an attack.'

I feel that shiver of fear again. 'They need to try him on some different drugs. When we see the consultant...'

'Whenever that might be. It's been about four weeks now since you saw Dr Jackson. We need to call the surgery again, ask Dr Jackson to chase it up.'

As usual, of course, Ben says *we* when he clearly means *I* need to do something.

If I Lost You 49

'Yes, I know. I'll call him again tomorrow,' I agree.

* * *

The next day, just as I'm driving into the car park at work, Barbara calls me.

'Jo?' she says. She sounds quite distressed. 'Have I caught you in time, before you start work?'

'I've just arrived, Barbara, but if it's something quick...'

'It's my arthritis. It's playing up something rotten, I can hardly move.'

'Oh, no, poor you.'

'I've called the surgery. The doctor's going to see me urgently. To get some more painkillers, I suppose, not that they'll probably do any good. Quarter to ten, the appointment is, but I can't get there by bus; there's not enough time now, even if I could walk to the bus stop.' There's a pause. 'I wondered if you'd be able to take me.'

I close my eyes. She sounds desperate. I consider suggesting she gets a taxi, but it's pretty obvious she can't afford to.

'I know it's a cheek to ask you,' she goes on in a rush. 'I just don't know what else to do.' She sounds alarmingly like she's on the point of tears. 'None of my neighbours seem to be at home. I don't think I can stand the pain much longer, and paracetamol doesn't touch it.'

'OK,' I say. 'Look, I'm going to have to talk to my boss, and, well, I'll probably have to take the morning off.' More time out of my holiday allowance. There's no way he'll let me just take a couple of hours off out of the goodness of his heart, and to be fair I can't expect him to. For just a moment, I consider calling Ben and asking him if he can take her, but I can already imagine what he'd say about it. And he'd have to drag the kids along with him. No, I'll keep this between Barbara and me. 'I'll pick you up as soon as I can get there.'

'Oh, you're an angel,' she says. 'I'm so grateful.'

Needless to say, Trevor isn't happy.

'Do you actually *want* to work here, Jo, or not?'

'Of course I do. I'm really sorry. It's an emergency.'

'I've never known a person have so many emergencies. What is it this time? Child with a scratch on their nose? Broken fingernail?'

'My, um, mother has an urgent doctor's appointment. She's crying in pain and she can't walk.'

'Strange, that, isn't it? Nobody else in the whole of Greater London can get a doctor's appointment within three months, never mind an urgent one. I'll deduct your pay.'

'I'd rather take a half day of my annual leave.'

'No.' He stares me down. 'You won't. We're busy; we can't afford to have people just going off on annual leave without any prior notice. You'll have the pay deducted. And for your information, Jo, if this happens any more, I'll have to give you a written warning.'

'Warning of what?' I ask shakily, as if I didn't know.

'Dismissal, what did you expect? I need workers who can actually work, not people who drift in and out when they feel like it.'

I'm feeling taut with anxiety as I drive to Barbara's flat to pick her up. I wish I'd suggested she got a taxi and let me pay for it. I really mustn't let her think it's OK to ask me to drive her around whenever she needs it. This is really not good; I shouldn't be doing it. Ben would say I've only known her five minutes, why do I think I should lose half a day's pay to take her to the doctor's when I've got enough appointments to manage already, for my son? And he'd be right; this is too much. It's not as if we're actually close; I've only met her three times.

But it's that emotional pull. She's my mother. I never thought I'd meet her at all, but now I have, can I turn my back on her when she needs help? When I arrive at her flat, she hobbles to the door, wincing with pain. Her face is pale and drawn, and she has to lean on me to walk to the lift. When I help her into the car, she's flinching and gasping with every movement, and I feel so concerned about her that I start to put my own anxieties about my job to one side. I'd do this for Mum or Dad if they needed me. I have to step up and do the same for my birth mother.

'How long have you been suffering like this?' I ask her as we pull away.

'Well, it's always there, the pain, but the trouble is, with rheumatoid arthritis, you get flare-ups, you see. I haven't had a flare-up as bad as this for a long time. I woke up in such terrible pain I didn't know what to do with myself.'

'It's lucky the doctor could see you so quickly.'

'To tell you the truth, I told the receptionist I was suicidal and I'd kill myself if the doctor couldn't help me.'

'No!' I take a quick look at her face. 'You wouldn't really, would you?'

'I don't suppose I would, to be honest. But it worked, didn't it? I got an urgent appointment.'

I don't know whether I'm more shocked that she would say such a thing to get an appointment, or that she's in enough pain to even think about it.

We drive the rest of the way to her doctor's surgery in silence, and I help her out of the car and into the reception area, where she sits down with obvious effort, grunting and gasping.

'Would you like me to come in with you?' I ask her as we wait for her name to be called.

She looks a bit uncomfortable. 'No, I don't think so. I wouldn't quite know how to explain it. The doctor's known me for a long time.'

'And he doesn't know you've got a daughter. I get it,' I reassure her. 'It's still early days; it feels strange to me, too. You could always pretend I'm just a friend.'

'Thanks, but I'll be OK.'

She's in with the doctor for a while, but at least she looks satisfied when she comes out, clutching a prescription.

'He said these are strong; they should do the job. Could you take me to the pharmacy?'

'OK. Did the doctor say any more about you having surgery?'

'He's already referred me to the hospital. I saw the consultant there last year, but he said I wasn't bad enough. How does he know what pain I'm going through? Dr Fuller says he's going to re-refer me. I'll probably have to wait another year for an appointment, though. Bloody NHS.' She looks at me sideways and adds, 'I suppose you go private.'

'You're joking, aren't you?' I say with a laugh. 'There's no way we could afford that.'

She looks surprised and falls silent as I help her stagger back out to the car.

By the time we've got her prescription and I've driven her home, I'm gasping for a cup of coffee.

'Come in,' she says. 'I'll put the kettle on.'

'Let me do it.'

It's the first time I've been in her kitchen. I suppose it's because she's not very mobile at the moment, but the mess in here is quite horrifying. While I'm waiting for the kettle to boil, I wash up the dirty plates and cups and give the surfaces a wipe down. The sink and cooker look like they could do with a good clean, too, but I don't want to go so far that I cause offence.

'Thanks,' she says as I carry the coffees in. She's on the sofa, her feet up on a stool, rubbing her knees.

'I'm very grateful to you for taking me today,' she says. 'I hope your boss didn't mind.'

'He does mind,' I say, my worries rushing back and making me feel suddenly sick. 'But I couldn't have let you struggle on your own.'

'I couldn't have got there,' she admits.

'Well, let's hope these tablets help. Until you get the hospital appointment, anyway.'

'Yes. If the NHS ever gets its bloody act together.'

She rants on about the NHS for a while, how it's gone downhill since she retired, and I switch off, thinking about Trevor's threat of giving me a written warning. What the hell am I supposed to do next time George has an asthma attack? If the school secretary calls me to say he's having a really bad attack, as has happened before, I can hardly wait until I've finished work to rush him to hospital. I feel pure panic going through me just at the thought of it.

'Are you all right?' Barbara has stopped talking and is looking at me with her head on one side, looking concerned.

'Oh, yes, sorry.' I don't want to talk about my work, so I just add, 'I'm just hoping George doesn't keep having such bad asthma attacks. As you say, the NHS is so overwhelmed.'

'Well, don't forget what I said, will you? I'd always be happy to come and sit with him while he's recovering, to save you having to take more time off work.'

'Thank you. I will bear that in mind.'

I know Ben wouldn't like it, and I really hope it doesn't come to it. But at least now, for the first time, I know I've got someone I could call on if I absolutely had to.

9

I manage to get back to the office in time to do an hour or so of work before having a quick lunch. Even though Trevor's deducting a whole morning's pay, I feel so anxious about the work getting behind, how much of that is my fault, and the threat Trevor made about giving me a warning letter, that I feel the need to show I'm making an effort. May and Pauline were almost gloating when Trevor was making his sarcastic comments this morning, and it wouldn't surprise me if one of them has been feeding him complaints about the impact of my absences on everyone's workload.

Nadia's unusually quiet for the rest of the day; she just shakes her head when I ask whether anything's wrong, so I get on with the work, letting my mind go back to Barbara and wondering if I was an idiot to rush out and help her this morning when, as Ben would undoubtedly remind me, I still hardly know her. I wonder again about her life. What the hell does she do all day, every day, in her flat on her own? She put the TV on as soon as we got indoors – it was a repeat of a quiz show. I suppose that's the answer; that's all she does. It must be so boring for her. She really doesn't have much of a life, and to be honest I feel a bit concerned about her. The flat was in a terrible state; it quite obviously hadn't been cleaned for ages. I wonder if she's putting on a brave face and if, in fact, her arthritis is worse than she says, even when she's not having a flare-up. Perhaps she's actually incapable of doing anything physical, at any time. She really needs someone to come in to help her and take care of her, but I bet social services won't stretch to that. I couldn't say anything, anyway; it would have felt like criticism, or interference.

* * *

'You're later than usual, aren't you?' Ben says when I walk in this evening.

'I had to stay a bit late – the work's getting behind again,' I tell him, sighing as the worry of Trevor's threat resurfaces.

'Did the others all stay late too? Or just you?' he asks, almost aggressively.

'Just me.'

'So is Trevor paying you overtime?'

'No, Ben; I stayed because the work's behind, and the reason it's behind is I keep having to take time off. For George, and... other things.'

I nearly tell him about Barbara's doctor's appointment, and about Trevor's threat to put me on a warning of dismissal. At one time we'd have talked things like this over, he'd have listened to me, sympathised with me, perhaps given some sensible advice. But now, all he says is, 'Well, what do you expect me to do? You know *I* can't take the time off.'

'I know you can't. I don't expect you to do anything, Ben.' I'm too weary to argue about it. 'Anyway, where are the kids?'

'Out in the garden, playing football.' We bought them a miniature goal for Christmas so they can practise shooting and saving together. 'Well, Molly's been playing but George has to keep sitting down. He's been really breathless, again. Did you remember to call the doctor?'

'No,' I snap. 'Did you? You were the one at home all day.'

I know I'm only snapping because I feel so bad about forgetting. How could I have forgotten? It was the most important thing I had to do today... until Barbara called me, then Trevor said those words about a warning letter and everything else went out of my mind.

'Just because I'm at home, it doesn't mean I'm not still working,' he retorts. 'I have to plan next term's lessons, I have the GCSEs to worry about—'

If I Lost You   55

'I'll call the surgery tomorrow,' I interrupt, walking past him to go out to the garden and check on our son.

'Hi, you two,' I shout as I head out of the back door. I'm relieved to see George is now actually participating, aiming a kick at the ball as I watch him. 'Who's winning?'

'Me,' Molly says, holding up her arms in triumph as George's ball goes flying way past the goal. 'I've scored four goals and George has only scored one. He's useless.'

'No, I'm not, Molly. I... keep getting... out of puff.'

He's struggling to speak, his skinny little body bent over, hands on his knees, as he fights for breath. I feel as if the wind's been knocked out of me, too, as I'm watching him, suddenly and painfully aware that he's getting steadily worse. He hasn't even been running around, just aiming an occasional kick at the football, but he's looking terrible. He's already turning to sit down on the garden bench again.

'Perhaps you'd both better come in for a drink now,' I suggest, trying to sound cheerful. 'It's getting colder.'

I go back inside, to find Ben starting to peel potatoes.

'Did you at least remember to call your mum about the inset day?' he asks sarcastically as I join him.

The kids have an extra day off after the end of the holiday, but Ben's got to go in to work, and sure enough I've forgotten this as well.

'I'll call her as soon as she gets in from work, OK?' I know I'm snapping, but I can't get past the image of George, bent double in the garden, trying to breathe.

'Do you think she'll be able to have the kids? It's a bit short notice now,' he says, frowning.

I wish he didn't make me feel like this is my fault. I wish I even had the energy to argue the point. Why can't we ever talk civilly about these things any more?

I wait till half past five and give Mum a quick call while Ben's finishing off the dinner.

'Oh, darling, I'm sorry. You know I'd like nothing better than to look after the children,' she says when I explain the situation. 'But I can't do it that day, unfortunately. I've got something else on.'

56 SHEILA NORTON

'Oh. Well, never mind.' She doesn't say what it is she'll be doing; it's unusual for anything to take precedence, for Mum, over spending time with her grandkids. But I don't ask – if she's not telling me, it must be something private. 'It's my fault, I should have asked you sooner.'

'Perhaps another time,' she says. 'But we're seeing you on Easter Sunday, aren't we? We're looking forward to it.'

'Me too.'

I put my phone down and turn to shake my head at Ben.

'Seems like you'll have to book another day off,' he says mildly.

'I can't.'

'Well, I know it's not ideal, but you surely haven't used up all your holiday allowance yet.'

'No, but it's quite short notice, isn't it, and I've had a few days off recently. Trevor's not going to be happy.'

He gives a little shrug. 'Sorry, but I don't see why you should worry much whether he's happy or not. He pays you a pittance, it's a totally unrewarding job and he can't complain about you legitimately taking your full holiday quota.'

'I'm supposed to give more notice, and quite often I can't. When George is ill, for instance.' I stop and swallow. I can't, I just can't bring myself to tell him about Trevor's threat. 'Actually,' I say, suddenly coming to a decision, 'I know what to do: I'll ask Barbara.'

'Barbara? I don't think so, Jo. You've only known her for five minutes.'

'I know, but she's mentioned several times already that she'd be happy to come and look after the children. And she was a nurse, remember? She nursed children with asthma. We can trust her with George.'

'No, I don't like the idea at all,' he says. 'We don't know her well enough. It's like asking a complete stranger into our house, asking them to look after our kids.'

'So come up with a better idea, Ben.' I'm shouting now. Lovely. The children have drifted into the lounge, staying close to each other, the way they do when they hear us arguing. I never used to let them hear us arguing but it seems to happen all the time now. 'Barbara's *not* a stranger, and the children already like her. Anyway, she'll probably feel pleased to repay the favour – after I took time off work today to help her—'

If I Lost You

That's blown it. We stare at each other in silence for a moment.

'So that's why you had to stay late at work,' he says. 'You weren't going to tell me, were you? Now I see why you can't have the day off for the kids next week. Barbara was more important, was she?'

'Don't be ridiculous, she's not more important. But she needed my help, and she's offered to help us in return, and I'm going to take her up on it. I'm going to give her a call after the kids are in bed.'

'I don't like it,' he repeats, but I don't even bother to respond. And when I call Barbara, she sounds so excited about coming to sit with the kids that I'm really glad I've decided to trust her. Ben's made his feelings clear, but basically he's just opted out of having any responsibility for what happens to his children on Tuesday. Frankly, I'm beginning to think I might as well be a single parent.

10

I call the doctor's surgery the next morning about chasing up George's hospital appointment. The receptionist, who, as always, sounds rushed and harassed, tells me she'll pass on the message to Dr Jackson, but as this was also what she promised last time, I don't feel particularly reassured, and decide I should perhaps skip the middleman and call the hospital myself. By the time I've negotiated the intricacies of the hospital's network of phone numbers for different appointment desks, I'm getting hot and bothered, cross and impatient, and I'm conscious of May and Pauline looking at me and checking their watches – anyone would think Trevor employed them purely to keep tabs on me. Eventually I get through to someone who assures me Dr Jackson's referral about George has been received and marked urgent and 'you should hear about an appointment very soon'. I'd like to debate the meaning of the words *urgent* and *very soon* but I'm now too stressed to spend any longer on the phone. I'll just have to call again if nothing happens.

* * *

Mum and Dad come over for dinner on Easter Sunday. I'm still wondering why Mum sounded odd on the phone, saying she had 'something else on' that prevented her being with the kids on the inset day, but when they turn up at midday, bringing Easter eggs for both the children, and a box of chocolates for me, there's so much excitement, with the kids chattering about what they've been doing over the holiday, that it's not till later that we get the chance to talk – but even then she doesn't mention it at all, so I still don't want to ask. I tell myself perhaps she simply has to work that day – it's not one of her usual days in the office, but to be fair, it's not really my business why she can't help out this time. The fact is, she can't and fortunately Barbara can, and that's all I need to know.

As always, Ben is polite and charming while Mum and Dad are with us – as he is whenever we're with anyone else. I'm grateful for this and it gives us a respite from the endless quarrelling, but at the same time it feels strange and fake, like we're just acting parts. Mum obviously senses it too, because while we're clearing up after dinner she asks if everything's all right.

'You're very quiet,' she says. 'Are you worried about anything, JoJo?'

I give a short laugh. 'I'm worried about everything, Mum.'

'What in particular?'

I don't want to mention Ben – our relationship. I feel almost ashamed to tell her that Ben and I are now so far from being happily married that we've both said, on separate occasions, that we'd happily split up if it weren't for the children. And I don't want to start her worrying about my job. Instead, I just fall back on the subject we usually disagree about but that I can't get off my mind:

'George.'

She tries not to sigh, but turns back to the sink, away from me, shaking her head slightly.

'He's fine, I keep telling you; you had childhood asthma yourself and you grew out of it by the time you were ten. He's got his inhalers; they work, so—'

'They don't *always* work.' I'm fighting the threat of tears. It's so frustrating that we have this disagreement every time we talk about George's condition. So upsetting that she doesn't understand, doesn't seem to believe me – worse, she seems to think I'm exaggerating his symptoms, even making an unnecessary fuss. 'You know we've had to rush him to hospital, Mum, too many times. It's not right. And I *told* you the doctor's worried now.'

'He's probably worried because you insist on taking George back to see him so often.'

'You don't see him when he's been outside, trying to run around like a normal five-year-old, and he's absolutely fighting for breath – all the time, Mum, not just when he has an attack. Haven't you noticed his cough?'

'All children get coughs, darling,' she says dismissively.

'Not constantly, not coughing and wheezing every time he tries to do anything. I told you, Dr Jackson's referred him to a paediatrician, urgently. I've had to chase it up because he wanted him seen within two weeks and it's already been four. He thinks it might not be just asthma.'

'He shouldn't be worrying you like that. Of course it's asthma. I know well enough what it's like, from seeing you have all those attacks when you were little. But as I've said before, you're just making matters worse by panicking him.'

'I don't. Nor does Ben. We're both worried, but we don't let George know that.'

'He'll be picking up the vibes, though, trust me. Look, he's my only grandson; don't you think I'd be worried myself if I thought it was anything worse? I know asthma is nasty – you had to go to hospital once or twice yourself when you were little – but you're really not doing him any favours by fussing so much over him.' She pauses, and then goes on, 'You're not doing Molly any favours either.'

'Oh, so now I'm a completely rubbish mother to *both* of my children, am I?' I shoot back. I knew I shouldn't have started on this subject. It never goes well. But I always hope that, just once, Mum might try to understand, might show some concern, instead of seeming to blame *me* for George's worsening condition.

'I'm not saying that, don't be silly. I'm just saying that, on your own admission, Molly has been a bit difficult sometimes recently. Answering you back, being stroppy, being mean to her brother. She feels left out, Jo.'

'I know she does. Don't you think I'm aware of how she feels? It's difficult, Mum, you don't understand.'

'I do,' she tries to soothe me. 'Come on, don't let's argue; the children

If I Lost You 61

will hear. All I'm saying is, try not to treat George like an invalid, fussing over him. He needs to be able to have fun like any other child.'

I close my eyes, exasperation robbing me of any further discussion.

'He can probably feel the tension in the house,' Mum goes on more quietly. 'That doesn't help.'

'What tension?' I shoot back.

'Between you and Ben. Don't look at me like that. I know you both make an effort while we're here, but there's such a chill in the air, it's a wonder we're not all turning to ice. I don't know what's going on, Jo, but you both need to buck up and sort it out; it's affecting your kids.'

'Mind your own business,' I snap, and then I instantly regret it, tears spurting to my eyes, but I can't bring myself to apologise.

And if Mum thinks there was a chill in the air before, it's even icier for the rest of the time she and Dad are here. For the first time ever, I'm not sorry to say goodbye to them. And I'm *glad* it's Barbara, not Mum, who's coming to look after the kids on Tuesday.

* * *

Tuesday comes around all too soon anyway. Ben and I are back at work and the kids have to come with me – earlier than our usual start – to pick up Barbara.

'Why can't Granny drive herself here?' Molly asks as I rush her and George into the car.

'She doesn't have a car. I don't think she's ever learnt to drive.'

The children both look shocked. They probably think all grown-ups automatically know how to drive.

'*I'm* going to learn to drive as soon as I'm old enough,' Molly says, after I've explained that it's necessary to have lessons, and pass a test.

'I'm not,' George says. 'I don't like doing tests.'

'You will want to, believe me, when you're older,' I tell him with a smile.

I'm glad to see Barbara's waiting for us outside the flats when we arrive, as I'm already in danger of being late for work again.

'I'll leave you our spare key,' I tell her, letting her into the house, 'just in case you need to go out – if there was an emergency of any sort.'

I don't specify what sort of emergency I'm thinking of, but I'm sure she knows – although, if George *were* to have a bad attack, it'd probably be quicker for me to rush home and take him to hospital than for her to call an ambulance. Perhaps I'm just being paranoid. It comes with the territory.

'OK. Thank you,' she says. 'We'll be fine, won't we, kids? We're going to have a fun day.'

'Yay!' George shouts.

'What kind of fun?' Molly asks. 'Can we play football in the garden?'

'Granny can't run around,' I warn them. 'Now, be very good, OK?' I give them both a kiss and turn to Barbara, adding, 'I'll give you a call in my lunch break, to check how things are going. Don't let them play you up.'

'They won't, don't worry,' she reassures me cheerfully, making me reflect – a bit late in the day – that she probably hasn't ever had much experience with five- and seven-year-olds. 'Go on, have a good day, don't be late.'

Of course, I *do* worry; I worry all day, picturing the worst possible scenarios going on at home. Nadia tries to reassure me that I'd have had a phone call if there were any problems, and that I have to start trusting Barbara with my kids if we're going to have a proper mother-and-daughter relationship. It still feels strange, remembering that Barbara's my mother, that she's grandmother to my children. It's all happened so quickly.

But when I call her at lunchtime she sounds fine, and she puts each of the children on the phone to have a quick chat. Molly tells me about a game they've been playing, and George says they went out in the garden, having another football competition, and Granny was referee but she had to stay sitting down. I feel relieved for a moment, until he adds that he had to sit down after a little while too because he couldn't stop coughing.

'But you're all right now, are you?' I ask him anxiously.

'Yes. Just tired.'

'Thank you so much,' I tell Barbara when I get home. 'I hope you're not too worn out. The kids can be a bit full-on.'

'They've been really good,' she says. 'I've enjoyed it. I'd be happy to help any time, Jo.'

When Ben gets in from work she's still here, still chatting, and he goes straight upstairs, ignoring us both, as if to underline the point that he didn't

If I Lost You   63

want Barbara here. But still, I ask her to stay for dinner. It's the least I can do, really, after she's helped me out so much today.

'My asthma is really annoying,' George says as he's getting into bed. 'I want to play football, Mummy, but I just keep on coughing and wheezing all the time.'

'I know, sweetie. I'm hoping we'll be able to get you some better medicine soon. But did you have a nice day with Granny?'

'Yes. I really liked her looking after us. She kept saying me and Molly are very lucky cos we've both got our own bedrooms. So I said sometimes Molly has to come into my room and one of us has to sleep on the floor. Like we did at Christmas when Grandma and Grandpa came, and you had to pull out the truckle bed for one of them, in Molly's room.'

Molly's listening from her room across the hall.

'I told Granny I don't like it when I have to go in with him,' she calls out. 'I told her he keeps talking and making a noise when I want to go to sleep, and he wouldn't sleep when Father Christmas was coming and I had to call you to come and tell him off.'

'You're a tell-tale, Molly,' George shouts back. 'Granny said you have to be nice to me cos I'm only five.'

'All right, both of you, that's enough now, time to go to sleep, please,' I say, kissing George goodnight and going into Molly's room. 'Don't wind him up, please, Molly,' I say softly.

'It's not fair,' she says, throwing herself down on her pillow. 'He gets away with everything because he's *only five* and he's *got asthma.*'

I sit down on her bed and pull her into my arms.

'That's not true, Mollipop. He *is* younger than you, and he *does* have asthma, but that doesn't mean he gets any special treatment. Daddy and I love you both just the same, you know that, don't you? You're our big girl, you'll always be special – you're *both* special in different ways.'

'Granny doesn't love us both the same, though. She likes George best.'

'I'm sure that's not true. Look, it was the first time she's looked after you both, and perhaps she was just a bit careful with him, because he's little, and he gets wheezy.'

She gives a little shrug, but she's still pouting. I kiss her goodnight, tell her I love her and go downstairs, sighing heavily. I hate having to admit it to myself, but Mum's right about this: Molly does feel resentful because of the extra concern we have to show to George. She's been a bit moody recently, a bit mean to her brother, but surely all children go through phases like this? I'm convinced it's perfectly normal. I can't worry about it; I simply haven't got room in my head for any more worries. If Barbara did show George any preferential treatment, I'm sure it was only when his breathing got bad. I'm not going to ask her; it would feel petty and would come across as not trusting her. And I do. Both kids seem to have been fine in her care today, she obviously loved looking after them and, OK, it might be a bit soon to have trusted her with them, but what choice did I have? Ben had washed his hands of the whole situation and – as usual – it was left to me to make a decision and take responsibility for it. Even if there had been a problem today with Barbara, I realise I probably wouldn't have wanted to tell him about it. That says it all, really, doesn't it?

11

Fortunately, in the morning Molly seems to have forgotten all about her gripes from last night and is more anxious about what I'm putting in her lunchbox for the first day back at school. But I still spend the whole day at work worrying about both children. I try to talk to Nadia about them; despite the fact that she's only in her early twenties and doesn't have any kids, she's a good listener and always seems to have something reassuring to offer. But today, again, she seems quiet and distracted. When I ask her if anything's wrong she just shakes her head, so I don't push it, but I can't help wondering if she's unwell: she's been uncharacteristically quiet for a while now. I know it sounds selfish, but I miss being able to chat to her. The other two women only talk among themselves and there's no way I'd share anything personal with them, since they've made it quite clear they resent me. Perhaps even Nadia's got fed up with me and my problems. The thought alarms me, makes me feel sad and guilty at the same time. I suppose it's always been a bit one-sided: I seem to have so many issues and she never seems to talk to me about hers, so I've just presumed she doesn't have any.

I'm still thinking about Nadia when I collect the children from school. I'm so busy trying to concentrate on Molly, telling me excitedly about an art project her class is working on, that it's a while before I notice George is unusually quiet and subdued.

'Are you all right, my Georgie boy?' I ask him, giving his shoulder a squeeze.

He shrugs.

'Did you have a good day?' I persist.

Another shrug.

'Anyway,' Molly interrupts, 'when we've all finished our paintings, we're going to put them all together to make, like, a *scene* and it'll go on the classroom wall, but it'll go *right round* the wall.'

'Wow!' I say with a smile. 'That sounds great. Come on, get in the car, then. Let's get home, shall we?' I look at George again as he fastens the strap on his seat, and decide he's probably just tired and I'm best to leave him alone.

But we've only been home for about half an hour when he starts to wheeze noisily. I give him his inhaler and it seems to calm things down, but later, as he's getting ready for bed, it starts again. Finally he settles down and sleeps soundly all night, only to wake up in the morning coughing and wheezing really badly.

'He seems to be getting worse again,' I say quietly to Ben. 'I wish that appointment with the paediatrician would hurry up.'

'Well, he certainly doesn't look well enough to go to school today.'

'No,' I agree, sighing.

'I'll drop Molly off, then,' he says, sounding like he's making a huge sacrifice, rather than just going one or two streets out of his way. If only getting Molly to school was all I had to worry about. If only. 'Come on, Molly. See you tonight,' he adds casually to me as he leaves, assuming it's perfectly fine for me to take yet another day off. Not even asking me if it'll be OK. After all, my job isn't important. It only pays for all our food, to say nothing of running my car, buying the kids' school uniforms, and, well, OK, his salary pays for everything else, pretty much. But that's hardly the point.

I stare out of the window as he drives off, wishing I didn't feel this resentment, wishing I'd at least told him about Trevor's threat to put me on a written warning. Then I make a sudden decision. Whether Ben likes it or

If I Lost You   67

not, I'm calling Barbara. As always, she answers straight away; I'm beginning to think she never sets foot out of her flat. And within minutes I'm gently shaking George awake, pulling his coat on over his PJs and taking him out to the car.

'Are we going to Granny's?' he says, perking up a bit.

'We're picking Granny up.' I don't think it's an option to take him to her flat; it would be quicker of course, but frankly, it's a mess; from what I've seen so far she doesn't seem to keep much food in, and there's nothing for him to do there. We pull into the car park at her flats and she's waiting for us outside, smiling widely.

'You had another silly old asthma attack?' she says casually to George as she gets in the car. 'Damned nuisance, aren't they? Never mind, Granny's going to look after you today.'

'Thanks so much, Barbara. Sorry it's such short notice. And I'm just going to have to drop you back at home and dash straight off – I'm already late.'

'Of course, don't worry about us, we'll be fine, won't we, Georgie?'

'Yes,' he says happily.

I drop them at the house and carry on to work, somehow managing to get there only about fifteen minutes late.

'Don't worry,' Nadia says. 'He hasn't noticed.'

'Thank goodness.'

'George not well again?'

'Another asthma attack.' I look at her now and realise she's not even really listening. She's staring at her computer screen but looks as if she's miles away. 'Are you OK, Nadia?' I ask her quietly. 'Are you...' I pause again and drop my voice to a whisper. 'Are you annoyed with me, about – you know – my timekeeping?'

But she looks up straight away, blinking as if she's just woken up.

'What? No – of course not, Jo. I totally get it – I feel really sorry for you, I mean for George.' She swallows, a flush coming to her face. 'I know I've been a bit quiet. It's nothing to do with you, honestly.'

'You're not feeling ill, are you?'

'No.' She's actually smiling now. 'No. I'm fine – more than fine, in a way. But... well, I'm in a bit of a... kind of... personal predicament.'

'Can I help at all? You've always been good to me, love, so if there's anything I can do, you must tell me.'

She shakes her head. 'No. It's something that only I can decide about. A matter of... a choice. A decision.' She looks up at me and there's something in her eyes – a kind of light – almost excitement. But at the same time, there's a sadness about the way she adds, very quietly, 'A matter of the heart.'

'Oh.' I don't know what to say. Nadia's married; she apparently married Ahmed very young. She's always seemed happy, often saying the only thing she regrets is that they haven't yet started a family. So I wonder what to make of her *matter of the heart* – but she turns back to her computer now anyway, looking as if she's already regretting saying anything, leaving me feeling that I can't ask any more questions. But I wonder about it for a while before going back to worrying about George's worsening asthma – and Molly's worsening attitude. And Ben's attitude too. To say nothing of my mum, the way we argued again recently. And Barbara, how hard her life seems to be, and how Ben seems determined not to trust her. And my job here, and how difficult it's getting to take time off. In short, I feel like my life right now is one huge worry.

* * *

'Is Daddy at home with George now?' Molly asks, later, when I pick her up from school.

'No. Granny's there. I had to go to work.'

'Oh, that's not fair. *I* want to stay at home with Granny.'

'Well, at least you're not the one having asthma attacks, Mollipop,' I point out.

But of course, I can't expect her to think this is any compensation. As soon as we get home, she runs into the lounge, demanding to know what George has been doing with Granny, what she's missed out on.

'Granny gave me chocolate buttons,' he brags.

I glance at Barbara. 'You didn't have to do that.'

'I told him to save some for Molly – didn't I, Georgie?' she says. 'But by

If I Lost You 69

the time I'd gone to the kitchen to make myself a cuppa, he'd eaten the lot. Naughty boy,' she adds, affectionately, giving him a cuddle.

Molly's pouting, blinking back tears while George is smirking at her. I feel like telling him off – he knows he's upsetting her – but to be honest, it's Barbara's fault for not putting some of the sweets aside for her.

'Sorry, Molly,' she says, cheerfully. 'But it's George who was ill, wasn't it – he needed a treat. You're OK, you've been to school.'

'I didn't *want* to go to school,' she retorts. 'It's not fair.'

'Molly...' I warn her, but frankly I agree with her, of course; it's not fair at all, but George is still smirking, and Molly flies at him, landing a slap on the side of his head so that he howls in pain, or protest, or both, and I have to pull her away before a full-blown fight ensues.

'Well, that wasn't very nice, Molly,' Barbara says. 'Your brother's only little.'

'I know, but it isn't fair,' she yells, red in the face with her anger. 'He gets everything, just because he's got stupid asthma, and I get nothing, and nobody cares about me.'

'That's not true, Molly.' I'm trying to stay calm, but I'm so upset, I feel almost sick. I've never seen her so angry and upset; even as a toddler she rarely had tantrums, but now she looks so furious, it's as if a tap has been turned on and all her distress is gushing out at once.

'He gets days off school just because he's tired. He gets to lie on the sofa watching TV whenever he wants, he hits me and pinches me and cries like a baby if I hit him back, and you *always* think it's my fault, never his fault, Mummy. You and Daddy always tell me off, and now Granny's telling me off too and it's *not fair.'*

She's crying now – loud heart-wrenching sobs that shake her little body as she turns away, shaking me off when I try to pull her into my arms. She pushes past me and runs out of the room, up the stairs, into her bedroom and the door slams.

I go to follow her, my own distress bringing me close to tears myself, but then I glance at George and see him cuddled up protectively with Barbara's arms around him – and he looks positively pleased with himself.

'She's always horrible to me,' he tells Barbara.

'Poor Georgie,' she says.

'All right, Barbara, I think that's enough,' I find myself snapping.

I head out into the hall to go up and check on Molly, but at that moment I hear Ben's key in the door. He takes in the look on my face, glances in the lounge and looks back at me again.

'She's been here all day with George?' he says, not bothering to keep his voice down.

'Yes. Barbara has kindly helped out again,' I say, trying to keep my tone even. Then I turn and call back to Barbara, 'I'll take you home now.'

She gets up, looking a bit disgruntled, hobbles to the door and takes an age getting her shoes and coat on, so I run upstairs quickly to see if Molly's still crying, but she's lying with her face to the wall, pretending to be asleep.

'Let's have a talk when I'm back from taking Granny home,' I say, but there's no response.

Ben's still standing in the hall, looking slightly bemused.

'Molly's been a bit upset,' I tell him. 'She just wants to be left alone. I'll talk to her when I get back.'

Barbara's quiet in the car.

'I don't want that to happen again,' I tell her firmly as I reverse off the driveway.

'What?' she asks innocently.

'Treating one of the children and not the other. Molly's already feeling left out – sidelined – as you just heard. And—'

'Sorry. It was just because George had been poorly. And I did tell him to save some for his sister.'

'Well, if you bring him a treat like that again, please keep some of the sweets aside yourself for Molly. OK?'

I suppose I'm angry – frustrated – with myself, as much as with her. What did I expect when I decided to let Barbara look after my kids? She's barely had any experience with kids before. It's my own fault for not giving her more detailed guidelines.

'Look,' I say, 'we're having a hard enough job trying to treat them both the same when it's almost impossible, given George's repeated problems.'

'Well, I'm sorry,' she says again. 'But Molly's a big girl. She should understand, shouldn't she?'

If I Lost You   71

'No, she shouldn't. She's only seven, she *can't* understand. She doesn't like her brother having these attacks, it frightens her, but she also doesn't like feeling like she's less loved – less special – than him, and I don't blame her. It's difficult, and I know a packet of sweets is nothing in itself, but this sort of thing just makes her feel, even more, that nobody cares as much about her as they do about George.' I pause. Barbara's sitting in silence, perhaps resenting what she sees as my ingratitude. 'Sorry to be so blunt. Thank you, I am grateful for today, really I am. But next time...'

'I'll make sure they share. You're right,' she says. 'I didn't think.'

'Thank you.'

I take a breath and give her a smile. I know that, in the scheme of things, it really wasn't such a terrible mistake. Am I just cross and upset because I've now had to acknowledge, myself, exactly how badly let down Molly is feeling?

'I won't let it happen again,' she says. 'I... don't want you to stop me coming round.' Her voice breaks a little as she goes on, 'I've been on my own for so long; I never expected to be part of a family again. I don't want to lose you now.'

We're pulling up outside her flats now and I lean over the handbrake and put an arm across her shoulders.

'You're not going to lose us. You are part of the family, OK? It's probably my fault. I should have made a few things clear to you. So now we've had a chat about it, we're all right, aren't we?'

'Yes. Thank you, dear.' She wipes her eyes. 'I'll see you soon, then, I hope.'

'Of course. Take care.'

And I drive back wondering how I've managed to go from anger to feeling almost guilty myself in the short time it's taken me to take her home.

12

The evening doesn't go well. Molly's still upstairs when I get home. Ben says she didn't want to talk to him, and he's preparing dinner, looking grumpy, saying he's annoyed that I asked Barbara to cover today without discussing it with him. I remind him again, wearily, about the facts of my miserable working life, before going up to see our daughter, who's still lying on her bed but is at least ready to talk.

'It's not fair,' she mutters.

'No, you're right, it's not. It's not fair that George has this horrible cough and breathlessness, either, though, is it?'

'No, but that's not *my* fault. I didn't make him have it.'

'I know, sweetie.' I pull her into my arms. 'Look, Granny isn't used to looking after children. And she did mean for you and George to share the chocolate buttons. I'll have a talk to George about it, and I've already spoken to Granny. She won't let it happen again.'

She shrugs. I know perfectly well that this wasn't all about the sweets. It goes deeper, but she's too little to have the words for it. She just knows – she's found out far too young – that life isn't fair, and I wish I could make it right for her, but I can't. George needs extra care, he needs time off school sometimes, and it often takes the attention away from her. All I can do, for now, is give her a kiss and tell her it's sausages for dinner – her favourite.

If I Lost You

But I also have a talk to George when I go back downstairs, because I'm quite sure he knew perfectly well what he was doing when he ate his sister's share. He pouts and complains again about Molly hitting him, but I can't let him get away with things like this just because we're all so worried about him.

* * *

He's quiet on the journey to school the next morning, and looks close to tears when I kiss him goodbye.

'What's wrong, Georgie?' I ask him.

'I don't want to go to school,' he says. 'I don't feel well.'

His breathing seems OK, so I'm inclined to think it's just because he had a day off yesterday. I really don't want him having more time off school than he needs to, for his own sake.

'Go on, you'll be fine when you see all your friends,' I try to encourage him, but he trails miserably across the playground after Molly, his head hanging.

I start to talk to Nadia about it while we're settling down to work, but I can see she's distracted, so I stop. We both work in silence for a few minutes, before she suddenly turns to me and says very quietly, with a little ghost of a smile, 'Can I... tell you something, Jo? In confidence?'

'Of course.' I lean closer across the desks. 'What is it?'

She drops her voice to little more than a whisper. I have to strain to hear her above May and Pauline's chatter on the other side of the office.

'I've met someone,' she says. 'I mean, a man. I've been seeing someone.'

I look up at her in surprise.

'Oh,' I say again, unsure of how to react. 'Is it... um, is it serious?'

'Yes,' she says, looking down at her desk. 'I know what you must think. But the thing is, Ahmed and I...' She sighs. 'Don't get me wrong, he's lovely. But, well, we just don't often... It's not like we're...' She sighs again, then goes on, 'Like I've told you, it was an arranged marriage. Our parents are all quite religious and they suggested it; we didn't have to agree, there was nothing forced about it, but we did, we wanted to, we liked each other.'

'But?' I encourage her gently.

'There's never been any passion,' she says flatly. 'Nothing like that. We don't have sex very often, so it's no wonder we couldn't get pregnant. We're... more like friends. But I've never wanted to hurt him.' She sighs. 'I met Zach in Tesco. I shop there every Saturday, so does he, and we got chatting. I knew straight away.'

'Knew what?'

'That he was the one,' she says, breaking into a smile. 'The one I should have waited for. I should never have married Ahmed. It's not as if I'm very religious – I only went along with it to please my parents. I was so young, only sixteen, and he was only eighteen – what did we know? We were like kids, playing house. It was fun at the time.'

'So how long have you been seeing Zach?'

'Not very long. But we haven't actually had the opportunity yet to,' she drops her voice again, 'spend a night together. And he's arranged something now, told his wife he's going to be away on business overnight.'

'So he's married too?' I look at her. She's still so young, so innocent in many ways. I feel sad for her, thinking about her agreeing to a loveless marriage at just sixteen, but I'm worried that this guy's taking advantage of her naïvety. 'Are you sure this Zach really cares about you, Nadia?'

'I know what you're thinking,' she says. 'But we've got to know each other really well – we have coffee together in Costa after we've shopped, every week. He's not just using me, whatever it sounds like. He's not like that. He's quite a bit older than me, sensible, says he's never cheated on his wife before but he loves me and wants to be with me.'

'So he should tell his wife about you. And sorry, but you should tell Ahmed, too. That's only fair, Nad.'

'I know. We will. But the thing is, his wife's pregnant, so he can't tell her until after the baby's born, it wouldn't be fair. And I'll tell Ahmed at the same time.' Her face drops. 'That's the only part that's worrying me.'

'I really don't think it's a good idea to go away overnight with Zach until you've both told your partners,' I warn her, but she adopts a sulky expression now, reminding me so much of Molly when I've told her something she doesn't like that I have to suppress a smile.

'We can't be expected to put our lives on hold,' she says indignantly. 'We love each other.'

If I Lost You   75

We don't get a chance to talk any more now because Trevor comes into the office, in an even worse mood than usual because he's lost some important data and wants someone to blame. But I think about Nadia and her new boyfriend for the rest of the morning. I don't know what to say to her; it obviously wouldn't be helpful to spell out what to me seems blindingly obvious: that this guy is almost certainly a rat, that he's got no intention of leaving his wife, and he's going to hurt her and probably wreck her marriage. OK, perhaps the marriage is a failure but this isn't the way she needs to end it. She's such a nice girl but she's so quiet and innocent, I never even hear her talk about going out with friends. All I want to do is protect her – but I can't. It's not my job, not my place. All I can do is warn her, and that's what I've done.

* * *

Soon after lunchtime, I have a phone call from the school.

'I'm so sorry to tell you George has had another asthma attack,' Miss Brent, the school secretary, tells me. She's the designated first-aider, and very efficient. 'His teacher gave him two puffs of his inhaler, and I've now given him another two, and he seems to be improving.'

'Thank you. So, he's not actually ill, and his breathing's settled now? Do you think he'll be OK to stay at school until three-fifteen?'

'I'd have thought so, but he seems a bit distressed. He's saying he wants to go home. Mrs Austin said he's looked unhappy all day.'

I lower my voice, keeping my head down over my phone, not wanting my colleagues to overhear. 'I'm sorry, but I'm really not able to take any time off, unless it's an emergency.' I feel terrible saying this. What kind of mother doesn't rush to take her child home when he's in distress?

'That's fine, Mrs Hudson,' she says calmly. 'I quite understand. I'll take him back to his class. I'm sure Mrs Austin will let him just sit quietly until the end of the afternoon.'

'Thank you.' I put my phone down, and as I return to my computer screen I see Nadia looking at me, sympathy in her eyes. She doesn't say anything; I'm sure she understands from the way I was almost whispering into the phone that I don't want to talk about it. I'm too ashamed. George is only just five – still my baby – and I feel like I'm letting him down. I hate this job.

He starts crying as soon as he sees me waiting for him in the playground when school finishes. I hold out my arms to him.

'I hear you got really breathless again today,' I say, stroking his hair. 'Are you all better now, sweetie?'

'No,' he mutters crossly through his tears. 'I'm not. I felt horrible all day and I wanted to come home.'

'Oh, baby, I'm sorry. We're going home now; you'll soon feel better.'

'No I won't,' he retorts.

'What's wrong with him?' Molly demands as she comes to join us.

'He had another asthma attack. He's probably tired,' I tell her.

'I'm *not* tired, I just feel horrible.' He goes into a coughing fit, his chest heaving pitifully. 'I want to go home,' he says eventually.

He walks slowly back to the car with me, still coughing, while Molly skips on ahead. I feel more worried about him every time I look at him. He's pale and looks distressed, struggling even to walk slowly because his breathing is so laboured. This is no good; it's not an asthma attack, or not like his usual ones – he must have something else wrong with him. I'm seriously wondering if I should take him back to Dr Jackson again, or even to A&E. I can't keep waiting for the paediatric appointment, which has now almost taken on the aspect of a fairy tale – something I've been told about but don't really believe in.

And then, when we get home, the fairy tale has come true: there's a letter from the NHS on the mat. His appointment is on Thursday. I have no idea how I'm going to get the time off to take him to the hospital, but I can't ask anyone else to cover this. It's too important, and I'm his mum; I don't care what Trevor says or does, I'll be taking George to the hospital myself.

13

George seems better now we're home, and fortunately the next day is Saturday. I've got a lot of housework and washing to catch up on, and I've organised a Tesco delivery. I'm just unpacking everything when Barbara calls me.

'Hi. Is everything OK?' I ask her.

'Well, not really. My knees are playing up again today.'

'Have you taken the painkillers?'

'Yes, but they always take a while to work, and they make me feel a bit woozy. The problem is, I was going to go out and get some shopping, but I don't think I can manage it.'

'Oh.' I look around me at the piles of groceries, meat, fruit and veg I've just had delivered. 'What do you need?'

'Well, everything, really. I mean, I've probably got enough for today, but I really need to stock up a bit. I was wondering if you could take me.'

I hesitate. I do feel sorry for her, but I've got a lot to do myself.

'It'd probably be easier if I just get you what you need and bring it over to you,' I suggest.

'Thanks, but I really do need to have a proper stock up this time. At Lidl or one of the other big shops. I've run out of nearly everything, and the thing is, even when my knees are OK, I can't carry much home with me.'

I think for a minute. How does she normally manage? Of course she can't carry a full load of shopping on her own. She must have to just buy enough for one day at a time. I could have offered to add what she needed to my Tesco order, and dropped it all round to her – that would have been easier.

'You're sure you've got enough for today?' I ask her, coming to a decision. 'Because if so, I'll take you tomorrow. I'm a bit busy today – I'm in the middle of stuff, and—'

'That would be lovely. Thank you so much, love.'

The warm glow evaporates pretty quickly, though, when Ben arrives back with the children. By now I've hoovered the whole house, the second lot of washing's drying, I've put all the shopping away, and I'm ready to greet the kids with a hug and a drink and biscuit and hear all about what they did in the park. I feel pleased with myself – but not for long.

'Will you be around tomorrow afternoon to stay with the kids?' I ask Ben once we're on our own in the kitchen, sipping coffee.

He gives me an odd look. 'No – what are you talking about? We're—'

'Look, I've had a call from Barbara,' I interrupt him. 'She's in a bad way again with her knees and she's asked if I could take her to do a big shop. I've said I'll pick her up about two, and...'

Ben's staring at me. I wish he wouldn't make me feel guilty every time I want to help my birth mother with anything. It's about time he accepted she's going to be part of my life.

'Is there a problem with that?' I ask him, trying not to snap.

'Well, only that I thought we were going to your mum and dad's tomorrow.'

Bugger. He's right – I promised, last weekend, that we'd go over there for Sunday dinner. It's not something we do too often – they tend to come to us fairly frequently instead – but I agreed to this because I felt bad, at the time, about arguing with Mum over George.

'Oh yes,' I mutter.

'You didn't forget, did you?' he says, looking smug about it.

'Just for a moment, I did, yes. I was busy when she called and I've had a lot on my mind, thinking about George's appointment and everything.'

'So you're going to call Barbara and cancel?'

If I Lost You   79

'Yes. I can take her this afternoon instead. If that's OK with you?'

'I suppose so.' He raises his eyebrows. 'I just hope she isn't expecting too much of you, Jo. I mean, once you start this – taking her shopping – is she going to be wanting you to do it every weekend? Because we're busy too.'

'I know. Look, she just wants to stock up properly for once, so that she doesn't have to keep going out every day for one or two items at a time. It makes sense. And she's been so good – coming to look after George at a moment's notice.'

'And upsetting Molly,' he says pointedly.

'We've moved on from that.' I'm trying my best to keep my patience. Ben seems determined to stop me doing anything with Barbara. 'Look, she's been a lifesaver. It's been getting more and more difficult for me to take time off.' Again, I don't mention the threat of the written warning.

'You need to think about looking for a different job,' he says.

'Oh yes. Like there are scores of jobs out there where I could work from nine till three, close enough to the school. It's all very well for you, you're working at a job you love, doing what you trained for, getting some satisfaction from it. I wish I could do the same. Perhaps I should just go back to running my classes – at least I was my own boss then.'

'That doesn't work now, with the children, with George having so many urgent issues. You know that.'

'And that's why I have to put up with working for Trevor. It's hardly because I *like* it.'

We've been over this ground so often, Ben just sighs and shakes his head, as if I'm being deliberately difficult, as if it's my fault that perfect, school-hours job opportunities aren't lined up out there just waiting for me to snap them up.

'You need a job where you can work from home,' he says, getting to his feet wearily, as if I've tried his patience quite enough for one day.

'Find me one, then,' I snap back.

I call Barbara and tell her I'm free this afternoon after all. We go to Lidl, she fills the trolley, and when we get to the checkout she pulls out some ten-pound notes. She's nineteen pounds fifty-two pence short. I put the difference on my card, and even as I do, even as she's promising to pay me back, I somehow know she probably won't. And I know I probably won't tell Ben.

* * *

Mum greets us the next day with hugs and a huge smile, as if our argument on Easter Sunday never happened, as if she's not even aware that we haven't spoken on the phone all week.

'It's so lovely to see you all. Come in, let's get the kettle on. Dinner's in the oven.'

This is how we are now, I realise sadly. It's always the same. We just pretend there isn't this huge difference between us, this obstacle that, these days, seems to prevent us having the happy mum-and-daughter relationship we always used to have. I go along with it because I love her and I don't want there to be a constant bad feeling between us, but knowing how she feels – that she thinks I'm overreacting to George's condition, making too much fuss, actually doing *harm* to both my children – hurts me, and it's hard to put it to the back of my mind.

It doesn't take long, though, for the usual scenario to begin. After we've had coffee, after the children have finished sharing their news and Mum and I are alone in the kitchen, preparing to dish up the dinner, she turns to me, looking serious. I try to forestall her.

'Mum – I hope we're not going to have the same conversation all over again.'

'What same conversation?' she says, with feigned innocence.

'You know. About George. Because I've got the appointment for him now, with the paediatrician. It's this week. So let's wait and see what he says, shall we?'

'Would you like me to take him for you?' she says immediately. 'I can get the day off. It'll save you having to ask Trevor—'

'No. Thank you, but I want to take him myself. I'll manage it somehow.'

She turns away for a moment, pretending to check the vegetables steaming on the hob, before looking back at me and saying, 'Well, we can compare notes afterwards, then. Because *I* saw somebody myself this week.'

If I Lost You 81

'You saw somebody?' I repeat. 'A doctor? What – for yourself?' I'm immediately alarmed. 'Is something wrong, Mum?'

'Not for myself. For you. About George.'

I'm so shocked, I actually take a step back. 'About George? What the hell? You can't – you're not allowed. You didn't say.'

'It was a just a chat with a friend of a friend. She doesn't know me, she doesn't know you or George. I just wanted someone's opinion – someone medical, outside the family.'

I can feel my face burning with rage; my arms and legs are trembling with it.

'*What*? You can't do that, Mum. You can't talk to some random *medical* person – was she even a proper doctor? – about George without even telling me. Discussing George's medical history – it's supposed to be confidential. I hope this doctor, or whoever she was, told you she couldn't talk to you about it.'

'Calm down, she didn't have his medical history, she didn't even know his name. I just asked her a few questions about asthma, about the best way to handle it, and she said—'

I've heard enough.

'I don't want to know what she said, OK? I'm really not happy that you did this, Mum – going behind my back, talking about George to someone we don't even know. How could she tell you anything without seeing him? How could she possibly know better than the doctors he's been seeing regularly? I suppose this was why you couldn't help out with the kids on the inset day – well, thanks for that!'

'You said Barbara covered it.'

'Yes, she did, and frankly it's a good job she's turned up, as she's been a lot more help than you've been.'

I regret this, of course, as soon as the words are out of my mouth, but I'm still too annoyed to take them back. We dish up the dinner in silence, and eat the meal barely looking at each other. Thankfully the children are chatty enough for it to go unnoticed. Afterwards I tell her to sit down while I load the dishwasher, and I make an excuse to leave early, saying that the kids need to get ready for school tomorrow.

'You're quiet,' Ben comments as we drive home. 'Everything all right?'

I give a snort in response, because it would take me too long to list all the things that aren't *all right*. In fact, I feel like there's only one person in my family who isn't worrying me at the moment, and that's the cat.

* * *

I feel miserable and anxious the next morning at work. I know I need to get the day off for George's hospital appointment on Thursday, and I know I'll have to ask Trevor – even though I'm sure he'll say it's too short notice.

'Talk to him straight away,' Nadia advises me. 'That'll give him a few days' notice; he can't complain about that.'

Unfortunately, he can. And he dresses up his complaint to make himself sound reasonable.

'I'm sorry to hear your son needs to see a specialist,' he says with a pretence at a sympathetic smile. 'I'm a parent myself, I'm not heartless, I can imagine how worrying it must be.'

Yes, you're a parent, I think grimly. *But you've got a wife to handle all the family and domestic issues. Same old story.*

'But,' he goes on, 'try to see it from my point of view. If everyone asked for time off whenever a member of their family had an appointment with a doctor—'

'Someone always does have to,' I interrupt desperately, 'and it's usually the mother. I can't send a five-year-old to hospital on his own. I'm giving you notice this time, aren't I?'

He shakes his head, as if in sorrow. 'Can't do it, Jo, sorry.'

'But it's only a morning. And I'm not asking for it as a favour, I'll take it out of my annual leave.'

'I can't allow that, unfortunately. Pauline's off this week. She booked it months ago. I can't have two of you off at the same time.'

'For one morning,' I repeat. 'If the consultant sees George quickly, I might not even need the whole morning.'

He just shakes his head again. 'Sorry I can't help.'

He walks off, back to his office, with a swagger. I feel, ridiculously, like throwing something at the back of his head. He's being deliberately diffi-

If I Lost You   83

cult about it, knowing full well that he's left me with no options. What am I supposed to do now?

'Take the day off sick,' Nadia whispers as I go back to my desk.

'He'll know. It'll be so obvious that I'm not really sick.'

'He can't sack you for having a day off sick, though. You don't need a sick note for just one day. Tell him you've got a really heavy period. He'll be too embarrassed to discuss it.'

Perhaps she's got a point. But whatever Trevor says or does, I'm determined that I'm taking Thursday morning off to take my son to the hospital myself, come what may.

'By the way,' Nadia suddenly goes on quietly, 'you know what I was telling you about, the other day?'

'The... other man?'

'Yes.' She hesitates, then goes on in a rush, 'I wondered if you'd do something for me.'

'What?' I ask warily.

'Would you mind if I tell Ahmed I'm coming to your place on Saturday night? I mean, you won't have to do anything or say anything, it's just, you know, so I've got an excuse for going out. I don't know what else to say. I don't usually go out without him, but he knows you...'

'I've only met him once, Nadia,' I protest.

'Yes, but he'll trust you, because you're... older, and a mum, and everything,' she says awkwardly. 'So I thought, if I say you've asked me to look after the children because you and Ben are going away for the night, then it would mean I'd have to stay the night at yours, and he'll be OK with that.'

'But what if he wanted to check?'

'He won't. He'll be OK about it. He likes me working with you.' She smiles. 'He thinks you're a good influence.'

I raise my eyebrows. I don't like this. I want to refuse. But Nadia's been good to me – she's the only person here who's always on my side, always sticking up for me, prepared to lie for me if necessary. I feel like I should be prepared to do the same for her, but...

'I really think you should wait until you've told Ahmed you don't want to be with him any more,' I say. 'I'm not sure you know this Zach well enough. If he really loved you, he'd leave his wife, even if she is pregnant. It'll be harder after the baby's born.'

Her smile drops. 'If you don't want to help me, I'll ask someone else.'

She's going to do this anyway, whatever I say. I sigh to myself. I feel for her – she obviously hasn't had much fun in her life, but she thinks she's in love and I just don't want her to get hurt.

'It's not that I don't want to help you. I'm just worried about you. Zach's older, and he's taking advantage of you – I'm not sure he's really what you think he is.'

'He loves me. He's waited for me to be ready – and I am,' she insists. She shrugs. 'I'll ask May, then.'

'No. Don't ask her. Look, can I think it over? I'll let you know before Saturday.'

'OK.' She smiles. 'Thanks, Jo. You're my best friend.'

This in itself is sad. She doesn't need someone of my age for a best friend. She should have other young women to talk to about these things; she should be going out and having fun, not wasting her life with someone who's just *nice* – and definitely not with someone older, married and surely about to end up hurting her. But what can I say? I can't even manage my own life; I'm hardly fit to judge anyone else.

14

Molly's already waiting for me in the playground when I arrive back at school this afternoon, and George is standing at his classroom door with Mrs Austin, who asks for a word with me, suggesting George waits outside with his sister.

'I've been worried about George since he came back last week after the holiday,' she says. 'He's not himself.'

'In what way?'

'Well, I – and Miss Brent – get the impression that George might be saying he's having asthma attacks when he isn't.'

'*What*?' I'm staring at her now, astounded. 'Sorry, but what on earth makes you think that?'

'Don't get me wrong, Mrs Hudson, we're taking it seriously, of course. But he really didn't seem to be having an asthma attack on Friday.'

'He wouldn't lie about it. He just wouldn't,' I protest. 'He knows how serious it is.'

'And he said he was having one again today.'

'I didn't get a call about that.'

'No. Because, honestly, it didn't seem like an asthma attack.' She pauses, and then goes on, looking more serious, 'But he really didn't look well. And that cough – it's really lingering, isn't it, and it's... I'm not a doctor, obviously, but it doesn't sound like an asthma type of cough. He only starts wheezing if he's been running around.'

'Oh. So you're not saying you think he's inventing his symptoms? Because I can assure you—'

'No, that wasn't what I meant. I'm just saying that George assumes it's always asthma when he feels ill. But if it's *not* asthma...' She pauses again, giving me a meaningful look.

'...then what is it?' I finish for her. 'Yes, well, I'm hoping I might get some answers on Thursday.'

'Yes, you're taking him for a hospital appointment, aren't you. That's why I thought I should tell you our concerns. I hope you get some answers, Mrs Hudson, because he really doesn't seem very well lately.'

'Thank you. And I'll keep you informed.'

George looks at me warily as I go out into the playground.

'What did Mrs Austin want to talk to you about?' he asks.

'Well,' I say, keeping my tone light, 'she was telling me that you thought you had another asthma attack today.'

'I *did* have one. I had to go to Miss Brent and she gave me my inhaler.'

'Poor Georgie.' I give him a hug. He's coughing again, and I feel a shiver of fear. What *is* wrong with him, if even the school staff don't think it's necessarily asthma? But at least they believe him – at least *they* don't think we're just making too much fuss. Even if my own mother does.

* * *

I'm at work the next day when I have another call from Barbara.

'I know you're at work, love, but I just wondered if you could do me a favour,' she begins.

I feel my heart sink.

'Barbara, I really can't take any more time off at the moment.'

'I know. But luckily my appointment is at four o'clock. Would you be able to drop me off after you've picked the children up? I really don't think my knees would stand for it – walking to the bus stop and—'

'Is it a doctor's appointment? Are you in a lot of pain again?' I ask her.

'No. I mean, yes, I'm in pain, I'm always in pain, love, but it's no worse

If I Lost You 87

than usual. No, I've got to go to the Job Centre. Can you believe it? The doctor has apparently decided to stop signing me off for disability benefit, just because he's given me different tablets, I suppose. How ridiculous. As if I'm capable of going to work! So I need to tell them – they need to understand I can't possibly—'

'OK,' I say quickly. 'I'll pick you up as soon as I've collected the kids. You can tell me all about it then.'

'Thank you, love. I appreciate it.'

I spend the rest of the day worrying about this, on top of everything else. I lose concentration on my work, making mistakes, taking longer over everything. Nadia asks if I'm all right but I just nod and carry on worrying. What am I supposed to think about Barbara's situation? She's obviously genuinely in a lot of pain, otherwise the doctor wouldn't have prescribed the stronger painkillers. So I suppose he thinks that, because the painkillers are helping her, she's now going to be able to work. I presume up till now he's just kept on signing her off work without questioning it. I've always believed everyone should work if they're able, so I find it difficult now to align my views with my sympathy for Barbara. She never looks very well, to be honest, and I presume that's because of the pain of her arthritis. But what if the doctor's right? Should I be colluding in keeping her from working?

Then I give myself a little shake. No, there's no way she'd be putting on an act. I've seen how much pain she's in when she walks. I shouldn't be doubting her – I should be supporting her.

We've got behind with the work again and, knowing I'm going to take Thursday off without permission, I make a concerted effort to get through as much as I can today. I haven't yet given Nadia my answer about Saturday evening but she doesn't chase me up on it so I figure I can put the decision off for another couple of days. I make sure I'm in plenty of time to collect the children this afternoon, and I warn them that we've got to pick up Barbara and take her to an appointment.

'What's an appointment?' Molly asks.

'A date and time that you have to go somewhere,' I explain, starting the car.

'Where's she got to go?'

88   SHEILA NORTON

'To a place where they sort out whether people can go to work, and try to find them a job if they can.'

'Is Granny going to go to work?' Molly squawks. 'I thought you said she wasn't well enough.'

'Well, yes, that is what I think. But we'll have to see what they say at the appointment.'

Barbara's waiting outside for us, as usual, and comes slowly towards the car as I get out to help her in. She's hobbling badly, using a stick.

'Hello, you two,' she says, turning to smile at the children once she's settled into her seat. 'How are you both?'

'All right, thank you,' Molly says.

'I'm tired. I wanted to go home,' George says.

'Aw, well, I hope we won't be too long,' she says.

Luckily there's a car park almost opposite the Job Centre.

'You can just drop me here and come back later, if you need to get the children home,' Barbara says. I've had to help her out of the car again and she's leaning heavily on her stick, struggling just from the effort of standing upright.

'No, I think I'd better stay with you. You can hardly walk. I thought the new tablets were helping?'

'Not as much as I'd hoped.' She doesn't argue as I take her arm, holding George's hand on the other side, and we slowly cross the road at the pedestrian lights.

'I don't think you'll be allowed to come in with me,' she says once we're inside, in the waiting area, and I've managed to find her a seat, 'not with the kids.'

I glance at the children, who are staring around the room, fascinated by the assortment of people in here – old, young, all of them presumably out of work. I have a momentary, frightening, image of myself sitting here with them all, desperately seeking a new job if Trevor actually carries his threat to its conclusion.

'No, you're probably right,' I concede.

Molly's looking at the posters on the wall, trying to read them.

'What sort of job do you want to do?' she asks Barbara. 'Would you like to work in an office, like Mummy?'

If I Lost You · 89

'Or be a teacher, like Daddy?' says George.

'Well...' Barbara looks stumped for words for a moment, but fortunately her name's being called out now and she struggles to her feet, hobbling slowly into the room she's being directed to.

The children then spend the next few minutes arguing with each other about what job they think Barbara ought to do. Molly's trying to make sensible suggestions and she's getting annoyed by George, who's deliberately coming out with outlandish ideas.

'Policeman,' he shouts.

'She's not a *man*, George,' Molly says. 'She'd have to be a police*woman*.'

'We just say *police officer*,' I tell her.

'Fireman,' George interrupts excitedly. 'I mean fire woman. Fire officer.'

'She couldn't climb up a ladder, could she?' Molly says with exasperation. 'Say something sensible, George. Like a librarian. That would be good, wouldn't it, Mummy? She could sit down, and just check the books in and out.'

'I don't actually think Granny will be able to get a job,' I warn them. 'She's too disabled.'

'What's de-stabled?' George asks.

'Disabled, stupid,' Molly says. 'It means you can't do stuff. Or you've got, like, a *condition*.'

'Molly called me stupid, Mummy,' George says, giving her a push.

'Ow! Don't push me, George. You *are* stupid, and now you're being a crybaby again.'

People in the room are looking at us – unsurprisingly. If we were at home I'd be raising my voice by now, probably sending them both to their rooms to calm down. But it's never that easy in public, besides which, I know they're both tired from school, missing their usual drink and biscuit, and they're bored.

'Behave yourselves, please,' I say in my quiet-but-deadly voice. 'Molly, don't call your brother stupid, please – he's not. George, stop crying, nobody's hurting you. Here's Granny now,' I add, with relief. 'We can go home.'

Barbara hobbles across the room to us, looking in surprise at George's red, tearstained face and Molly's scowling, resentful one.

'What's all this about?' she says. 'Who's upset you?'

'Molly,' George says, wiping his eyes.

'George,' Molly says. 'He pushed me.'

'She called me stupid.'

'All right,' I say, forgetting to keep the volume down this time. 'That's enough. Outside, both of you.'

None of us say any more until we're back in the car. Then I turn to Barbara and ask her quietly how she got on.

'Well, the girl who interviewed me seemed to think it's pretty obvious I can't be expected to work. But she says her hands are tied if the doctor doesn't sign me off again. If he doesn't, I'll have to sign on for the dole.'

'Jobseeker's Allowance. Then they'd expect you to *look* for work, at least.'

'Well, that's not going to happen,' she says, surprisingly confidently. 'Because I'm going back to the surgery, and I'm going to show the doctor how bad I still am, and he'll sign me off sick again.'

I'm not sure how to respond to this. I just hope she's right. We drive most of the way back to Barbara's place in silence now, until, just as we turn into her road, George asks, 'What are you going to be, Granny? I said a fire officer, but—'

'I said a librarian. I think that's the best, don't you, Granny?' Molly interrupts him.

Barbara turns round and smiles at them both. 'I think I'm just going to be a granny, that's all, if that's all right with you both?'

'Yay!' George shouts.

'But that's not a *job*,' Molly says.

Fortunately I'm now pulling up outside Barbara's flat and I get out of the car to help her out, so there's no need for the conversation to go any further – until we set off again for home, at least, and by now the children are both more interested in the subject of biscuits.

'You're late, aren't you?' Ben says, opening the front door before I've even had a chance to put the key in. He must have heard the car pull up. I wasn't expecting him to be home yet.

'Yes. Barbara asked me to take her to the Job Centre.'

'The *Job* Centre?' He raises his eyebrows in surprise. 'She's looking for a job?'

'She might be a fire officer,' George says eagerly.

'No she's *not,* George,' Molly says. 'She says she only wants to be a granny, remember?'

'She was called in for an appointment,' I say, 'to check that she gets the right benefits. She just needs her doctor's confirmation again, that's all.'

I'm not meeting Ben's eyes as I hang up my coat and head for the kitchen. Why not? Why can't I be honest with him and admit I'm wondering exactly what I'm sure he's thinking: that perhaps there *are* sitting-down jobs that Barbara could do, and could have been doing already, even with her arthritis. I feel disloyal even wondering about it myself, so I don't want to hear Ben echoing my own thoughts. She's had a hard life, she's in a lot of pain; if she needs to be on benefits now to get by, then she should have them, and I'm happy to support her.

15

George collapses on the sofa after dinner and the cat jumps up to lie on his lap. He's still coughing, looking like it's wearing him out.

'George, you can't have the cat lying on your chest while you're coughing like that,' Ben says at once, walking into the lounge and lifting Ebony off him.

'But, Daddy, he makes me feel better,' George complains. 'Mummy says—'

Ben turns to me, barely able to control his annoyance. 'It'd be a good idea if you mention the cat to this paediatrician you're seeing on Thursday.'

'Yes, OK, I will. But until anyone says—'

'It can't be helping him, having a furry animal lying on top of him,' he interrupts crossly. 'I don't care what you say.'

'All right, Ben.' I get it, I know he's worried, just as much as I am, but talking like this in front of George is really not good, or helpful. 'Leave it, please. I'll discuss it at the appointment, OK?'

'I wish I'd tried to put something in place to get the morning off myself, to come with you, but it's too close to the GCSEs, and there's no cover.'

'It's fine. It doesn't need both of us. I've said I'll take him.'

'Is Trevor all right about it?'

'Yes.'

If I Lost You   93

I'm outright lying to him now, but I've had enough for today. I don't want any more arguments or discussions about Trevor and how I should look for another job. I haven't got the energy. I'm too tired, too worried, too sad about everything.

'Mrs Austin told me today that even *she*'s wondering whether it's asthma,' I tell him once we're out of the children's earshot.

'Did she?' He frowns at me. 'Well, if it's not even asthma, we don't actually know at all if the cat might be causing it, whatever it is.'

I give up.

* * *

'I don't want to go to school,' George starts complaining as soon as he comes downstairs for breakfast the next morning. 'I was coughing all night, I couldn't sleep.'

My heart sinks. 'Come on, George. You'll be having tomorrow morning off anyway, to go to the hospital.'

'But it's PE today, Mummy. I don't want to do it, I always end up having to sit out because I get out of breath, and sometimes people laugh at me.'

'Perhaps we should ask for him to be excluded from PE,' Ben suggests.

'They always let him sit out if he can't keep going. Let's see what the doctor says tomorrow, George, OK? Come on. You'll be all right when you get there.'

'OK,' he says in a little, sad voice. I feel mean enough as it is, without the look of martyrdom on his face when we finally leave the house, but I'm relieved to see that he walks into class without any further protest.

It takes me longer than usual to get from the school to my work. I'm probably only five minutes or so late by the time I arrive, but unfortunately Trevor happens to be in the office as I come in, and he's in a bad mood. He makes a great show of looking at his watch, before turning to stare at me as I sit down at my desk, flustered, still in my jacket.

'Isn't it strange, ladies,' he says, addressing Nadia and May, 'how you all manage to turn up here, every day, well before nine o'clock, and work a full day without being constantly interrupted by phone calls from your families and having to take time off for so-called emergencies? And yet your *friend* here, who only works part-time, seems to have trouble telling the time, even when she deigns to give us the pleasure of her company for more than half a day at a time? I'd find that *very annoying* if I were in your shoes, having to work twice as hard to compensate for somebody else's lack of commitment to the job.'

'That's not fair, Trevor,' Nadia says. 'Jo's got young children, the rest of us haven't. And you know her son often has to go to hospital.'

'So does her mother, it seems. And I don't suppose she's the only one of you who's got a mother.'

I wriggle out of my coat while I'm turning on my computer. I can feel my face burning with humiliation as well as the smart of unfairness. Five minutes, for God's sake! I know I'm not the only one who's occasionally held up by traffic. Pauline's on leave this week, but I can feel May looking at me, probably thinking Trevor's got a point, that they're all having to cover for me by picking up my work. It's not exactly true, but we do share the work, so however hard I try to catch up, I know it makes it harder for us all if anyone's not here. I know Trevor's deliberately trying to show me up and turn the others against me, and I'd like to answer him back, but that would only make matters worse, so I just keep my head down over my work until he stalks out of the room, muttering angrily to himself.

'Thank you for sticking up for me,' I say to Nadia after he's gone. 'Five minutes, honestly. The traffic was awful.'

'He's just in a bad mood. It's not really about you,' Nadia says quietly. 'Apparently he's lost one of our clients, and head office have been having a go at him.'

'He'll take it out on me, though, whether I'm at fault or not,' I say grimly.

'We all just need to keep our heads down today.'

'He's got a point, though, hasn't he,' May bursts out suddenly. 'I mean, it's not really fair. The rest of us all have to get here on time every day. We all have problems with the traffic, it's not just you.'

'I know, I know, I'm sorry,' I say. 'It's just – I have to drop the children at school.'

'You're not the only person in the world who's had children,' May retorts. 'We've all been there. You just have to organise your time properly.

If I Lost You 95

And if your son or your mother keep needing you to do things for them, perhaps you should stay at home and put your family first.'

'That's a horrible thing to say,' Nadia exclaims. 'I don't know what your problem is. None of us come to work for the fun of it; we need the money. Jo always makes up for whatever time she's had to take off, or she takes it out of her annual leave. And she works twice as hard as you or Pauline do. It's not *just* about being here early, if all you do when you get here is sit at your desks gossiping about your husbands.'

May gives a gasp of indignation. But I'm just looking down at my lap, trying to fight the urge to put my head on my desk and cry. It's good of Nadia to be so supportive, and everything she says is true, but it hurts to have my fears confirmed: to have it spelt out that our other two colleagues have been resenting me, thinking I'm not pulling my weight. And it's only going to add fuel to the fire if Trevor's listening to all this from his office. I do exactly as Nadia has suggested, keeping my head down and getting on with my work all day. I don't stop for tea or even take a lunch break, and when it's time to leave for the school run, I wait till the last possible minute.

'Jo,' Nadia says quietly just as I'm logging off, 'have you given it any more thought?'

'What?' I ask distractedly.

'What I asked you about.' She lowers her voice. 'Letting me say I'm staying over at yours, babysitting, on Saturday.'

'Oh.' I haven't, of course, given it any thought. I haven't had a free minute to think about anything, let alone someone else's problem. I don't like this, and I want to say no. In fact I'm just about to – to make up some excuse to get out of it – when I think about how she stuck up for me yet again this morning, how nice it was of her to be so supportive. How nice she *always* is. And I look at the clock – I'm cutting it fine; I'm going to be late for the kids – and I close my eyes and just say it.

'OK. OK, yes, whatever.'

'Oh, thank you so much,' she says, and the light, the excitement in her eyes, reminds me for a moment of how it felt to be twenty-two and imagining yourself to be in love. She drops her voice again so that the others can't hear, and adds, 'I hope it goes OK tomorrow. Don't worry – I've got your back, if anything's said.'

'Thanks, love.'

* * *

All evening I keep thinking about what I've promised Nadia – what I wish I *hadn't* promised. I wonder how to mention it to Ben, but then realise I don't have to – he never needs to know. It seems Nadia's husband will believe anything she tells him, as long as it involves me – the older, trustable woman. I find myself feeling sorry for him. OK, so it might not be a good marriage, but it sounds dull rather than being particularly horrible. I can understand why it's not enough for Nadia but I'd bet anything she's jumping out of the frying pan into the fire with this Zach.

'What are you thinking about?' Ben asks me suddenly. 'You look like you're miles away. Are you worried about George's appointment tomorrow?'

'Well, yes, I am a bit,' I say, quickly putting Nadia and her love life out of my mind. 'But on the other hand, I'm glad we're finally getting to see somebody who might understand what's wrong. Whether it really is asthma and he just needs different meds.'

'Or not,' Ben says sombrely. 'What... I mean, have you got any thoughts about what it might be, if it *isn't* asthma?'

'Of course I haven't,' I say, a little abruptly. 'I'm not a doctor. Even Dr Jackson didn't seem to be able to suggest anything. That's why we're seeing a specialist.'

He raises his eyebrows at my tone, and I regret it, but I know I'm only being snappy because the thought of what's wrong with George if it isn't asthma is too scary to contemplate. I wonder whether Ben – who might be a science teacher but isn't a doctor any more than I am – has any thoughts on it himself, but he doesn't say anything and I don't want to ask him.

'Well then,' he says, throwing down the tea towel and heading off to turn on the TV, 'I guess we'll just have to see what happens tomorrow.'

16

The next morning, as soon as Ben's left to drop Molly off at school, I call Trevor to tell him I've been sick.

'I hope you're not pregnant,' he comments rudely.

'Perhaps I want to be,' I shoot back. Not that I do, obviously, but how can he be allowed to say things like that?

'Have you got a sick note from your doctor?'

'No. I don't need to, just for one day, as I'm sure you know.' I've decided my excuse will be more realistic if I take the whole day off.

Needless to say, he doesn't wish me better. We both know I'm lying, but he can't prove it. I'm uncomfortable with it – I don't like inventing illness. But what the hell can I do, when Trevor's being so unreasonable?

A little later, George and I are on the tube, heading to the hospital where the paediatrician's based, when I suddenly become aware of somebody further up the carriage staring at me. I look up, just as the woman who was watching me turns away. She's fumbling with something in her bag. For a moment, away from our usual setting, I can't think where I recognise her from, but within seconds I realise it's Pauline, from work. She's on her annual leave, probably off to meet friends or visit her adult children. She's seen me, and I'm supposed to be sick – but at least she wasn't there when I asked Trevor for the morning off and he refused. I wonder, briefly, about trying to talk to her – to concoct some story, in case she mentions seeing me when she comes back next week. I could say I was going to the hospital myself because I felt so sick. But no – that just sounds ridiculous, especially as I've got George with me. Just as I'm debating this the train comes to a stop at the next station and Pauline gets out, and she's on the platform, walking towards the exit before I can think it through any further. What's she going to do, anyway – tell Trevor she's seen me on a train? Why would she? She doesn't even know I'm supposed to be throwing up at home.

'I don't want to see a new doctor,' George says, and I just sigh and give him what I hope is a reassuring smile. The nearer we get to the hospital, the more anxious I'm getting myself, and I don't want George to pick up on it.

* * *

Dr Taylor turns out to be a lovely man. He talks to George as much as he talks to me.

'So, how are you, George?' he asks.

'All right,' George says quietly, looking at the floor. 'I didn't want to come.'

'Oh, why's that?'

He shrugs awkwardly. 'I feel all right today. But sometimes I don't.'

'What happens when you don't feel right?' Dr Taylor asks gently.

'I have asthma attacks. I have them in the middle of the night sometimes, and when I'm playing, and I have them a lot when I'm at school. Specially in PE.'

'What happens in PE when you get an attack?'

'I can't breathe. I have to sit out, and sometimes people laugh at me.'

'Oh, no. That's not nice, is it, George,' he says sympathetically. He turns to me. 'How long has he been treated for asthma?'

'Since he was three.'

'And his GP says in his referral that George has been tested for allergies and nothing was found.'

'That's right. My husband seems to think the cat might be—'

If I Lost You

99

'Daddy doesn't think I should have Ebony on my lap,' George interrupts.

'Ah, well, I think if George was allergic to cats it would have shown up on the tests.'

'Yes,' I say, smiling for a moment. Then I remember why we're really here, and go on, 'But even with his inhalers, and his tablets, George isn't getting any better.'

'He's still having frequent attacks?'

'Yes. But...' I frown. Are the attacks actually more frequent, or are they just... different? 'He's got this awful cough – it never seems to clear up. We've talked to the pharmacist, and tried different types of cough medicine, but nothing touches it. He wheezes mostly when he's running around – that's when he gets really short of breath. He actually goes a funny colour.'

'Blueish?' Dr Taylor suggests.

'Well, yes, I suppose so. But it's the cough that never really lets up. He's got it all the time, not just when he's wheezing or having a full-blown attack. And, well, he's just so tired all the time, too.'

'I'm not surprised, if he's constantly coughing. And if any form of exercise makes him wheeze – that's enough to make anyone tired, eh, George?'

George nods, looking pleased that the doctor seems to understand.

'I get very tired,' he confirms. 'Sometimes I can't sleep because I keep coughing, and sometimes I wake up wheezing and have to have my inhaler.'

'And does the inhaler help?'

'Usually,' I say. 'It calms the wheezing, but the cough...'

'The cough doesn't go away.' Dr Taylor nods. 'So, your GP's now wondering if it's really asthma or something else. As you know, asthma can be quite serious – I see from his notes that George has had to be rushed to hospital on several occasions. But of course, asthma isn't the only condition that can cause these kinds of symptoms. I take it he's been vaccinated against whooping cough?'

'Yes.'

'Good. So we need to work out what else it might be if it *isn't* asthma.

Jump up for me, would you, George, so I can have a look at you? Would you mind taking your shirt off for me? Thanks, buddy.'

He smiles at George and makes a thing about warming up his stethoscope before placing it on his chest. I look at my boy – my sweet child, so little, so skinny and pale – and, as if I'm seeing him for the first time, I suddenly realise: he's *too* skinny, *too* pale. He's shorter than nearly all the other kids in his class. My heart misses a beat. Should I have been worried about this? I've always thought he was just small for his age.

'He's quite small for his age, isn't he,' the doctor says, as if he's been following my thoughts. 'Does he eat well?'

'Yes. Well, normally. You know, like all kids, he can be fussy, but he's got a pretty good appetite.' I know I'm trying to convince the doctor George is just a normal little boy, that there's nothing abnormal about his height, or his weight, or his poor skinny, pale little body, even though I can see quite plainly, as he's being examined, that George's chest muscles seem to have to pull too hard with every breath. Am I trying to convince the doctor there's nothing out of the ordinary about my son – or convince myself?

Dr Taylor glances at me, and I see the concern in his eyes, despite his smile and his reassuring tone, as he says, 'Well, we're going to have to get some tests done, before we know whether there's anything other than asthma going on.'

'What kind of tests? And what do you *think* might be going on, doctor?'

'I'll have to take some blood from him, I'm sorry to say – we can get that done today. And then I'll get him seen at the Lung Function Unit at Great Ormond Street. They'll do some lung tests on him and report back to me before I see you both again – or they might actually take George over as their patient.'

'So you can't tell me anything more today?'

'I'm afraid not. But what you can be doing in the meantime is filling in this questionnaire.' He hands me a couple of printed sheets, the first of which is headed *Family and Medical Questionnaire*. 'That'll be extremely useful in helping us toward a diagnosis.'

'You think it's something inherited? I had childhood asthma myself,' I tell him eagerly, 'but I grew out of it.'

'That's one possibility, of course – put it down on the sheet,' he encour-

If I Lost You

ages me. 'But I don't think it's *necessarily* something inherited. We just need to rule everything out.'

'But... you don't think it's just asthma?' I persist.

He looks me squarely in the eyes. I can see the sympathy there. I guess he's probably a father himself.

'At the moment, Mrs Hudson, I don't know anything for sure. But I'm concerned enough to think it's quite possible it could be something other than asthma, yes. Until we get these tests done – urgently, I hope – we're best to keep treating it as asthma. That certainly can't do any harm. And let George rest when he needs to. The school should be told that. PE is good for him, of course, but if he's tired, coughing, wheezing or distressed at all, he should be sitting out. Would you like me to write you a note for the school?'

'No. No, they're being very good, they won't disagree with that.'

George, fortunately, has lost interest in the conversation now and is putting his shirt back on, and looking at me impatiently, wanting to go.

'Get his bloods taken now. Follow the signs outside, or the nurse will show you the way,' he says kindly. 'And you'll hear from the Lung Function Unit—'

'Doctor Taylor,' I interrupt him, my voice shaking as I start to get to my feet. 'Tell me honestly: do you think it's something serious?'

He looks back, straight into my eyes.

'It might be.' Then he stands up to take my hand, managing a little smile before adding, 'But let's not think like that yet. It could equally well still be asthma.'

* * *

'What was he talking to you about?' George asks. 'I didn't understand.'

We're sitting in the café at the hospital, having hot chocolate and a toasted teacake. It's the treat I promised him while he was crying about having his blood taken. I don't know how to answer him now; I'm struggling even to make a show of eating and drinking. I'm still feeling too shaky, too conscious of the look in Dr Taylor's eyes as he replied to my question about whether George's condition could be serious – and his response, uttered kindly but sombrely, as if he wanted me to know, to understand and take on board the likelihood of it. *It might be.*

'Oh, just about how difficult it is to decide why you're coughing so much,' I finally manage.

'Did he say it's Ebony's fault, like Daddy does?'

'No. He says it's definitely not Ebony's fault.'

'Good.' He smiles. 'Can we take a treat home for Molly, please, Mummy? It's not fair if she gets left out.'

'That'd be nice,' I agree, giving him a shaky smile. My little boy – my brave little soldier whose thin, pale body I see every day but looked at today, for the first time, through the eyes of somebody who understands, who knows he should be bigger, sturdier, have more energy at five years old and who suspects it's *something serious.*

Then I give myself a little shake. I can't do this – I can't give in to my darkest, scariest thoughts. Didn't Dr Jackson also say it might equally still be asthma? George needs me to be strong, to be cheerful and reassuring and keep up a pretence of normality. He needs me to be positive. *I* need to be positive. I take a bite of my teacake, forcing myself to pretend to enjoy it.

* * *

I parked the car close to the tube station when we set off, so that I can drop George back at school on the way home. I feel strangely at a loss. I should be going back to work – I would be, if Trevor wasn't being so difficult. As it is, I've got to spend the rest of the day at home on my own, trying to keep busy, trying to keep the fear at bay. I put the hoover round and then decide to clean the windows, and the physical activity helps to calm me slightly. Before I've even finished, it's time to go back for the children.

'We got you a Kit Kat, Molly,' George tells her when she comes out of her classroom, 'because we had hot chocolate at the hospital, didn't we, Mummy? And it wouldn't have been fair if you didn't get a treat too.'

'Thank you,' Molly says, looking surprised. 'What did your doctor say?'

'Not much,' he says with a shrug. 'But I had to have a needle stuck in my arm and they filled up a tube with all my blood.'

Molly gasps, looking horrified but fascinated at the same time. 'All your blood?'

'Not all of it,' I say, smiling at them both. 'Only a little bit.'

'Why?' Molly says, but George just shrugs and proceeds to describe how much it hurt, having the needle in his arm, and how he was told he was really brave, the bravest boy they'd had all week, and was given a sticker to prove it.

And as I listen to him chattering away, with no sign of his cough at the moment, no wheezing, no obvious signs of tiredness or that scary blue tinge to his skin, my terror starts to ebb away a little. Surely it can't be anything serious? He seems perfectly OK... He's perfectly OK most of the time, isn't he? It'll surely turn out to simply be asthma. He'll grow out of it. It'll be fine. That's what I'm going to believe: it'll all be fine.

17

'How did you get on with George at the hospital?' Ben asks as soon as he comes in.

I give him a very brief summary, deliberately missing out the part about it possibly being something serious. I'll tell him that later, after the kids are in bed. However positive I'm trying to be, I'm too afraid I'll start crying if I actually have to say those words out loud.

'So he still thinks it's probably asthma?' Ben says, sounding exasperated. 'So it was just Dr Jackson being over-cautious?'

'Possibly. But it's always best to have the opinion of a specialist, isn't it. Anyway, George needs to have some further tests.' I lower my voice. 'I'll tell you more later.'

He nods in agreement and goes to talk to the children. I can hear George telling the story of his blood test all over again, and Ben laughing and saying how brave he must have been, and I know he won't be laughing when I tell him the full story. But I'm unprepared for exactly how he does react when finally, after dinner and when I'm sure both children are asleep, I sit down next to him, turn down the volume on the TV and repeat what Dr Taylor told me.

'So what does he think it is, if it isn't asthma?' Ben demands.

'I don't know. I don't think he knows himself yet.'

If I Lost You   105

'Well, that's not bloody good enough, is it? He's *paid* to know. What's the point in seeing a specialist if he doesn't know what the hell he's doing?'

'Ben, be reasonable. I've told you: George has to have some tests done before they can make a diagnosis. He's got to go to Great Ormond Street for them. We have to think positive.'

'Do we?' he retorts angrily. 'Well, it doesn't *sound* very positive to me – all that about how he's small for his age and everything – what's he implying? That we don't feed him properly? That we're not looking after him?'

'No. He didn't say anything of the sort. Calm down, Ben.'

'Calm down? You're telling me this guy thinks there's something seriously wrong with my son—'

'*Our* son,' I correct him, wiping tears from my eyes. 'And he only said it *might* be serious, but it might equally well not be.'

'In other words, he doesn't know. Right. So we need to go private, that's obvious. Find someone better qualified. Get these tests done quicker.'

'They won't be done any faster, Ben. He's assured me it will be urgent.'

'Like this appointment was supposed to be urgent, and still you had to chase it up? It's no good waiting for the NHS, Jo, they couldn't care less if our son lives or—'

'Stop it!' I shout, giving up now on the fight to hold back the tears as well as the struggle to stay calm. 'Don't talk like that. The tests *will* be urgent, he's promised me, and he *is* properly qualified; we'd probably get the same doctor and the same tests if we forked out all the money in the world.'

'So you're not prepared to pay whatever it takes to save George's life,' he says.

'We haven't even *got* whatever it would take. But it's irrelevant. If his life was actually in danger he'd have been admitted to hospital there and then. Look, you're upset – so am I. But we need to stay positive. Yes, Ben, we do, for George's sake. We need to have these tests done and then find out what's actually wrong, before we make any more decisions.'

'Well, if the tests aren't done quickly, I'll—'

'They will be. Dr Taylor promised me, and I'll keep on top of it, all right? I'll chase it up if we don't hear anything.'

He nods, still looking disgruntled. 'Have it your way, as usual,' he mutters.

I just shake my head and get up to make a cup of tea. I know our marriage hasn't exactly been a bed of roses lately, but I'd have hoped that, in the face of something like this, we might have been able to present a united front. I'd hoped we might actually have hugged each other, tried to comfort each other. But no – all we've done is argue again. I really do wonder why we're still together – and I'm shocked to realise the thought doesn't even upset me. I'm getting resigned to it.

* * *

As soon as I arrive at work the next day, Trevor calls me into his office.

'I presume you're feeling better?' he says, an edge of sarcasm to his voice.

'Yes, thank you.'

'Well enough to take your son to his hospital appointment, were you? But not well enough to come to work.'

'No,' I say. 'I told you, I was sick. I couldn't take him.'

He passes his phone across the desk to me. 'Funny, that,' he smirks. 'Because I could have sworn this was you. On the tube yesterday morning. With a child. You were taking your son to his appointment, weren't you: the appointment I *didn't* give you time off for.'

It's a photo showing, as he says, a picture of me and George on the tube. It's a bit fuzzy because it's been zoomed in, but there's absolutely no doubt, no point whatsoever in denying, that it's me.

'Where did this come from?' I demand shakily, passing the phone back to him. But of course, I know the answer perfectly well. Pauline was on the tube, in the same carriage as me, and I'd seen her fumbling with something in her bag. It was her phone. That nasty, spiteful cow has taken a photo of me and sent it to Trevor. I'm so shocked that someone – anyone – could actually hate me enough to do this, that I've completely lost the ability to say anything else.

Trevor hands me an envelope, pretending now to look apologetic.

'Your written warning,' he says. 'It's a pity. I'd been thinking that

If I Lost You

perhaps the warning of giving you this might have been enough; I'm not an unreasonable man, and I'd thought perhaps I'd hold fire for a while and see if things improved. But now, well, you've left me no choice, frankly. By rights, I should have given you this and a second one already and we'd now be talking about instant dismissal.'

The word *dismissal* makes me shudder, and somehow I recover my voice.

'I *had* to take him. I'm sorry, but I had no alternative.'

'I might have been more generous,' he says, ignoring this, 'if you hadn't already been so unreliable, so often, but frankly the situation simply hasn't been fair to your colleagues, which has been clearly demonstrated by the fact that someone has had to, very reluctantly I might add, forward this *evidence* to me.'

'Reluctantly? I'm sure she was delighted to do it.'

'I don't expect there to be any unpleasantness with your colleagues, as a result of someone having provided this evidence,' he warns me, leaning across the desk now and fixing me with a threatening look. 'I hope that's understood.'

Evidence. I snarl inwardly as I get up and shuffle off back to my office in disgrace. Who does he think he is – chief inspector of the Met? Head of the CID?

'Are you OK?' Nadia asks, looking at me in concern.

'Not really.' I wave the envelope at her. 'Trevor has been "not unreasonable" enough to give me this, because *somebody* – who I mustn't be unpleasant about – has been unpleasant enough to take a photo of me and George on the tube and send it to him.'

I put my head in my hands, trying not to cry. Oh, God, what do I sound like? I feel like I've degenerated over the last couple of months into a naughty schoolgirl who's hated by the rest of the class.

I rip open the brown envelope and pull the sheet of paper out. I can feel May's eyes on me across the room. I wouldn't be surprised if she's in on this too – she's just as much of a bitch as her nasty, bitchy friend. But if anything, this just makes me even more determined to read the damned thing out, in front of her, rather than take it home to read, as if I'm ashamed of it.

First Written Warning, the paper's headed.

Dear Mrs Hudson

I am writing to inform you that, following numerous verbal warnings, a first Written Warning is hereby placed on your file, for the following reasons: persistent poor timekeeping and short-notice absences. If there are further incidences of either of these behaviours while this notice is on your file, you will receive a Second Written Warning. If you wish to appeal against this decision, you will need to do so within seven days.

Kind regards,

Trevor Milligan, General Manager

In the circumstances, it's probably weird that the first words I can utter are '*Kind regards*? Is he having a laugh?'

But to my annoyance, however hard I try to keep up a pretence of treating the whole thing with contempt, my eyes start to fill up with tears. Nadia jumps to her feet to put an arm around me.

'Ah, don't cry, love. He's an idiot, a nasty piece of work. He won't fire you. He needs you too much, he knows that. You're the best worker here.'

'It's just one thing on top of another,' I mutter. 'Sorry. I'm all right.'

'How did it go at the hospital?' she asks gently. But I just shake my head. I can't talk about it – even to Nadia – let alone with the smirking madam across the room from us listening in.

We need to get on with our work. But I've seriously got to start looking for another job now.

18

Saturday morning. I turn over in bed, relieved to know there's no work today. I haven't mentioned the warning letter to Ben, and I realise I probably won't; there's enough antagonism between us already. Keeping up my attempt to be cheerful and positive, I smile and agree when he suggests he takes the kids to the park after breakfast, and I sit down to call Mum. I'm still trying to keep my tone cheerful as I describe the hospital appointment, and she interrupts as soon as I tell her Dr Taylor said it was still quite likely George's problem was asthma.

'Of course it is,' she says. 'Didn't I tell you? It's obvious it's asthma.'

'But Mum, he also said that it *might* be something more serious. That's why he wants George to have these lung tests done.'

'He's probably just getting the tests done to keep you happy,' she insists, laughing. Actually *laughing*, when all I need is to be taken seriously and perhaps shown a bit of sympathy by my mother. 'Because you insist on thinking the worst, making a big issue out of it, when it's perfectly clear it's childhood asthma and he'll grow out of it, like most children.'

'Dr Jackson wouldn't have sent me to a paediatrician,' I insist, 'if he didn't think it *might* be something else. It was his suggestion that it might be something else – not mine. Why are you so determined to believe I'm being an over-fussy mother? Why can't you support me in this?'

'Because,' she says, sounding like the effort of being patient with me is straining her to her limits, 'I'd know if there was something seriously wrong with my grandson. He's a perfectly healthy little boy who's, unfortunately, got childhood asthma. That's it.'

'You don't want to think about it, do you?' I suddenly realise. 'That's what this is – you're in denial. You'd rather close your eyes to it than face facts. Well, I'd like to do that too, Mum, but I can't. I've got to acknowledge that there might be something seriously wrong, but I've still got to try to stay positive, and I just wish there was someone, anyone, in this family who'd support me in that.'

I don't feel proud of myself for hanging up on her. But, if anything, the conversation has strengthened my resolve to put my own feelings to one side and cope with this situation as well as I can. Ben's too angry, Mum's in denial; I'll handle it on my own. Then I have another thought: perhaps I'll try talking to Barbara, instead. I haven't spoken to her since taking her shopping last weekend and perhaps she'll be a bit more sympathetic than Mum was.

She picks up straight away as usual, and seems pleased to hear from me. She's silent throughout my description of the appointment with Dr Taylor, and when I finish speaking, she simply says, 'Poor George. And poor you. You must feel so worried, love.'

'I am,' I say, sighing with relief that, at last, somebody seems to be on my side. 'But I'm trying not to show George I'm worried, obviously. And until we get the tests done on his lungs, we don't know anything for sure. We're hoping, of course, that it is still asthma, nothing worse.'

'Of course. Let's hope that's how it turns out. Well, it sounds like George is in good hands; the doctor sounds very thorough.'

'Yes. Thank you, Barbara.'

'I'm just wondering,' she says quickly before I can end the call, 'if you and Ben would like an evening off. You must both feel so stressed – what if I come over to babysit for you tonight and you can go out for a little drink or a meal together?'

'Oh.' This is so unexpected that I can't even reply straight away.

'It'll do you both good,' she goes on, 'and I'd love to spend an evening with the children. What do you think?'

If I Lost You

'Really? You wouldn't mind?'

'Of course I wouldn't. You've done enough for me, haven't you, giving me lifts and dinners, and helping me with the shopping.' She pauses. 'Speaking of which, I could really do with a few more things from the supermarket this weekend.'

I laugh. 'Well, OK, I think that'd be a good bargain; I'll take you shopping this afternoon, and you babysit for us later.'

'Deal,' she agrees.

I feel better as I hang up, thinking about having an evening out. I can't remember when Ben and I last went out together. Perhaps it'll give us a chance to talk things over more calmly.

'It doesn't have to be an expensive meal,' I say when Ben and the children are finally home from the park and I tell him about Barbara's offer. 'In fact, why don't we eat here and just go out for a couple of drinks?'

'One of us will have to take Barbara home afterwards.'

'She could stay overnight.'

He raises his eyebrows. 'Really?'

'Well, why not? It's only fair, then she won't have to stay up late waiting for us to get home.'

'The kids will have to sleep in the same room.'

'That's all right. Just for one night, they won't mind.'

'OK, then.' He looks back at me. I'm sure he's as aware as I am that we need to have a proper, calmer talk together. 'If you think the children will be all right with it. Does she know this latest stuff about George?'

'Yes, I've told her. And I'm sure they'll both be pleased to have Granny looking after them again.' George will, anyway.

'And you can trust her, can you? After what happened before, when she upset Molly?'

'I'm sure she's got the message now about that.'

'OK,' he says again. He doesn't sound particularly happy about it, but let's face it, neither of us are feeling happy at the moment. I'm just hoping that we'll be able to discuss our feelings a bit more honestly tonight without having to worry about the children overhearing.

'How was George while you were out?' I ask while we're getting lunch ready.

He shakes his head, sighing. 'We tried to play football, but he couldn't chase after the ball at all. He was so breathless, he could hardly even walk. It's not right, Jo. It wasn't an asthma attack – he wasn't wheezing this time, just out of breath. I'm telling you, we need this dealt with urgently. And can't we get him some medicine for that cough?'

'He's had medicine. We've tried every type the pharmacist can suggest,' I remind him wearily. 'You shouldn't have been encouraging him to run after the ball if he was feeling breathless.'

'I'm trying to give him a normal childhood,' he retorts.

'Well, that might not be possible. Not until we know more. Don't look at me like that,' I add. 'I'm just trying to be realistic and do the best thing for George at the same time.'

'So am I,' he says, sounding hurt. 'Of course I am, but… it's not easy.'

This is the point where we should be in each other's arms, comforting each other, agreeing to work together to do the best for our son. But he turns away from me, and the moment is gone.

* * *

I take Barbara to Lidl again and, as before, at the checkout she pulls a wad of notes out of her purse and, again, she's slightly short. She acts surprised, looking guilty as I stump up the difference, and says she'll pay me back as soon as her benefits are paid in. This reminds me to ask her whether she's heard any more from the Job Centre.

'My doctor agreed to sign me off again,' she says. 'He says the practice manager looked at my case, that's why I got sent to the Job Centre, but *he* thinks it's ridiculous expecting me to look for a job in my condition. At my age.'

'But it's quite a few years yet until you get your state pension, isn't it?'

'About six. I know I'm fortunate to have my NHS pension, but that's not much. Not enough to live on.'

I'm surprised. I always thought the NHS pension was supposed to be pretty good, but perhaps it's not enough on its own.

By the time we get back to her place and I've helped her unpack everything, I decide I might as well take her straight home with me, ready for this evening. As I pull up outside the house, Barbara touches my hand and says, quietly, 'Don't worry. I won't say anything to George about his hospital appointment. It's probably best for him if we keep off the subject for now, isn't it?'

'It is, yes – thank you.' Again, I'm touched by her concern and the gentle way she's showing her support for me – so unlike the implied criticism from my own mum and the blame game going on between Ben and me.

The kids both seem pleased to see their granny again.

'She won't just be looking after you, this time, George,' Molly tells him smugly. 'She's going to be here for both of us, OK?'

'OK,' he says cheerfully. 'And you've got to sleep in my room, remember. It's your turn on the floor.'

'Actually, you can both sleep in Molly's room. We can pull out the truckle bed, and Granny can have your bed, George. So there's no need for anyone to sleep on the floor.'

'Well, it *will* be your turn on the floor next time Grandma and Grandpa stay over,' George crows to Molly, determined to have the last word, but she ignores him.

I make us all a quick meal of fish and chips, and as usual Barbara clears her plate and tells me it was delicious. I'm acutely aware that she probably doesn't feed herself very well while she's on her own. I should really invite her for dinner more often. After we've cleared up, I tell the children to get into their PJs and give them strict instructions about going to bed soon, with no fuss or arguments.

'Don't let them play you up,' I tell Barbara. 'Make sure they clean their teeth, and give George his preventer inhaler. We won't be late, but call me if there are any problems, OK?'

'There won't be,' she says cheerfully. 'Have a nice time.'

Ben and I walk to the pub a couple of streets away, neither of us talking until we're settled at a table with a drink each in front of us.

'Well,' I say, hoping to get a conversation started, 'it's a long time since we did anything like this.'

'We don't often get the opportunity, do we? And it's not something we can afford to do too often, either.'

'That's true.' I think about his insistence, the other day, that we should pay privately to get George's condition diagnosed more quickly, and wonder again where he thought we'd get the money from. I take a swallow of my wine and decide to jump straight in to the conversation we need to have. 'Ben, we can't afford to pay privately for—'

'I know,' he interrupts. 'I was just... angry.'

'With me? Or with the NHS?'

'Both.' He runs a hand across his face. 'OK, sorry, I know it's not your fault, I guess it's not anyone's fault, but why can't we get this sorted out *now*? Not just urgently, but *now*. You think I'm being unreasonable, but who wouldn't be, when it's their child's health at stake?'

'I know, I feel exactly the same, Ben, it's not just you. But I'm determined to stay positive, for George's sake as well as for ours. And I do believe Dr Taylor's doing his best – I do have faith in him.'

'Well, we'll just have to see, won't we.'

'Yes.' I take another sip of my drink before adding, quietly, 'But let's not lose hope already. There's still every likelihood it's just asthma – perhaps it's a bad type, perhaps he needs more medication.' I pause, before adding, 'My mum seems to think we're making a fuss about nothing.'

'Does she?' he says, looking surprised. 'I'd have thought she'd be really supportive at a time like this.'

'Well, she's not,' I say a little bitterly. 'Not like Barbara.'

'I must admit, it was good of Barbara to offer to babysit tonight.'

'Yes. She really is a kind little soul, Ben. I know you think I'm doing too much for her, perhaps too soon, but we've built up quite a rapport already. I feel so sorry for her, and she's been very helpful to us.'

He shrugs. 'Fair enough. If it makes you happy.'

'It does.'

By the time we've finished our second drink we're talking together more easily and calmly than we've done for months. We've both admitted our marriage is in danger of breaking down, and have agreed once again to try to patch things up as best we can, however temporarily it might be, for the sake of the children, especially while we're going through this crisis with George. It's a massive improvement and I don't want to ruin it all by telling him about the warning letter I've got on my file at work; hopefully things

If I Lost You

will improve there now, especially if I can call upon Barbara again some-times to help out, and meanwhile I'm determined to start looking out for jobs where I can work from home. There's no point in worrying Ben unnec-essarily at this stage.

We arrive home well after ten-thirty, and we're surprised to see the light is still on in the lounge. I push open the door, to find Barbara still sitting on one of the sofas, with the TV on, showing a film with the sound down very low.

'I thought you'd have gone to bed,' I begin, then glance across the room – where both children, in their PJs, are on the other sofa, with a blanket over them and Ebony lying between them. They're not asleep.

'You're still up,' Ben exclaims, behind me.

'Sorry,' Barbara says. 'They're all right, though.'

They both scramble up and run to hug us.

'Why aren't you in bed?' I ask them.

'We went,' Molly says. 'We were in bed, weren't we, George, and then there was this knock on the door and the man was shouting.'

'He waked us up,' George joins in. 'And we was scared so we came downstairs, and I needed my inhaler cos I got wheezy.'

'What man shouting?' Ben's asking, staring from one of them to the other and then back at Barbara. 'What happened?'

'Why don't we get the children back upstairs to bed now,' Barbara suggests calmly, 'and then I can explain. Don't worry, children, Mummy and Daddy are home now and we'll sort it all out. You can go to sleep now.'

I shepherd both kids up to Molly's bedroom and settle them into bed, my mind racing with questions about who the shouting man might have been. Whatever's happened, though, I think they'll both be asleep within minutes. When I get back downstairs, Ben and Barbara are sitting in silence in the lounge, waiting for me. Ben has a face like thunder, and I can already sense it's me he's angry with.

'What is it?' I ask, looking from one of them to the other. 'Who was it that came to the door, Barbara? Was it a neighbour? Or—'

'It was, apparently, Ahmed,' Ben says. 'Husband of your friend Nadia.'

'Oh.' I clap my hand to my mouth. 'Oh my God. I totally forgot. It was tonight...'

'Yes. Tonight,' he says, sarcasm dripping from him as he continues to aim his icy stare at me, 'when Nadia was apparently supposed to be babysitting for us.'

'I'm sorry, Jo,' Barbara says, giving me a helpless shrug. 'I didn't know what to say. I didn't even know who Nadia was. He said he'd tried to call her and her phone was off, and he tried to call you – so did I – but you didn't pick up.'

'Oh, I didn't hear... it was noisy in the pub, my phone was in my bag.' This bothers me more than anything else. Why didn't I take my phone out and leave it on the table? What if Barbara had had a problem with one of the children? What's the matter with me? It could have been urgent.

'But anyway, he knew where you lived,' Barbara's going on, 'so—'

'He's been here before,' I confirm, as if this detail matters at all in the scheme of things. 'They both came for drinks at Christmas.'

'He came to let her know her sister was in hospital.'

'Oh my God,' I say again. 'What did you say?'

'Well, what could I say? I told him I didn't even know Nadia, and there must have been a mix-up. I said I was babysitting, so perhaps you'd forgotten you'd asked Nadia already. But he didn't look at all happy about it.'

'No,' I say faintly. 'No, he wouldn't have been.' I glance at Ben, then turn away quickly from the look on his face. 'I'm so sorry, Barbara. It's completely my fault.'

'So,' Ben says in that same icy tone, 'what *is* this, Jo? Was Nadia using you – using the excuse of babysitting for our children – as a cover for doing something she didn't want her husband to know about?'

I nod, miserably. 'And then I forgot. There's been... a lot on my mind. I wouldn't have gone out if I'd remembered. I'd have been here to talk to Ahmed—'

'And what would you have said, if we'd been here?' Ben challenges me. 'Pretended Nadia changed her mind about babysitting and went off some-where, forgetting to tell her husband? You'd have lied for her, would you? Covered up for her?'

'Look, I obviously didn't think he'd turn up here. OK, she asked me to

If I Lost You 117

cover for her, I didn't like doing it but I gave in because she's been decent to me, the only person at work who has. I don't like what she's doing, but—'

'But now you've got to deal with it,' he says. 'What if he's left a message on your phone, asking you where Nadia is? What's the matter with you – haven't we got enough worries of our own without offering to get involved in other people's messy affairs?' He gets up and heads for the stairs. 'I'm going to bed.'

19

The weekend is spoilt. I take Barbara home soon after breakfast, apologising to her all over again on the way for what happened last night.

'Oh, don't worry about me,' she says carelessly. 'It was no skin off my nose. It's you I'm worried about. Ben seemed pretty unhappy about it all. Is he giving you a hard time?'

'It's just one more thing,' I explain with a sigh, 'on top of everything else. The worry about George. And to be honest, Ben and I haven't been getting on, anyway. Not for quite some time. We've even talked about splitting up.'

'I'm really sorry to hear that,' she says. She touches my hand again, lightly, as it rests on the steering wheel, and I'm grateful that she's not saying too much. It wouldn't take a lot to set me off crying again.

I cried myself to sleep last night as it was. I'd checked my phone and, yes, there was a message from Ahmed, demanding to know where his wife was. What could I do? I quickly messaged Nadia to tell her she needed to get in touch with him right away, and I haven't heard anything since. I just hope she looked at her phone as soon as she woke up, if she was too busy with Zach to do so last night.

I feel like I've let everyone down: Ben, the kids, because they must have been scared when this all kicked off last night, and even Nadia. However much I dislike what she's doing, I did agree to cover for her. But more than any of this, I was crying because of George, my fears for him and the fact that I feel so powerless to help him until I know what his diagnosis is. And I'm determined not to cry, or show my anxiety, when I'm with him.

Sunday passes quietly. The children are both tired after their late night, Ben's barely talking to me again, and to be honest I'm not sorry. I've apologised for last night and I don't know what else he expects of me, so I can't be bothered to try. The weather's as miserable as I feel, so I put a silly film on the TV and settle down with both kids and Ebony on the sofa.

'Don't let the cat lie on George's chest,' Ben snaps when he comes into the room after finishing his marking.

'Dr Taylor said the cat won't hurt me, Daddy,' George immediately pipes up.

'Yes, he did; I forgot to tell you that, Ben,' I agree. 'I asked him specifically about it, and he said there was absolutely no reason—'

'But he doesn't have to live here and see how badly George reacts, does he,' he retorts crossly.

'He's not reacting to the *cat*,' I insist. I should let it go, but honestly, it's ridiculous how determined he is to blame poor Ebony, despite the best medical opinion. He glares at me and walks back out of the room.

'What's the matter with Daddy?' Molly asks. 'Why do you keep arguing, Mummy?'

'We're not arguing, we're just disagreeing,' I lie.

'That's what me and George do,' she says. 'But you call it arguing.'

And I can't really say anything to that.

* * *

I go into work on Monday with a heavy heart, thinking about Nadia and what I'm going to say to her. I haven't heard anything back from her in response to my message yesterday, or anything more from Ahmed.

'I'm so sorry,' I begin as soon as I sit down at my desk. 'What happened? Did you call him? Did you come up with an excuse? And did you see your sister, is she OK?'

To my surprise, she just smiles.

'Don't worry, Jo. It's fine. Yes, my sister's all right; it was a false alarm. She's pregnant – her baby's due any day now – and she went into hospital but it turned out to be false labour, apparently.'

'But what about Ahmed? He was shouting, apparently; he must have been angry. What did you tell him?'

'Oh, I decided to tell him the truth,' she says calmly. I feel my mouth drop open in surprise. 'I think he suspected, so I thought why keep lying and pretending? I'm going to move out. I'll get a room somewhere – Zach's going to pay for it for me – until his wife's had the baby, then he's going to tell her, and we'll move in together.' She hugs herself as if she can't contain her excitement. 'It's going to be wonderful. It's *so* romantic, he loves me so much, and now he'll be able to come to my room and see me whenever he wants.'

'But what did Ahmed say? Was he angry, or upset?'

She shrugs and I feel a pang of sympathy for the poor man who's being dumped so unceremoniously, with apparently such a lack of feeling. 'He'll be OK. Like I said, he's a nice guy, Jo, but just not for me. He'll meet someone else. Sorry about him coming to your house, though. Hope it wasn't too embarrassing.'

I shake my head. I worried all day yesterday about this situation, and here she is, cheerfully dismissing the whole thing – and dismissing her own marriage – as if it was just a minor inconvenience. I decide that's the last time I'll get involved in anyone else's affairs. I've got enough worries of my own.

I keep my head down, conscious all the time of needing to prove to Trevor that I'm doing more than my share of work, conscious more than anything of the warning letter in its envelope in my drawer.

* * *

George comes out of school this afternoon looking shattered again, Molly's irritated by him because he walks so slowly back to the car, and Ben, when he comes home, pretends to be cheerful in front of the kids while being monosyllabic with me. I'm tired of this, tired of the endless worry, the endless strain, the weight of everything on my shoulders. I want the

If I Lost You 121

appointment for George's tests to come urgently just as much as Ben does, but it's only been a couple of days – I have to be reasonable, I can't start chasing it yet.

A couple of days later, George wakes up in a really bad way with his breathing again. His asthma inhaler isn't helping much, his cough's wearing him out and by the time I've managed to calm him down enough for him to lie back down and fall into a restless sleep, Ben's already left for work and there's no way George is going to be going to school. I don't even hesitate this time before calling Barbara, and within minutes I've carried George out to the car, rushed Molly in beside him and we're driving over to pick Barbara up.

'Are you really sure you're OK about staying with him all day again?' I check with her as we arrive home. 'He's better now, just very tired.'

'Never mind, Georgie, you can have a sleep on the sofa when we get indoors,' she tells him cheerfully. 'Don't worry, love,' she adds to me. 'Go on, get yourself and Molly off to school and work or you'll be late.'

I'm so grateful to her, I don't want to say that, actually, we already are late – very late – again. I haven't even got time to think about this too much as I hurry to deliver Molly to her classroom door, apologise to her teacher and head on to my work as fast as I can – I'm far too concerned about George.

In fact, my thoughts have been so focused on George that when I arrive at work I don't even check my watch for the time. It's quiet in our office when I walk in; thank God, at least Trevor isn't in here. But the others are all watching me – Nadia with a worried expression, the other two looking like they're trying not to smirk.

'What's up?' I ask Nadia, and then, as I sit down at my desk, I add, 'What's this?'

It's another brown envelope with my name on it. And I don't really need to ask, I just rip it open. It's my second warning letter.

'Trevor's just brought it in,' Nadia says quietly as I rip it open. 'Jo...'

But I'm already pulling the folded piece of paper out of the envelope and opening it up.

'Are you all right?' she asks.

'No, I'm not.' This is more than I can take. I march out of our room, trying to ignore the looks I'm getting from May and Pauline, and head straight down the corridor to Trevor's office. His door's open and I don't bother knocking.

'I'm here to appeal,' I snap, waving the letter in the air.

Trevor's secretary, Ramona, who shares his office (and it's widely rumoured within the company that that's not all she shares), almost falls off her chair in surprise.

'Excuse me,' she says, blinking her false eyelashes at me, but I ignore her.

'It says in this,' I bark at Trevor, waving the letter in the air, 'that I've got seven days to appeal. Well, I'm *not* waiting seven days. It's not fair, I don't deserve it.'

'You've been warned countless times,' he responds with a heavy sigh. 'You've already been given one warning letter. And today it was at least half past nine before you deigned to appear. Apart from anything else, it's setting a bad example to the other employees.'

'I work twice as hard as those two.' I manage to stop myself. It won't help to start casting aspersions about my colleagues, however much I'd like to. I take a deep breath and try to continue more calmly, 'I do more than my share of the work. I always make up any time I miss, and it's only ever because of emergencies.'

'Of which you seem to have a disproportionate number,' he says. 'It's not that I don't sympathise with your situation, Jo, but it's just not good for discipline to have one employee waltzing in and out of the office at will, while everyone else manages to keep to their contracted hours.'

'A bit of consideration might be nice. If you really sympathised.' I've run out of steam now and I feel ridiculously close to tears. It's not as if I can promise I'll never be late again. I have no idea from one day to the next whether everything's going to go smoothly or if I'm going to suddenly need emergency childcare or to rush to the hospital. How do other parents manage this? Why *am* I the only one who doesn't seem to be able to hold it all together? Perhaps it *is* me – perhaps there's something fundamentally wrong with me.

'The warning will stay on your file for three months, after which it will

If I Lost You　　123

be removed if there are no further incidents,' Trevor goes on, dismissing me with a nod. 'I think that's more than reasonable.'

I wish I wasn't just hanging my head and walking out of his office in defeat. I wish I could tell him to stuff his job. I wish I could tell Miss Fluttering Eyelashes to wipe that superior look off her face, that we all know she doesn't need to beg to keep *her* job; she wouldn't get a written warning even if she turned up at lunchtime every day for a month. I wish I could think of better arguments, that I could stay and fight instead of slinking away like a sad case. But frankly I just haven't got the energy.

20

I decide to work through my lunch break, to make a point, but then I end up wondering why I'm bothering. Trevor's fixated on the time I arrive in the morning, rather than the length of time I work or the amount of work I actually do, so I've just got to pull out all the stops in future to get here before nine. I send a quick message to Barbara to check how George is, and she reassures me that he seems fine now, so I keep working all day until it's time to pick up Molly. She's in a cheerful mood, telling me her teacher's asked them all to write down as many things as possible at home beginning with 'b'.

'I've already thought of *bed* and *baby*,' she says.

'We haven't got a baby at home,' I say, smiling.

'Well, I can say George is a baby, cos he's only five. Oh!' she adds, suddenly laughing. '*Brother* is a "b" word too, isn't it. But I'm not sure how to spell it.'

'I'll help you. Or perhaps Granny will.'

'Oh yes, I'll ask Granny.'

As soon as we arrive home, she rushes indoors, dropping her school bag, calling out for George and Barbara.

'Granny, how do you spell *brother* and can you help me think of some

If I Lost You   125

more "b" words?' There's a pause, and then, from the hallway I hear her go on, 'Are you better now, George? You look better.'

'Yes, I just had to stay on the sofa all day, though, cos I feel too tired to do anything.'

I follow Molly into the lounge. George does look a little better, thank goodness. He's sitting up on the sofa now, Ebony sprawled across his lap, and he's got Pop Up Pirate set up on the coffee table.

'I'm glad you're better,' Molly tells him, and I feel proud of her for being nice to him instead of being resentful of the attention he's getting, like she so often is. 'But I need "b" words, Granny. I need to make a list.'

'All right, Molly, in a minute,' Barbara says. 'When George and I have finished this game.'

'I'm going to win,' George says.

Molly follows me out of the lounge into the kitchen.

'It's not fair,' she says. 'George has been at home all day with Granny. I want her to do something with me, now, but she won't.'

'I'm sure she will, sweetie. Just let them finish their game.'

She trudges sulkily back to the lounge, but five minutes later she's back again, looking even crosser. 'It's *not* fair. They've started another game now, Mummy, and George says Granny's got to play with him because he's ill. But he's not ill now, is he? Granny never wants to do anything with me.'

I go back into the lounge myself, where, sure enough, Barbara and George are involved in a highly fraught game of Pop Up Pirate.

'This is great fun,' Barbara enthuses, looking up at me, laughing. 'Kids today have such a lot of toys, don't they?'

'Yes, they do. Um... Barbara, would you mind just having a break from the game for a minute? Molly wants to talk to you.'

'Oh.' Barbara looks genuinely surprised. 'Yes, of course. What is it, Molly?'

Molly sits down on the other side of her and asks if she can help her come up with some more 'b' words. Barbara puts her head on one side and thinks for a minute.

'What about *bathroom*. Or *bath*?' she suggests. 'And have you got *books*?'

Molly writes these down eagerly.

'*Bananas*?' Barbara goes on. '*Beach*?'

'We haven't got a beach here.' Molly laughs. 'It's supposed to be things at home.'

I leave them to it, noticing as I go out of the room that George is sulking now. Well, he's had more than his share of Granny's attention today. It's good to see Molly looking more cheerful.

I wait until both kids have gone upstairs to play before I talk to Barbara again.

'Thanks for doing that with Molly, earlier,' I say. 'As I said before, she gets a bit resentful of the attention George gets.'

'I can see how that happens. I just feel so sorry for poor little Georgie.'

'We all do, of course.' I look at her for a moment, thinking about what she's told me of her working days. 'Did you used to nurse many children who had similar symptoms to George?'

She nods. 'Yes, lots of kids came in with bad asthma; they had to go on nebulisers and get hooked up to the machines to measure their oxygen levels.'

'But... did you see many who had *other* things, similar to asthma but...' I hesitate. 'But worse?'

She nods. 'Yes, of course.'

I feel my pulse quicken. Does she have an idea what George's condition might be? Is she frightened to tell me?

'What sort of conditions?' I ask her very quietly.

'Oh, all sorts,' she says, starting to turn away, but I stop her.

'Tell me,' I insist. 'What sort of conditions?' There's a moment of silence, where we meet each other's eyes, before I utter the word we all dread, the word neither Ben nor I, and not even the doctors, so far, have uttered. 'Cancer?'

She continues to meet my eyes as she replies equally quietly, 'Yes, of course, cancers, and... other things.'

'Do you think George has cancer?' I ask in a whisper, but she looks away now, shaking her head.

'I can't answer that, Jo. I'm not a doctor. I was just a nurse. I just looked after them.'

'But do you *think*, as a... as a mother, as a grandmother... do you *think* that's

If I Lost You   127

what's wrong with him? Please, Barbara, tell me if you do. Nobody's said it, but I get the feeling they're thinking it, and I need to know. I *need to know*.' I end on a low wail of distress – the distress I've been keeping to myself, swallowing it back, refusing to let it surface, plastering on a smile, because everyone needs me to keep cheerful and positive – and inside I'm not. Inside I'm just scared.

She puts an arm around me.

'Just give him lots of love and cuddles,' she says softly. 'That's all we can do.'

This is why she's been giving George more of her time and attention. It's not, as Molly obviously thinks, because she prefers him and doesn't love her – it's because she thinks he won't be with us for long. My head spins. For a moment I think I'm going to faint. Is this what they think – Dr Jackson, Dr Taylor, even perhaps George's teachers? Do they all think this, but nobody's dared to tell us yet? They're keeping us waiting until they have actual proof from the test results, then they're going to sit down and tell us what they've been suspecting all along?

'No,' I whisper. 'It can't be, I can't let that happen, that's not it, it can't be. It's just asthma, they said it still could be just asthma.'

'Of course it could,' she soothes me.

But I know what she really thinks, now. And I'm terrified.

* * *

When Ben comes home I still feel sick from the shock of guessing what Barbara thinks. I can hardly eat, and doubt I'll be able to sleep tonight. But I don't tell him. I can't; I don't want to say it, not to Ben, not to anyone. I figure that it's my burden to carry for now, until we find out – until we know anything for sure. But I do talk to Molly at bedtime.

'You mustn't get upset if Granny fusses over George a bit, sweetie. It's only because he gets ill.'

'I know that,' she says impatiently. 'I don't like it when he has an asthma attack. But it does make me feel sad that Granny doesn't like me as much as him.'

'Oh, sweetheart, she *does* love you. We all love you. Haven't I told you that mummies and daddies love all their children just the same, however different the children might be, and whatever they do?'

'I know *you* do, and Daddy does. But I don't think Granny does.' She pauses, then goes on, 'Perhaps she would if I was the one that got ill.'

'No, it's just that it's when George is ill that we sometimes *need* Granny, to help look after him, that's all.'

She shrugs and I lean across the bed to kiss her goodnight. My big girl: she acts so grown-up at times, but she's still only seven, still not old enough, really, to be grappling with complex issues like whether she's loved less than her brother. And definitely not old enough to cope with being told what might be wrong with him. If his diagnosis turns out to be serious, I can't imagine how I'm going to be able to tell her. I sit down on my own bed and close my eyes, and find myself muttering the first prayer I've said for many years. If there's a God, and He's listening, He's surely got to make my little boy be OK, hasn't He? I swallow back the tears as I beg Him, promising all those things we all promise when we want something so desperately, so viscerally that we'd give the earth for it if only we could. Nothing else matters as much as this. My baby can't be allowed to die from cancer. He. Just. Can't.

21

The following Monday, I'm just getting back to work after eating my lunchtime sandwich at my desk when my phone starts to flash and vibrate with a call. I've started keeping it on silent at work to avoid giving Trevor any more reasons to criticise me, although I leave it where I can see it on my desk in case there's an urgent call from the school. But this isn't the school – and, thank God, it isn't Barbara either, needing a lift to a doctor. It's Mum. But when I answer the call, she's struggling not to cry.

'It's your dad,' she says. 'He's in hospital, JoJo. He's had a heart attack.'

I jump to my feet so fast I knock my chair over.

'Are you OK?' Nadia's asking me anxiously, but I just shake my head, leaving the chair on its side and managing, through my own tears, to tell Mum I'm on my way, confirm which hospital it is and stuff the phone into my bag.

'I've got to go. It's my dad,' is all I can say, and Nadia immediately understands. She gets up and puts her arms around me, telling me to take a deep breath, that I shouldn't drive until I can be calm, that it'll only make matters worse if I have an accident on the way to the hospital. And I know she's right, obviously, but I can't stop to calm down, I can't stop to have a cup of strong tea first as she's suggesting, I can't stop to tell Trevor—

Except that, *fuck it*, he's just walked into the office.

'Where are you going?' he asks, standing still and staring at me.

'It's my dad, he's—' but he's interrupting me already.

'Oh, your *dad* this time, is it?' he sneers. 'Well, at least that makes a change from your mum, your kids, your so-called *sickness*—'

'Trevor,' I interrupt him back, and if nothing else, my anger with him has managed to stop me, and my voice, from shaking. 'My dad's in hospital. And I'm going, right now, whatever you say, and I know I'm on my final warning but I couldn't give a shit, because quite frankly you can stuff your job where the sun doesn't shine.'

If the circumstances were only different, I might have enjoyed the look not only on his face but on those of the two bitches on the other side of the office too.

* * *

I find Mum waiting at Dad's bedside, gripping his hand, crying as she looks up at me. Dad looks pale and shaken but he gives me a little flicker of a smile. Mum starts to fill me in on what happened, but before she's got very far, a doctor comes in and tells us Dad's going to need surgery to have a stent fitted, but that he should then make a full recovery. Mum and I hug each other, crying again with relief.

'It was lucky you recognised the heart attack for what it was,' the doctor tells her, 'and that the ambulance got him to hospital quickly.'

It's not until a little later, while we're still waiting by Dad's bedside in A&E, that I realise I haven't told Ben what's happened yet. And I haven't made any arrangements for picking up the children. I message him but, of course, he's taking a class and won't see the message in time to do anything about it.

'I've just got to make a call,' I tell Mum, and head out into the corridor for a moment.

I try a couple of numbers of other mums at the school – mums I know from the early days when we were all first-time mothers and on maternity leave, when we had the luxury of time for friendships – but when neither of them pick up, I call Barbara.

'Hi,' I say in relief when she answers. 'Listen, I need a huge favour. I need you to call a taxi – I'll pay for it; if you have to stop at a cash point I'll give back the money just as soon as I can – and I need you to go to the children's school and be outside their classrooms for three-fifteen. It's Daffodil class for George, and Tulip for Molly, OK? I'm going to call the school and explain it's an emergency, or they won't let you take them. And...' I tell her about our key safe on the side wall of the house, give her the number, make sure she's written it down. 'Can you take them home and stay with them until Ben gets home? I'm trying to let him know, but he's taking a class.' I pause for breath. 'Can you do that for me, Barbara? I'm so sorry.'

'Course I can,' she says straight away. 'What's up, are you stuck at work?'

'No. I'm...' I feel tears threatening again. I can hardly get the words out. 'I'm at A&E with Mum. My dad's had a heart attack. I need to stay with Mum, I don't know how long for. And I don't know what to tell the children – Ben will have to talk to them. Please can you try to, well, just try to reassure them somehow? I'm sorry,' I say again, beginning to break down.

'Leave it with me,' she says firmly. 'I'll look after them, don't you worry about a thing. You get back to your dad and, well, I hope he's all right, love.'

I thank her again, hang up, make the necessary call to the school office so that the kids' teachers know their granny will be collecting them, and almost trip over my own feet in my haste to get back to Mum.

'Have you got someone to pick up the children?' she guesses, and I just nod. Thank God for Barbara. I'm beginning to wonder how I used to cope with all these emergencies before she turned up. Thank God I've got someone I can depend on now. I might not have known Barbara for too long, and at first perhaps I wasn't too sure about her; she might be my birth mother but she was still a stranger to me when we met. But I know her now; she loves my kids, I trust her with them, trust her enough to let her collect them from school, enough to let herself into my house and stay there with them. Realising this fills me with relief, as if a weight's been lifted off me.

The doctor comes back before long and tells us Dad's been stabilised with the drugs they're pumping into him, and he's being taken to a coronary ward, where they'll keep him overnight and operate on him first thing in the morning. They say it's a simple procedure to put in the stent, and it'll *do the trick*, but that the most important thing then will be to get his blood pressure down. They'll be keeping him in for a few more days to make sure they send him home on the best medication for that, and he'll have lots of advice about diet and exercise after he's rested and recovered. Dad looks a bit resigned at the mention of diet and exercise, but I think he's been sufficiently scared by this episode – as have Mum and I – to take all the advice on board.

Ben calls me just as we're following the porter taking Dad to a ward.

'I've just got your message,' he says, panic in his voice. 'I'm sorry, Jo, I was in class. How's your dad? I mean, is he... OK?'

'Yes. Well, the doctor thinks he will be. He's got to have an op in the morning. And he's got to get his blood pressure down, and he'll be on some other tablets, but...'

'But he'll be OK. Thank God.' He pauses, then goes on in a rush, 'Barbara's here with the kids.'

'Yes, I had to ask her – I couldn't think who else could pick them up.'

'I know. I realise that. It's fine,' he soothes me. His voice wobbles a bit as he goes on; he loves my parents almost as much as I do. 'As long as Harry's OK, that's all that matters. I presume you're going to stay there with Liz?'

'At least for tonight, yes.'

'So you'll need your overnight things. A change of clothes. Phone charger.'

'Oh, I didn't even give that any thought. I rushed straight here from work.'

'Of course you did. Was Trevor all right about it?'

I grimace but keep my voice even. 'Yes. Look, I can borrow a few things from Mum, just for tonight.'

'No, I can bring you whatever you need, as Barbara's here with the kids. I'll get everything together now. Let me know when you're back at their house and I'll come straight there.'

'OK. Thanks, Ben.'

While I've been talking we've arrived at the ward and Dad's already being transferred to a bed. He looks exhausted, and once he's settled in the bed he gives us both a tired smile and tells us we should go home.

'I don't want to leave you yet,' Mum argues. 'We'll stay until it's time for you to go to sleep.'

If I Lost You   133

'I'm going to sleep now,' he says. 'I can't keep my eyes open. Go on, I'm going to be fine now, Lizzie. I'm in the best place, being looked after. Thanks to you.'

Mum still insists we stay until he's actually fallen asleep, and at that point even the ward sister tells us we both look shattered and we ought to go home and rest.

'If there's any change at all, I'll call you, I promise,' she says. 'But he's going to be OK now, love. We'll make sure of it. And you can come back bright and early tomorrow to see him before he goes to theatre, OK?'

We thank her and make our way out to the car park, and I follow Mum back to her place so that I can watch her and make sure she's driving carefully. I wouldn't mind betting she's crying to herself in the car – I know I am. It's a reaction, now the worst of the shock has passed.

I'm cooking dinner for us both when Ben arrives with my overnight bag. I ask him in for a cup of coffee before he drives back again.

'You can stay for dinner, Ben,' Mum says. 'Jo's cooked enough to feed an army.'

'Thanks, but I think I ought to get back and help Barbara with the children,' he says.

'Are they both all right?' I ask anxiously. 'Is George OK?'

'Yes,' he says. 'Don't worry.' He raises his eyebrows at me. 'Barbara's fussing over him as usual; he's lapping it up. Look, I've brought you enough clothes for another three or four days, so you can stay as long as Liz needs you to. We'll be fine at home, now; if Barbara can't stay, I can get some cover organised so that I can get away early for the kids if necessary.'

'Thanks,' I say. I'm aware that this is the most civilised we've been with each other since our date night at the pub. Sad that it has to be something like this that's brought it about.

'It sounds like Ben thinks Barbara fusses too much over George,' Mum comments a little later as we're eating dinner.

'Oh, I wouldn't say that,' I lie.

'Really? I must admit I've got the same impression, from things you've said.'

'Have you? You haven't said anything.'

Mum shakes her head. 'No. I haven't wanted to interfere.'

'But now?' I encourage her.

She hesitates, twirling pasta around her fork, looking at me thoughtfully. 'Well, look, I've kept quiet because I know it's been so important for you, finally meeting your birth mother, and I understand that, honestly. But it seems to me that ever since Barbara turned up, you've been getting more and more anxious about George.'

'That's ridiculous, Mum,' I protest, putting down my fork and staring at her. 'I was anxious about George already, before I ever heard from Barbara.'

'Of course,' she soothes me. 'I know that; we've all been anxious about him, obviously. But I wonder if it's Barbara that's been feeding you these ideas about him being worse, having something more serious than asthma, and because she was a nurse, you listen to her. You believe whatever she says.'

'What? Of course she hasn't. It was Dr Jackson who *fed* me the *idea*, as you put it. He was worried enough to send the urgent referral.'

'Maybe so that everything *more serious* can be ruled out, to satisfy you finally that it's just asthma?'

I stare at her, blinking in shock. 'Mum, you know what the paediatrician told me – he thinks it's quite likely to be something more serious. He wouldn't be sending us to Great Ormond Street for tests, they wouldn't be wasting NHS time and money if they didn't think there was a strong possibility of this being...'

I swallow, shaking my head. I'm finding it almost impossible to continue this conversation. It's frankly unbelievable to me that my lovely mum would actually think I'm just being paranoid – an over-fussy mother – that I'm being somehow encouraged by Barbara to make too much fuss of my little boy – and to what end?

'You think I'm just *inventing* his symptoms? Imagining them? Trying to get attention for myself, or what? Come on, tell me – why would I be doing this, putting myself through it, for heaven's sake? I'm worried sick. So's Ben. We're both stressed out of our minds. I didn't need Barbara to tell me to take this seriously – it *is* serious, Mum. Don't you care?'

She looks back at me, shaking her head, hurt.

'Of course I care. I love George just as much as you do. But I'm worried he's getting spoilt, and that he's playing up to all this fuss. Don't tell me he's not happy to have all this time off school? Staying at home, being pampered by his granny, and being taken to all these appointments, being made to feel special and important. And how does all this affect poor Molly? She's going to resent it. You've already told me she's feeling left out.'

For a few minutes I can't even answer her. Ridiculous though her insistence is that the doctors are apparently willing to go through a charade of appointments and tests merely to prove that I'm – what? An over-fussy mother? Or suffering from Munchausen's by proxy? – and however much I tell myself that Mum's in denial because she's too frightened to accept the idea of her grandson being seriously ill, I'm aware that she's right about this. Yes, George is lapping up the extra fuss he's getting from Barbara, and yes, Molly does resent it.

'I'm very much aware of how difficult all this is for Molly,' I say finally, deciding it's pointless going on with the argument – pointless, and not the right time, with my poor dad languishing in hospital. 'I talk to her about it. She understands. It's not easy, Mum.'

'I'm sure it's not,' she soothes me. We're both silent for a minute, and then she goes on, 'I shouldn't have said anything, I'm sorry. Let's just forget it.'

'It's not that easy, now I know how you feel.'

We spend an uncomfortable evening together, the television filling in the silences between us. I go to bed in their spare room feeling disgruntled, and then lie awake feeling guilty. My dad's just had a heart attack; we should be concentrating on him, not arguing with each other like this. I toss and turn for most of the night, and as I finally drift off to sleep I promise myself I'll apologise to her in the morning and let matters rest.

22

I get up early in the morning to take Mum a cup of tea in bed.

'I'm sorry, Mum,' I tell her. 'I shouldn't have taken offence at what you said yesterday. But if you were with George all the time, you'd see how unwell he is, how worrying it is. I realise it's something you don't want to acknowledge, or face up to, but—'

'I'm not afraid to face facts at all. If I'd been afraid to face the truth yesterday, and realise your dad was having a heart attack, he wouldn't be having an operation today, he'd be—'

'All right, yes, I'm sorry,' I stop her, alarmed by the tears that have sprung into her eyes now, tears I've caused by my own insistence on trying to get through to her. Why didn't I just back off and leave the subject alone? 'Mum, please don't cry. Let's drop it. I don't want to argue any more.'

'Nor do I. Not while your poor dad's lying there in hospital.'

'I know,' I agree. 'Let's put it down to both of us being stressed, OK?' I lean over and hug her. 'I'll go and start some breakfast. I know you want to get to the hospital early.'

* * *

Dad looks quite perky when we turn up at his bedside.

If I Lost You   137

'Well, I'm all prepped and ready to go under the knife,' he jokes. 'I'll come back a new man.'

'I'd be happy to have the old one back, thanks very much,' Mum says, leaning over and kissing him. 'It's supposed to be quite a straightforward op, Harry. I've been reading it up on Google.'

'Ah, Dr Google,' says a voice behind us. 'He'll be putting us out of business before long.' A tall, distinguished-looking man holds out his hand to Mum, smiling. 'I'm Vijay Chowdhury, your husband's consultant. I've already discussed the planned surgery with your husband. Is there anything you'd like to ask me?'

'I don't think so, thank you,' Mum says. 'I mean, I presume this is necessary to prevent him having another heart attack.'

'We certainly hope so. But he'll be on medication for life, too, to protect his heart, and, as I'm sure you've already been told, keeping his blood pressure down will be most important: we'll have to keep a close check on that, reviewing his medication until it's stable.'

'We'll do whatever's necessary, Mr Chowdhury. We certainly don't want a repeat of this.'

'Of course. So, we'll be taking him up to theatre in about an hour's time, and I'll leave you to relax now.'

'He seems very nice,' Mum says after he's gone.

'I don't care how nice he is,' I say, 'as long as he knows what he's doing.'

'I'm sure he does; he's supposed to be the top heart surgeon here,' Dad says. 'The anaesthetist's been round to see me already too. He seems very nice as well.'

I'm sure it's just because I'm so nervous for Dad, but I can't help wishing they both didn't attach so much importance to whether or not the doctors are *nice*.

The time passes quickly, and pretty soon we're giving Dad a kiss as he's wheeled off to theatre. Mum and I look at each other and both agree that we should go to the hospital's branch of Costa to ease the wait with coffee and croissants, but once they're in front of us, neither of us feel much like eating.

'It's supposed to be a very straightforward op,' I remind Mum again, and she nods, almost enthusiastically, to cover how I know she's really feeling.

It's going to be a long day.

* * *

Eventually, back from recovery, Dad gives us a sleepy smile and a thumbs-up before going straight back to sleep.

'He's probably going to sleep for most of the day,' a nurse tells us. 'Why don't you pop off home for a break and come back this evening? He'll be more with-it by then.'

Fortunately it's not too far from the hospital back to Mum and Dad's place, so we follow her advice. We sit in the lounge together and chat, companionably enough, about this and that, avoiding any mention of Barbara, or George's illness, but I'm still struggling to get Mum's comments from last night out of my mind. I'm sure she realises this and probably regrets having said anything, but it can't be unsaid now. At about half past five, just as I'm about to get up and prepare some dinner for us, I have a phone call – it's from Ben's number but to my surprise and delight it's Molly, with George in the background demanding his turn almost as soon as she starts to speak.

'I miss you, Mummy, when are you coming home?' she begins. Then, before I've had a chance to answer, and presumably remembering her manners, she adds, 'Is Grandpa better now?'

'He's going to be better, darling, now he's had an operation,' I tell her. 'I miss you too, so much. But I need to stay with Grandma for a little bit longer. I'll be home as soon as I can. Are you both being good for Daddy?'

'Well, *I* am, but I can't speak for George,' she says. And then, 'Ouch! Don't hit me, George – I'm telling Daddy! *Daddeee!* George hit me.'

'I didn't hit her.' It's George on the phone now. Presumably Molly's run off to complain about him to her father. 'I *am* being good, Mummy.' He sounds close to tears. 'I want you to come home.'

'I will, very soon, Georgie. Don't cry. You've got Daddy there, haven't you. And Granny?'

If I Lost You   139

'Yes. I liked it yesterday cos Granny got us pizzas from the pizza shop. But Daddy cooked dinner tonight and it was horrid.'

I laugh. 'I'm sure it wasn't. Put Molly back on the phone now, please, Georgie. I'll see you soon. I love you.'

Molly sounds sulky now. 'I wish you'd come home, Mummy. George is being *unbearable*. He won't let Granny play with me at all, and he keeps crying and being like a baby so that Granny cuddles him, and Daddy's getting cross all the time.'

'Oh dear.' I can just imagine the atmosphere at home, but it's hard to know how much of this is true and how much is Molly being miserable because she's missing me. 'Well, I'll be back soon; please try to be nice to your brother. He's only little and he's upset about me not being there.'

'So am I. But *I'm* not making such a fuss, and nobody tries to be nice to *me*. It's not fair, Mummy.' She sounds like she's going to start crying, and my heart feels like it's about to break for her. She's right, once again. It *isn't* fair and I hope Ben's reminding Barbara about trying to treat both kids the same – but, of course, I'm also worried that George might be feeling ill while I'm not there.

'Is Daddy there, sweetie?' I ask her. 'Let me have a word with him now. Please don't be upset, I'll be home very soon and I love you both very much, OK? Try to be a big girl for me now.'

'I don't like being the big girl all the time,' she says sadly. 'Here's Daddy.'

'I'm in the middle of washing up,' Ben says, sounding stressed. 'Is everything OK? How did Harry's op go?'

'Well, he's back on the ward and the nurse said it all went OK. We've left him to sleep it off and we're going back later – perhaps we can see a doctor then, or tomorrow morning.' I pause, then go on. 'Ben, please give the kids lots of cuddles. They both sound so upset.'

'Of course I will. I am. They miss you, obviously. And frankly, it's difficult: Barbara's spoiling George so much; if we're not careful she's going to turn him into a little brat before we even get any diagnosis on his illness.'

'That's a horrible thing to say.'

'Well, I'm sorry, but it's true. Whatever this illness is, it's not right that she lets him do whatever he likes. I'd like to send her home now, frankly, but the kids want her here, and I must admit it was helpful that she picked them up again today – I couldn't get away early enough.'

'Well, there you go. I'm glad she's there to help.'

He sighs and lowers his voice.

'You know as well as I do that Barbara spoils him. He plays up to it and Molly was already feeling left out and resentful, before Barbara even came on the scene.'

'I know, I know all this, Ben, but I've spoken to Molly about it; she understands, OK?'

'Perhaps she *says* she does, because she doesn't want us to get cross with her. But the frustration's coming out at school instead.'

'What are you talking about? She's doing well at school.'

'Well, I wasn't going to tell you this until you got home, but here it is: her teacher sent me a message today – she knows you're away, obviously. She says she's noticed a change in Molly at school. Her behaviour is giving them cause for concern.'

'Cause for concern?' I repeat. '*Molly*?'

'Yes. Our good girl, Molly – our *big girl*, as we keep calling her. She's not a big girl, though, is she – she's only seven, not big enough at all to understand what's going on. She's confused, she's upset, she's playing up at school, and it's all because George is getting spoilt, while our poor daughter has to look on, being ignored, wondering what she's done wrong, why she isn't liked, why she's treated differently. It's not good enough, Jo, and it can't go on. It *mustn't* go on. It's having an effect, a detrimental effect, on both of our kids, and it's my fault as much as yours, because it's only now I'm spending more time with them that I'm realising quite how bad it's got.' He stops, takes a breath and goes on at his normal volume, 'I'm sorry. That should have waited until you got home. Give Harry and Liz my love.' And he hangs up.

I sit for a moment, my phone still in my hand, aware my mouth is open in shock.

'Are you all right, darling?' Mum asks. 'Are the children OK?'

I shake my head, then nod, then shake my head again.

'I don't know. I don't know what Ben's talking about,' I say. I know I'm lying, of course – I know perfectly well what he's talking about. I've been worried about it myself, but I had no idea it was affecting Molly's behaviour at school.

'I heard you mention Molly,' Mum prompts me.

'Well, apparently her teacher's concerned about her behaviour. I'm shocked – she's always been so good at school.'

'Poor Molly,' Mum says quietly.

It's like a red rag to a bull. 'What do you mean, poor Molly? I *know* it's been tough for her – I'm not stupid. I know George gets a lot of extra attention; it's inevitable, when one child gets ill and the other one's perfectly healthy, and of course she gets upset sometimes, she gets jealous and yes, she plays up at home, but I talk to her about it and she understands. I can't believe it affects her school work, or her school behaviour, that's ridiculous. There must be something else going on, someone at school bullying her.'

'But Ben thinks Barbara's spoiling George, too, doesn't he? Leaving Molly out. That's making the situation even worse. Because I suppose Barbara believes all this talk about something being seriously wrong with George, too. As I've already said, I can't help wondering if it's Barbara's influence on you that's making *you* so susceptible to the idea of it. Perhaps she misses her nursing career and she's turned George into her little patient, enjoying it, giving him all the fuss and attention and pretending to be a medical expert. In fact I'd be careful, if I were you – she could even be doing something to *make* him ill.'

'*What*?' I gasp. I can't actually believe what I'm hearing now. Has my mother completely lost the plot? Has the shock of Dad being rushed into hospital turned her head? 'You can't say that; you don't even know her. Of course she's not making George ill. She's just being kind and sympathetic, which to be honest is more than you seem to have been able to offer.' I get to my feet shakily and start to head for the door. 'If you don't mind, Mum, I'd like you to stay out of this altogether if you can't say anything more helpful.'

It's only as I start to leave the room that I realise I'm crying. I hate this, hate the fact that we're arguing again, hate having raised my voice at her when I'm supposed to be here to help her, to comfort her during such a difficult time. I can't understand what's got into her. I was careful with her feelings when I first wanted to meet up with my birth mother; I knew she might feel hurt or worried about it but no, she encouraged me. I promised I'd never call Barbara my mother because I still think of Mum as that; she's the one who brought me up, who's always loved me unconditionally without ever placing any demands on me. I promised her, too, that she'd always come first with me, always remain my real mum. But she's obviously jealous of the part Barbara's playing in my life, and the children's lives, to the extent that she seems determined to turn me against her, at the same time as insisting George's illness is all in our minds and it's Barbara's fault. So now it's not me who's got Munchausen's by proxy, it's Barbara. If it wasn't so ridiculous and so horribly upsetting, it'd be almost laughable.

I hesitate in the hallway, my annoyance and frustration suddenly getting the better of me. Mum doesn't seem to care; she doesn't care that she's upset me, she doesn't care about my worries, with George's illness, and now Molly's behaviour, to say nothing of the state of my marriage. She has no idea of the fact that I've just made myself unemployed in my haste to rush to her side when she needed me – when *Dad* needed me. I know she's having a tough time herself but I don't deserve to be spoken to the way she's been doing. Why does nobody seem to care what *I'm* going through?

I step back into the lounge, where she's sitting, perfectly calmly, flicking through a newspaper, and I'm overcome with rage and self-pity.

'I know you're jealous of Barbara, jealous of the time I'm spending with her,' I snap. 'But there's a reason for that: she's being more of a mother to me, frankly, and more of a grandma to the children than you are these days. So you might as well get used to it.'

As soon as the words are out of my mouth I want to take them back; I want to throw myself into her arms and apologise, tell her I love her and hear her say she loves me too. But I don't. I just go into the kitchen and start peeling potatoes. And we're barely talking when we sit down for dinner.

23

Dad's sitting up in bed when we go back to the hospital later.

'How are you feeling?' Mum asks him anxiously.

'Absolutely fine,' he reassures her. 'I should feel fine, shouldn't I, after all the sleep I've had.'

'You needed it, Dad,' I say. 'You have to get over the anaesthetic.'

'Has the surgeon been back to see you?' Mum asks.

'Yes. He came just a little while ago, before he went off duty. He says he's happy with how it went, and now I just have to rest. They want to keep me in for another day or two to get the drug regimen sorted out. I'd rather come home, obviously, but—'

'But not till they're happy for you to leave,' Mum says firmly.

They chat for a while about how he's got to take time off work once he's home, and how Mum's going to stay at home and look after him, and how they've both decided now to take early retirement. I sit quietly, letting them talk, wishing I could bring myself to say something to Mum – to say I'm sorry, to get things right between us again. But even as I'm thinking this, I rebel against it. I'm too cross with her.

When Dad starts to look tired, we kiss him goodbye and Mum promises to come back in the morning. I just tell him to keep resting and do as he's told, and that I'll see him soon.

'I might go home tomorrow,' I say as I'm driving Mum home again.

'I thought you would. That's fine.'

'I'll only go if you'll definitely be OK.'

'Of course I'm OK,' she retorts quite sharply. 'The children need you. Go home.'

The stinging tone makes me blink back tears. I can't believe we're behaving like this with each other, especially while Dad's in hospital recovering from such a major, traumatic event. I feel ashamed and want more than anything to reach out and hug her. But I don't. I can't. When we get back, I go to my room and pack my bag. I'm going home first thing in the morning. Perhaps Mum and I just need some time apart. Perhaps the stress of the last two days has got to us both.

It'll actually be a relief to say goodbye to her tomorrow.

* * *

As I drive home the next morning, reality starts to hit for the first time since I ran out of the office, having insulted my boss and told him to stuff his job. I'm now out of work. I could go back and offer heartfelt apologies, plead that the shock and emotion about my dad's heart attack had affected me to such an extent that I didn't know what I was saying. But the truth is, I don't even want to try. I've had enough. Trevor's browbeaten me into submission. I simply can't work any longer in a job where I'm being watched – not just by him but by two of my colleagues too – where I can't even ask for time off for a family emergency, even without pay, even if I make up the time I've missed. It's draconian, and I'm just not prepared to put up with it any more.

I give Nadia a call as soon as I get home, while I'm still sitting in the car on the driveway.

'How's your dad?' she asks. Her tone is strange: different, flat, almost as if she's not really interested.

I start to tell her, briefly, about his operation, but I sense she's not even listening, so I stop, and ask, 'Are you OK, Nad?'

'No,' she says, quite abruptly. 'Not really.'

'What's wrong?'

She gives a little snort. 'Just about everything, if you must know.'

If I Lost You 145

My heart gives a lurch. I'm worried for her. I'm guessing it's not working out with Zach, that she's made a mistake. But then, to be honest, it's better if it's happened now, rather than further down the line.

'Is it Zach?' I ask her gently.

'Of course it's Zach, you don't have to gloat. I know you warned me, so OK, you were right – are you satisfied?' she snaps.

I almost drop my phone, I'm so taken aback.

'Hey, OK, calm down, come on – tell me what went wrong. It's not my fault,' I can't help adding.

'Yes it is: of course it's your fault. If you hadn't forgotten to cover for me when I spent the night with him, if you'd been there when Ahmed went to your door, you could have come up with an excuse and I'd have got away with it. Now I've split up with Zach because he put me in this *disgusting* room in, like, some drug dealer's place, with a horrible broken bed and no shower or anything, and he said that's all he can afford and I should have been grateful. And thanks to you, Ahmed won't take me back. I can't believe you let me down like that, after all the times I've stuck up for you at work.'

'I'm sorry,' I find myself saying, although to be honest I think it's a bit rich that she wants to blame me for the way it's all turned out, when I tried to warn her against this course of events in the first place. 'Did you really *want* to go back to Ahmed?'

'Yes. But now I've got to move back in with my mum and dad, and they're both furious with me because I broke my marriage vows, blah-de-blah, and they keep quoting the Quran at me and want me to wear a head-scarf and I hate it – all of it. I wish I'd never told you about Zach in the first place, then I wouldn't be in this mess.'

'Hang on. This is not all down to me, Nadia. I told you it was risky; I didn't want to cover for you anyway. I can't believe you're blaming me for all this. At least you've got a home to go back to with your parents. If I were you, I'd be grateful for that and put up with them being cross with you for a while. They'll come round and forgive you, I'm sure.'

'Oh, there's no point talking to you. You don't understand; you're just like my fucking parents,' she snaps – and hangs up on me.

I sit for a minute, staring at my phone. I can't believe this from Nadia –

sweet, kind-natured Nadia who was the only person at work I could talk to, the only one who seemed to sympathise with me. I feel, pathetically, like crying again. I called her to confirm that I wasn't going back to work, and to suggest we kept in touch, but now my one work friendship's in tatters too. May and Pauline are probably rubbing their hands together in delight at never having to see me again, Trevor's probably busy compiling my dismissal letter and no doubt telling Ramona, while he's getting his hands under her skirt, how relieved he is to be rid of me.

I'm still trying to swallow back the indignation and self-pity as I let myself into the house – and stop dead in the hallway, aware that someone's in the lounge, with the TV on. Of course, Barbara's here. She's obviously stayed for a couple of nights, as it wouldn't have been worth Ben taking her home and picking her up again. And I haven't yet told anyone I was coming home. I look into the room and try to give her a smile.

'Hi.' That's about all I can manage to say. I feel shattered, wiped out emotionally.

'Oh, hello,' she says cheerfully, struggling to her feet. 'Want a cup of tea? I didn't realise you were coming back today. How's your dad? You look exhausted, you poor thing. You sit down, I'll go and put the kettle on.'

'Oh, Barbara,' I say, sinking onto the sofa and closing my eyes. 'Thank you. Thank you so much.' And before I know it, I'm crying again – big, noisy sobs that shake my body and huge fat tears that run down my face and drip onto my clothes, and I just can't stop now I've started. Barbara's sat down next to me, her arms are round me and she's telling me not to try to talk, just to cry it out, it'll do me good, I'll feel better for it. And eventually I shudder to a stop.

'I'm so sorry,' I start to say, but she stops me, shaking her head.

'Don't be sorry. *I'm* sorry, love. Is it your dad?'

'No, God, no, he's going to be OK, the op was a success. It's not that.' I feel even worse now – she's given me sympathy because she thinks my dad's passed away, and I don't deserve it, I'm just being pathetic, feeling sorry for myself. But even as I'm trying to tell myself to buck up, stop it, pull myself together, I still want to cry. I still can't help myself blurting out, pathetically, 'It's just *everything*. Everything's so awful and nobody's on my side.'

If I Lost You 147

'I am,' she says. 'Tell me. Whatever it is, whoever's hurt you, I'll listen. Get it off your chest, come on.'

So I do. I tell her how I argued with Mum about George's illness, and about Molly's behaviour – managing to avoid including the fact that Mum seems to blame Barbara herself as much as she blames me. I tell her how awful everything is between me and Ben. I tell her I've walked out of my job after two warning letters which I still haven't mentioned to Ben; the two women at work who seem to hate me; and, the final straw, Nadia blaming me for the collapse of her marriage, the marriage that only last week she was so desperate to walk away from.

'I just can't get my head around the fact that my mum refuses to take George's illness seriously,' I say, going back to the first thing – the worst thing – on the list. 'I get that she doesn't want to face it – neither do I. But she'd rather believe I'm deliberately exaggerating it, to get attention or something. She really thinks the doctors are just going along with these appointments and tests to keep me happy. It's so ridiculous, I should be laughing at it, but I can't, because... because it's *hurtful*. Because it makes it feel like it's my fault he's ill, that he's playing up to it. And that it's my fault Molly's got issues at school, that she's feeling left out and being difficult – and Ben thinks that too. Everybody thinks every bloody thing that's wrong with my family is *my fault*.'

'Well, I don't,' Barbara says firmly. 'I know we haven't known each other long, love, but I know already how much you love your kids. I know how much you love your mum and dad, too. I said to myself when we first got together: *Barb, you'll never take the place of her adoptive parents, and you mustn't even try, it wouldn't be right.* I'm just... an *extra* parent, if you like. Whenever you need one, OK? And it feels to me like you could do with a bit of extra love and support right now. So come on, dry your eyes while I go and put the kettle on. And I'll stay as long as you need me to, as long as it helps you to have me around.'

'OK,' I agree, sniffing. 'OK, thank you. I... honestly don't know what I'd do without you. How I managed before.' I reach out and give her a grateful hug. 'You seem to be the only person who believes in me.'

'Course I do,' she says. 'You're my daughter.'

24

Ben looks at me in surprise when he arrives home from work – having seen my car on the drive.

'I didn't expect you home yet.'

Then he catches sight of Barbara in the lounge, cuddled up with George on the sofa, and adds, 'She's still here?'

'Yes. She's... helping me.'

He raises his eyebrows in question, but I don't elaborate. I don't want to tell him about it – any of it: not the argument with Mum, not the fact that I've abandoned my job, not the issue with Nadia.

'Do you want me to take her home now?' he asks.

'No. She can stay another night, can't she, Ben? Please. I'm so tired, I could really do with her help, what with all the scare about Dad.'

'Yes,' he says, finally looking more sympathetic. 'It's been a scary time, hasn't it. Was your mum OK for you to leave her, already? I thought you'd probably want to stay with her for a bit longer.'

'She's fine. She said she didn't need me.' It's not even a lie. 'She thought it'd be better for me to get back to the children.'

'So tell me more about your dad,' Ben says. 'Did the surgeon say he's optimistic about his recovery?'

If I Lost You 149

'Yes. But he's got to make some serious lifestyle changes, once he's home and rested for a while.'

'Well, I'm really glad he's going to be OK.'

He goes into the lounge to see the children, returning a few minutes later with a worried frown.

'Molly doesn't seem very happy, again. Have you spoken to her yet?' he asks. 'About what we discussed on the phone?'

I don't remember it being much of a discussion. More of a lecture. But I just shake my head, wearily.

'No. I'll talk to her at bedtime. She was so excited to see me when I picked them up from school, I didn't want to upset her then.'

She was excited, in fact, until we got home and she realised Barbara was still here. She's looked sulky ever since, whereas George is loving all the extra attention. I know I need to talk to her – I don't need Ben to remind me.

'Fair enough, but it needs to be dealt with, Jo, and if you can't do it, I will.'

'I will, OK? I've said I will.'

* * *

'I didn't want George in my room again,' Molly says, looking close to tears when I go upstairs to see her at bedtime. George is in the bathroom, taking longer than necessary cleaning his teeth because he wanted to stay downstairs with Barbara instead of going to bed, so I've got a good opportunity to talk to Molly while we're on our own. 'Why can't Granny sleep downstairs on the sofa?' she goes on.

'That's not very kind, Mollipop.'

'She's not kind to me.'

I pull her towards me and hold her close.

'Molly, what's all this about? Daddy says your teacher's mentioned she's had to tell you off a few times recently. Why?'

She shrugs. 'I don't know. She's just picking on me.'

'But she said you've been answering her back. That's not like you at all. Are you unhappy at school for some reason?'

'I'm unhappy *everywhere*.'

'But why? What's making you unhappy, sweetie? Tell me, and I'll try to make it right.'

'You can't,' she cries. 'You can't make it right because everything's wrong, and I know it's my fault but I don't know why.'

'What? Nothing's your fault. Oh, baby, please don't cry.' I try to wipe her tears, but I feel so distressed at seeing her so unhappy, I could almost start crying again myself.

'Nobody likes me,' she sobs. 'Granny doesn't like me, George *hates* me, Daddy gets cross with me and you went away. Now my teacher hates me and my friends don't like me any more either.'

'Come here.' I sit down on her bed and pull her onto my lap. 'None of that is true, Mollipop. Well, only that I went away – but I had to. You know it was an emergency; your grandpa was in hospital.'

'You didn't even tell me you were going. You just sent Granny to the school and I didn't like it. I didn't want to get in the taxi with her, I was scared, and she said I was being silly.'

'Oh, sweetie, I'm so sorry – I couldn't tell you, it was so sudden, but I sent a message to your school so that your teacher would know. And I expect Granny was just worried about what to do when you didn't want to get in the taxi.'

'She doesn't like me,' Molly insists. 'She only likes George; she hugs him and fusses over him all the time and he looks at me like *this*.' She makes her face into a horrible, smug smirk and I know she's right, unfortunately – I've seen George doing it.

'I'm going to talk to George about that,' I promise her, stroking her hair back from her tearstained little face. 'But none of the rest of it is true. You know Daddy and I love you.'

'But you and Daddy keep having arguments. I can hear you when I'm in bed. Are you going to get a divorce?' she asks, looking at me with her big brown eyes full of anxiety.

'No, of course we're not.' I'm crossing my fingers as I tell her this. At one time I was pretty sure that was the way we were headed, but right now – with all the worry about George – I don't think either of us would want to put ourselves, let alone the children, through anything else. 'All

If I Lost You 151

mummies and daddies have arguments sometimes. It doesn't mean we're going to get divorced. And what makes you think your friends don't like you?'

She shrugs. 'Because Mrs Wallis keeps telling me off. Sophie says she doesn't like me any more because I'm naughty. But I'm not naughty, Mummy, I just don't always listen to what Mrs Wallis says because I'm thinking about something else, so she tells me off and I say it's not fair and she says I'm being rude.'

This is all delivered on one breath, without looking at me, because Molly's obviously ashamed of what's happened. But now I see it all, so clearly, so very clearly that I just want to hold her tight, smother her with kisses and never let her go.

'You're thinking about other things in the classroom while you're supposed to be listening to your teacher? Thinking about things you're worried about?'

She nods. 'I try not to, but I can't help it. I think about George being mean to me, and if it's all my fault because I should just try to be nicer to George because I know his asthma is bad and I don't want to be horrible to him because he's little. But *he's* horrible to *me,* Mummy, and Granny doesn't like me as much as George, so I must really be horrible, mustn't I, because she's a grown-up so she wouldn't think it if it wasn't true.'

Her poor little face is screwed up in frustration and anxiety, and all I can do is hold her and kiss her and rock her in my arms until she runs out of words and just sits here on my lap, tears streaming down her face.

'You should have talked to me about all this, way before now,' I tell her gently. 'You're *not* horrible, Molly, and nobody thinks you are – *nobody.* Granny's just different with George because of his asthma, that's all. You know she used to be a nurse, so she's used to being extra-specially kind to people who are sometimes poorly. And I'm sure she doesn't realise how upset you are.'

'Don't tell her,' she begs.

'No, all right, I won't if you don't want me to, but perhaps she needs to understand.'

'No, don't, Mummy. Don't tell George either, or he'll call me a tell-tale and a cry-baby.'

'Oh, Molly.' I hold her close again, inhaling the floral scent of her silky dark hair. 'We all love you, darling. Don't ever think like that again, OK?'

'OK,' she says, giving me a hesitant little half-smile.

But I don't know how much she believes me, and the whole conversation has worried me so much that I know we've all got to start making a concerted effort to show her she's not loved any less than her brother – no matter how worried we are about him. It's got to come from Barbara; I need to remind her again. But it's got to come from Ben, too. And most of all, of course, it has to come from me.

* * *

'Well, did you talk to her?' Ben asks once I'm finally back downstairs after tucking George into bed too. Barbara's gone up to have a bath and he's obviously grabbed the opportunity for us to talk without her listening. 'Did she tell you about the school thing? About answering her teacher back?'

'Yes. She's been upset about school, but that's only part of it, Ben.' I take a deep breath, preparing myself to list all of Molly's anxieties to him, but he doesn't give me a chance.

'Of course that's only part of it. I keep telling you, don't I – the biggest problem is Barbara, and the way she favours George.'

'Shh, keep your voice down.'

'She's in the bathroom, and frankly I don't even care if she hears me. It needs saying, Jo, and if you're not prepared to say it to her, I will. She's spoiling George and upsetting Molly, and—'

'I know.'

He looks at me in surprise.

'You know? You agree with me? So what are you going to do about it? Or do you want me to talk to her?'

'No. I will. I've already spoken to her about it, but yes, I'll have another word with her. But honestly, Ben, I get it. I mean, she shouldn't be making Molly feel left out, but I get why she's making a fuss over George. He really isn't well – he looks awful, most of the time now—'

'We're *all* worried sick about George. In fact, the next thing I was going

If I Lost You   153

to say to you was we need to chase up this appointment, for these tests he's supposed to be having urgently.'

'I'm going to do that tomorrow, OK? But anyway,' I go on, 'that isn't the only thing worrying Molly.'

'So what else is?'

'Hearing us arguing all the time. And here we go again. She's worried we're going to get a divorce.'

Ben gives me a very direct look, without saying anything for a full minute.

'I know what you're thinking,' I say, quietly. 'I know we've discussed it, but we agreed we should try to make it work while the kids are still little. And I think, now, with the situation with George...'

'Yes. You're right.' He lets out a long breath, looking down at the floor, before adding in a slightly shaky voice, 'Do you think the consultant was right, Jo? Do you think we have to be prepared for... for George's condition to be something really bad?'

I can't answer for a moment. I just sit here, swallowing back the threat of tears yet again, trying not to picture my little boy in some hospital bed, hooked up to God knows how many tubes and drips, surrounded by doctors and nurses who look up at us with sorrow and pity in their eyes. No, I can't, I just can't allow this to happen. We can't lose him, not at only five years old, not to some terrible disease that even the doctors seem too frightened to mention. It's not going to happen, it won't, I'm not going to allow it, I'll do anything, whatever it takes. We'll pay – we'll beg, borrow or steal whatever we need.

'Should we consider going private?' Ben says again.

'If necessary, yes.' Where did that come from? Was that really me – the person with no job, no money, no prospects, saying we should find what might amount to thousands of pounds to try to save our son? Well, of course we must. Whatever it takes – we'll sell the house if we have to. 'If we have to, that's what we'll do,' I say more firmly. 'But... we're not there yet.'

'Chase up that appointment, then,' he says, snappily, as if everything's my fault.

But I don't have to. Because the next morning, George's appointment arrives in the post, on an email and in a text message for good measure. It's for the Friday of next week.

25

As next Friday approaches, George seems to be getting more and more breathless each passing day. He's been sent home from school early twice this week because he was wheezing and coughing so much and his inhaler didn't seem to be helping a lot. I've told Ben that Barbara's been bringing him home, because he still thinks I'm at work – but I'm glad she's got a reason to stay on here. Ben doesn't like it, but I feel like I'd be lost, right now, without her support. She's the only one who knows the extent of my worries: about the job, and Nadia, and my mum, and she's kept my confidence about all of it, merely asking me occasionally if I'm feeling OK. I've already emailed Trevor to officially give him my resignation; I'm hoping that, because I've got in quickly, before he's sent me a dismissal letter, I won't have a black mark against my name for the rest of my life, but somehow I don't think he'll give in without a fight. Meanwhile Barbara's helping me with the children, and I've talked to her again about being careful not to let Molly feel left out. She seems to have taken it on board now. But the night before the appointment at Great Ormond Street, neither Ben nor I sleep much. I feel like I've been awake all night; in fact, I've just managed to doze off when I hear Ben going into the shower.

'Couldn't sleep,' he says when I mutter and cover my eyes as he turns on the light.

'I've only just *gone* to sleep.'

'Sorry.' He sighs and sits down on the edge of the bed. 'Were you lying awake listening for George's breathing, like I was?'

'Yes. It's what I do every night, Ben.' Then I stop, shaking my head. We're not going to start competing with each other over who's the most frightened for our son. We both are. We're petrified.

We're both going to the hospital with George this morning. Ben's taken the morning off, saying it was even more important for him to come to this appointment than to be with one of his GCSE classes just a few days before their exam.

'Has Trevor agreed to you taking the time off?' he asked me yesterday.

'Yes.' I'm so used to lying to him now, it's quite worrying how easily it slipped off my tongue. If he knew that all I've done this week, apart from going back and forth to the school, was to search for job vacancies online while Barbara pottered around the house, keeping things tidy for me, I can't imagine what he'd say.

It's an early morning appointment, so we drop Molly off at school on the way to park at a tube station. She's quiet, looking anxious as she says goodbye to me outside her classroom.

'Will you be back in time to meet me this afternoon, Mummy?' she asks. 'I don't want to go in a taxi with Granny again.'

'I'll be back, sweetheart,' I reassure her, but she clings to me as I kiss her goodbye.

'Is George going to be all right?' she says very quietly. 'His asthma's getting worse, isn't it? Will the doctors make him better? Will he have to stay in hospital?'

'We're going to see one of the very best doctors in London. Maybe even the whole world,' I add, just to make her feel less worried. 'I'm sure they'll soon have him feeling better.'

Of course, I'm not really sure of this at all – I'm not sure of anything any more. But she gives me a little smile and I send her into class with a thumbs-up and a reminder to try to listen to her teacher rather than thinking about anything else.

Neither Ben nor I talk much on the journey to Great Ormond Street.

If I Lost You   157

When I glance at him during the tube journey, I'm shocked by how pale he looks and the dark circles around his eyes, and I wonder if I look the same. Then I look at George – and my heart feels like it's about to break. I can see his little chest heaving, even through his T-shirt, with his laboured breathing. Have I got so used to this, now, that I normally hardly even notice it? He looks anxious, but he hasn't complained, this time, about having another hospital visit. I'm sure he wants someone to help him feel better as much as we do.

Fortunately, we don't have to wait very long until we're called in to see the doctor, who tells us she's called Mariana Fischer and she's a paediatric respiratory consultant. She seems reassuringly unfazed by everything we tell her, merely nodding sympathetically, smiling at George and asking him about school as well as about his symptoms.

'As Dr Taylor suggested,' she says, turning back to Ben and me, 'I'm going to do a few tests on George first. Then I want to ask you a few questions, if that's OK?'

'Of course, whatever you need to do,' Ben says.

The tests take a while and mostly involve George having to blow into things while she takes measurements. She does her best to make this fun for him, but he struggles with them, coughing and wheezing while he tries to follow her instructions. She then measures his height and gets him to stand on the scales, all the while smiling kindly at him but saying very little. Ben and I exchange nervous glances – it's impossible to know what she's thinking.

Finally, she suggests George plays in the toy corner on the other side of the consulting room, while she turns to us and runs through a list of questions: about any other conditions George might have, and then about the condition of our house, whether either of us smoke, or have any respiratory issues ourselves or in our family, and whether we keep birds, chickens or animals of any kind.

'We have a cat,' Ben says at once.

The doctor makes a note of this and Ben gives me a meaningful look.

'We had him tested for allergies, when he first started having asthma – or whatever this is,' I tell her quickly. 'But he's not allergic.'

'OK,' she says quietly, laying her pen down on the desk. 'Well, first of all

I have to tell you that this isn't asthma. And don't worry, I'm pretty sure your cat isn't to blame.'

'Then what is it?' Ben demands.

'Is it... serious?' My voice is shaking. I glance at George, but he's too involved with Lego to be taking any notice of us.

'Yes. I think it is.'

I feel the room start to spin – I have to put my head down. Ben's swearing under his breath.

'I think what we've got here,' Dr Fischer goes on, 'is interstitial lung disease. It's not common, but it's particularly rare in children. I've only seen a few cases. It's hard to diagnose.'

'He's been getting worse,' Ben says.

'Yes. And I can see from his size and weight, for his age, that he has what we call failure to thrive. His chest muscles are pulling inwards from struggling to make his lungs work. And his skin tone is slightly blue, isn't it?'

Neither of us responds. Neither of us has wanted to admit this, telling ourselves he was just naturally a little pale.

'And have you noticed his fingers?' the doctor goes on quietly. 'They're growing a little wider and more rounded at the ends – we call it clubbing. It's one of the symptoms.'

'I thought that was just the natural shape his fingers were developing,' I admit. 'It never occurred to me that it might mean anything – I'd have got him checked out sooner.'

'This isn't your fault, or your GP's fault. This condition is so unusual in children, and it's nearly always misdiagnosed as asthma at first – sometimes for years – even by the most experienced doctors.'

'So what do we do now?' Ben says. 'How do we cure this thing? Do we get different inhalers for him? Or tablets, or—'

Dr Fischer looks from one of us to the other for a moment, before she says, very slowly, as if to make sure we're listening, 'You both need to know, and understand, there is currently no cure for this disease.'

'No cure?' I repeat in a whisper. My head spins again. No. No, I can't accept this. We've found the answer, we know what's wrong with our baby boy – and there's *no cure*?

If I Lost You

'There must be something we can do,' Ben retorts, so loudly that I'm afraid George is going to hear, but fortunately there's music playing from one of the toys in the toy corner.

'What are you saying?' I whisper. 'Is this... is it...?' I can't get the words out. How can I? How can any mother possibly be expected to ask whether her child is going to die? 'Is it, like a cancer, that's going to get worse and worse until...' I put my hands over my face. No, I still can't say it.

'It's not a cancer, or anything similar to a cancer; it only affects the lungs,' she says gently. 'But it can be... life-limiting. We can't cure it, but we can try to treat it, and the treatment, we hope, will help George to enjoy a better life.'

There's something unspoken here. Something like *a better life, for as long as his life might last.*

'What sort of treatment are we talking about?' Ben asks, and the doctor goes on to describe steroids and drugs that would suppress George's immune system. She talks about the side effects he might get from the drugs, and how we'll have to try several different treatment options to find which give him the best results with the least problems, and how we'll need to bring him back for check-ups but some of these will be with our own GP, and how important it is for him to have all his vaccinations, and to avoid being in smoky environments.

I try to concentrate, but my brain is struggling to take it all in. I look at my little boy, innocently playing with the toys, and wonder how this can be allowed to happen. What did we do wrong? Why is this happening to us? *It's not fair.*

'Why did this happen?' I ask the doctor abruptly.

'I don't know,' she admits. 'There's no obvious reason, from what you've told me about his history, or the family's history. It's often impossible to pinpoint a reason for this disease. There might even have been a problem with George's lungs before he was born.'

'Tell me straight, doctor,' Ben interrupts her suddenly. 'Is he going to get better?'

'No. This disease isn't going to go away. But we can help you, help your son, to *feel* better. If the medications don't work, he might need oxygen

160 SHEILA NORTON

therapy. He might even need a ventilator at some point. Or he could, at worst, end up as a candidate for a lung transplant.'

'And if none of these things work?' Ben insists, almost angrily. I want to tell him not to ask. I don't want to hear this. I want to believe, for as long as I can, that George is going to be OK. But I can't speak. I sit in stunned silence, waiting to know the worst.

'Sometimes nothing works,' she admits. 'Sometimes patients don't survive.'

26

Ben and I don't talk about it on the journey home – not to each other, not to George. We somehow manage to respond to George's chatter about which toys he liked in the toy corner, and which ones were babyish. I manage to keep up the cheerful mummy pretence as I deliver him back to school, while Ben goes back to work and I pretend to return to my non-existent job.

'What did they say at the hospital?' Barbara asks me warily. She must be able to see from my face, from my silence, that it isn't good news.

'It's something very rare,' I say. I don't even want to go into detail. It hasn't sunk in with me properly yet – I don't feel ready to talk about it to anyone else, even to Barbara. Even to my parents, I think with a sudden jolt, as I realise they're going to want to know about this. How's my mum going to take it? She's finally going to have to give up her insistence that I'm imagining all this, that I'm inventing George's worsening symptoms for some nefarious purpose of my own.

'How rare?' Barbara asks me, looking puzzled. 'Has it got a name? I might have come across it when I was nursing.'

'Oh, I suppose you might. But the doctor said she's hardly seen any cases herself.'

I tell her what it's called, and she looks back at me blankly, before shrugging and saying perhaps it's a new type of asthma, and I can't, I just can't go into it, explaining it all, how serious it is, how George is now on some steroid medication but we don't even know if it'll be effective or not. I want to close my eyes and wake up later to find this has all gone away, that it was all a bad dream and we have two healthy little children and everything's OK, nobody's going to die. Oh, please God, nobody's going to die.

'Don't cry,' Barbara says, pulling me closer to her. 'Come on, the doctors know what's wrong now, they'll know how to make him better.'

'Yes,' I say, wiping my eyes. 'OK.'

I make some lunch but can't eat mine. I need to get back online to keep up the job search, but when I open my laptop, I find myself doing Google searches for George's condition in the hope that Dr Fischer missed something vital – something she doesn't know about, a potential cure that's only just been found, a new treatment that's in trial and proving successful. But there's nothing other than the things she told us. Nothing other than bad news.

'Shall I go and meet the children for you?' Barbara offers when it's time for school to finish.

'No, I'll go.' I need to get up, make an effort, try to put on my happy mummy face again. 'You can come with me if you like? For the ride?'

'That'd be nice. Yes, I'll come, dear.'

'Perhaps we'll stop off at the café the children like,' I suggest. Anything to prolong the pretence that there's nothing wrong. To keep pretending to be happy mummy for as long as I can. We didn't stop for a hot chocolate treat with George after the hospital appointment – Ben and I were both too shell-shocked. *Daddy needs to get back to work*, I told George. So they're both excited when I tell them we'll have the treat now instead.

'Is Granny coming for the café treat?' George asks, holding her hand as we walk back to the car.

'Of course.'

By the time we arrive home after having cakes and hot chocolate, which I really shouldn't be buying while I've got no money going into my account and I can't bring myself yet to go and sign on as unemployed, Ben's already home, wondering where we've been.

'To treat the kids at the café, sorry. But you're a bit early, aren't you?'

If I Lost You   163

'No, not really,' he says. He sounds strange – I'd almost say shifty, as if there's something he's not telling me. Perhaps it's just work worries – the GCSEs beginning on Monday – but I can't exactly push him to open up to me, considering how much I'm keeping to myself at the moment.

'Have you called your parents yet?' he asks.

'No. I'll do it after the kids are asleep.'

'I presume you told Barbara. What did she say?'

'I don't think she understands how serious it is. I didn't go into detail.'

'Probably just as well,' he mutters.

If he says anything about Barbara spoiling George even more now, I think I'll scream. I want to spoil him myself; I want to fuss over him and baby him, hold him and never let him go. But I know, I'm not stupid, I know we mustn't frighten him, or upset Molly. I know we've got to be the adults, the parents, the people who hold it all together and can't fall apart. Knowing it is the easy part.

We've finished dinner and the kids are winding down in front of the TV with Barbara when I realise Ebony hasn't been in for his food yet. It's a sunny day, the evenings stay light now until late, so I'm not unduly worried, but he's normally hungry by this time. I go to the back door and call him, but he doesn't come rushing in. I guess he's found something interesting down the garden, and the cat flap's open for him to come in when he's ready, so I don't think about it again until much later, long after the children have gone to bed. Even then, I don't spend too long calling him and looking for him again, as I know I've got to call Mum first. I'm horribly aware that I haven't checked in with her at all since I left, in a bad mood, after Dad's heart attack. After we argued so badly. And now I've got to give her dreadful news.

'How's Dad?' I ask as soon as she answers the call. 'I take it he's home from hospital now?'

'Yes. He's doing well. Behaving himself and taking lots of rest.'

'Good. Give him our love.'

There's an uncomfortable pause, then she says, her words tumbling over each other in her haste to get them out, 'I'm sorry if I upset you, with what I said when you were here.'

'Well, I'm sorry too that we argued.' I hesitate for a second, then go on quickly. 'But to be honest, you did upset me, yes.'

'I'm sorry. I'd never want to hurt you, darling, but—'

'Mum, I need to tell you something,' I interrupt her quickly. 'It's about George, so please don't say any more until I've told you.'

'OK,' she says. 'What is it? Another asthma attack?'

'It's not asthma.' I'm talking over her, loudly, shouting her down as she tries to protest, even now, that I'm imagining things or exaggerating. 'Mum, it's *not* asthma, we've been to Great Ormond Street today, to see a paediatric lung specialist, and she's done some tests on George, and asked us questions, and she's sure of what it is, and I don't want it to be this – but I've got to trust her, haven't I? I've got to get the right treatment for George. She's the right doctor, the one who can give him the best chance.'

I'm crying yet again; I can hardly get my words out and I have to stop to blow my nose.

'Best chance?' Mum echoes. Her voice sounds faint, as if she's on the other side of the world. 'What is it that she thinks he's got?'

'It's called childhood interstitial lung disease, and it's very rare. And he's going to be on steroids to see if they help, and if not there are other treatments she can try.'

'But hopefully the steroids will work? They'll stop his cough, and all the wheezing and—'

'We're hoping they'll help to control his symptoms. But they're not a cure.'

There's a long silence. Then, 'So what is the cure?'

'There isn't one,' I say, sniffing. 'There's no cure.'

'That's ridiculous,' Mum says. 'There must be. We'll take him to a private hospital – Dad and I will pay. Whatever it takes. If there's an operation, or—'

'Mum, there isn't. Dr Fischer is the most qualified specialist there is – she'd tell us exactly the same thing if we saw her privately. The only operation would be a... a last resort. A lung transplant, if he could even get one.' I swallow and go on, 'If it ever gets to that stage. But we have to try to think positively, for George's sake. We have to believe the drug treatment will help him.'

'But it won't cure him,' she repeats quietly, as if she's trying to convince herself.

'No.' I can't be cross with her any more; I'm not. This must be even more of a shock to her than it was to us, because she was so determined to close her eyes to the idea of George having anything seriously wrong with him. 'I'm sorry, Mum – sorry to have to give you this news, on top of what you've been through with Dad. Are you going to be all right?'

'Of course,' she says. I picture her giving herself a little shake, standing up straight, squaring her shoulders, and I almost wish I hadn't had to tell her. I almost wish I could have let her go on believing her only grandson was just having the occasional asthma attack and would probably grow out of it. 'But, well, perhaps there's still a chance this doctor's got it wrong, don't you think, JoJo? I still think it seems exactly like asthma.'

She's still in denial; I can't really blame her now. We say goodbye after I've promised to call her more often, sent love to my dad and promised to go over to see them again soon. I'm glad to have got past that horrible atmosphere between us, but I only wish it hadn't been something like this that pushed me into making up with her.

'Are you all right, love?' Barbara asks me when I go into the lounge, throwing myself down on the sofa and staring at the TV without actually seeing it.

'Not really.'

'Come here.' She pulls me into a hug and I stay leaning against her. She doesn't say anything else – she doesn't need to. I'm just glad she's here.

* * *

'Where's Ebony?' George asks in the morning, looking down at the cat's food bowl – still full of untouched food from last evening.

'He didn't come in last night,' I say, picking up the bowl to dispose of the food. 'I'll give him another call now; he must be really hungry.'

It's not like him. He nearly always comes in at night. I'm trying not to worry, trying not to let the kids see I'm concerned, but it rained during the night and I was sure he'd be indoors by the time we came down for breakfast.

'He's probably found a nice mouse to chase,' Ben says cheerfully to the children, although we both know Ebony's never been much of a hunter.

I put my shoes on and walk around the garden, calling him, shaking a packet of cat treats to attract him back.

'Has he run away?' Molly asks when I come back inside without him. Her voice wobbles and I try to give her a reassuring smile.

'I'm sure he hasn't.'

'Let's go out and look for him, George,' she says. It's Saturday; they're both still in their PJs. I tell them to finish their breakfast and get dressed first, and as soon as they're both ready they go out in the garden, shouting and calling for Ebony.

'It's not like him,' I say again to Ben. 'I'm wondering if I should knock at the neighbours' doors or put a message on the WhatsApp group, in case he's got locked in one of their sheds or something.'

He sighs. 'OK, listen. As far as the kids are concerned, he's gone missing, all right?'

I stare at him. 'What are you talking about? Where is he, then?'

'In a good home.'

'What? What good home? How do you...?'

Then I look at his face again, and I know. I know what he's done. I stand up. I want to hit him; I've never hit anybody in my life – even the realisation that I want to is enough to make me howl. Barbara's staring at us both with her mouth open and perhaps it's her presence that stops me.

'I'm only thinking of our son,' Ben begins, but I shout him down.

'No, you're not. You're thinking of yourself, trying to make yourself feel better, thinking it's something you can control – but you can't, you can't control this, Ben, neither of us can.'

'The doctor mentioned animals – she actually asked us—'

'And she actually said the cat was fine. Where is he? What have you done with him? When did you *give him away*?'

'Yesterday afternoon,' he admits, beginning to sound less sure of himself. 'I got home a bit early. I had a free period but I couldn't work, I was too upset, I wanted to see George – but you were all out. One of the teaching assistants has been talking about adopting a cat, so I called her.'

'You sneaked Ebony out of the house while we were out.' I'm so

If I Lost You 167

disgusted I feel like I might be sick. 'What were you going to do? Let the children wonder forever what happened to him? That cat is your son's best friend. He's his comfort when he's not well. Can't you get it into your thick head? What you've done isn't going to help George, it's going to make him ten times worse.'

As if on cue, the back door's flung open and the children pile in.

'We can't find him,' Molly says.

I look at George. He's crying and wheezing at the same time, holding onto the door frame as if his thin little frame needs its support.

'Has he run away, Mummy?' he croaks 'Why? Why won't he come back?'

'It's OK, George.' I pull both children towards me. 'Daddy's going to go and get him.'

'Do you know where he is?' Molly says, looking at Ben hopefully.

He nods, trying to force a smile, trying to say something, but I talk over him. 'We've had a phone call; someone's found him.'

'Can we come with you to get him back, Daddy?' Molly shouts excitedly.

'No,' he says. 'I'd better go on my own.'

'Yes, why don't you two get Ebony's bed all ready for him, and put some food in his dish, and fresh water?' I suggest, and they scurry to get their coats off, arguing over which toys they're going to lay out for the cat as a welcome-home present.

I can't even look at Ben as he walks to the door to get his car keys.

'Remember the cat carrier,' I say.

'It's still in my car,' he mutters, and leaves without another word.

27

Barbara hasn't said anything; she still doesn't, after Ben goes out, and I'm grateful for it. He's home within about half an hour, looking sheepish, not meeting my eyes as he lets the cat out of the carrier and the kids duly make a big fuss of him. I can't bring myself to ask whether his colleague was upset at being asked to hand him back – I'm afraid I don't even care. That's Ben's problem. Perhaps he'll help her find a cat at the adoption centre.

'I'm going to have to explain George's condition to him – and to Molly – soon,' I find myself saying to Barbara during the afternoon while Ben's in the garden. 'I don't know what to say – how much to tell him.'

'What does Ben say?' she asks.

'We haven't discussed it. We're not exactly talking much at the moment. As you've probably noticed.'

'He'll want an input, though, won't he.' She pauses, looking at me thoughtfully before going on, 'But I'd say George is a bit too little to spell it all out to him.'

'Yes. I agree.'

'Why don't you just tell him it's not asthma but another thing – you can give him the name if he wants it but he won't remember it; it's too long and difficult. And tell him that's why he's got new medication, and hopefully it'll help him.'

If I Lost You   169

'Yes. That sounds sensible. I've got to tell his teacher, too. I'll put it in an email – the full facts,' I add with a sigh.

'If you'd rather talk to her in person, I can come with you when you pick them up on Monday, and keep them both occupied in the playground.'

'Oh, thank you. Yes, that would be better.' I look at her, suddenly doubtful. 'That's if you're still going to be with us on Monday?'

'Why wouldn't I be? As long as you need me.'

'Well, yes, but I presume you'll want to be getting home soon.'

'What for?' she says with a snort of laughter.

I frown. I can't deny I've been grateful to have her around, but I presumed she'd be making plans to go back any time now.

'Well – it's your home,' I say with a little false laugh. 'You'll be glad to get back to your own bed, won't you?'

'Not really. George's bed's really comfy – much nicer than mine. And you've got a lovely home,' she adds wistfully.

'Well, yes, it's nice, but it's not very big.'

'It's the biggest house *I've* ever been in.'

I suppose this brings me up a bit short. Ben and I think of it as quite a small house – not that we don't appreciate how lucky we are to have it, in today's climate. But it certainly isn't grand, or particularly spacious, especially when there are two little kids running around in it. Molly's bedroom is just about big enough to have the truckle bed out, next to her own bed, but George's room is the typical 'box room', with no space for anything other than his bed, a child-size wardrobe and small chest of drawers. I dream sometimes about being able to afford to move to a four-bedroom house, perhaps detached, with a bigger garden, but I know it's never likely to happen.

'Well, I'm glad you've found it comfortable,' I say. 'But obviously, the children will be happier once they've got their own rooms again.'

'Why?' she says, sounding genuinely surprised. 'Lots of kids share bedrooms. Your two have been very lucky, having a room each, but it's a luxury.'

'Not really. Molly finds it hard to sleep with George in her room. And anyway...' Why am I feeling the need to justify this? 'It's what we want for them,' I add firmly.

'So I suppose you want to get rid of me.' She's trying to make it sound like a joke, but I'm worried, now, that there's a part of her that's actually serious. She really would like to stay – perhaps forever.

'Of course I don't want to get rid of you, don't be silly. You've been such a help to me, and to the kids, especially during these last few days. But, well, everyone has to go home eventually, don't they? We'll still see each other all the time.'

She doesn't respond to this, and I decide it's probably best to leave her to mull it over and realise she can't expect to outstay her welcome.

* * *

George wakes up coughing and wheezing during the night.

'He's woke me up again,' Molly complains when I go into the bedroom.

'He can't help it, Mollipop. Perhaps we'll get you back into your own bedroom soon.'

'Good,' she says. 'Will Granny be going home?'

'I don't want her to go home,' George protests. 'I like her being here.'

'Let's not argue about it now. Come on, we're all tired, and you seem a bit better now.'

'I still feel wheezy. Why did that doctor say it's not asthma, Mummy?'

This really isn't the time I wanted to have this conversation. But I've always tried to answer the children's questions as they come up.

'Because it turns out it isn't, Georgie,' I say. 'It's something else, very similar, but it needs different medicines from the ones you had when we thought it was asthma.'

I watch his little face screw up in confusion.

'So what do I say at school if I think I'm having an asthma attack?'

'You can just say you feel wheezy. I'm going to tell Mrs Austin about it.'

'Will the medicine make George better?' Molly asks. She sounds anxious – more anxious even than George, who seems to have accepted my explanation and is now complaining that he's tired and wants to go back to sleep.

If I Lost You   171

'We hope so. If it doesn't, though, there are others he can have.' I'm trying to keep my voice level and calm. I kiss them both goodnight and go back to bed, telling myself I've done the best I can to explain it to them – for now. I'm sure there'll be more questions, and I'll just have to answer them as and when they crop up. It's not going to be easy, and Ben seems to have opted out at the moment. It's as if, because his ridiculous decision to give the cat away wasn't the right thing to do, he's not prepared to contribute any more.

Or perhaps I'm just being unfair; I know he's struggling, just as I am. I only wish I felt that we were in it together, comforting each other the way we should be. I'm going to miss Barbara when she does go home.

* * *

'Are you still looking for another job?' Barbara asks me on the Monday morning, after Ben's gone to work. I'm dressed as if I'm going into the office, for Ben's benefit, but I'm sitting here, sipping a cup of tea, waiting for Molly to finish cleaning her teeth.

'Yes.' I sigh. 'Well, not strictly speaking. I mean, I haven't looked very hard yet – I've had other things on my mind.'

'I wondered if you'd decided to give up work. You know, be a stay-at-home mum, especially now George needs you more.'

I shake my head. She has no idea. 'No. Unfortunately, we're not wealthy enough for me to do that.'

'Can't you go back to doing what you did before – the classes you told me about?'

'I wish I could, honestly. I was so much happier doing that. But it's difficult now, with George needing me so often. It's not fair to clients to keep cancelling classes at short notice.'

'But you've got me, now. I could always look after George when he's not well.'

I look at her in surprise. 'I couldn't ask that of you. It would be too often. Ben's right – so's my mum – I can't go back to doing the classes until the kids are older.' The word *older* almost trips me up; I utter it in a kind of gasp, as the thought flits unwillingly through my mind: *if George even gets older*. I shudder and dismiss the thought before it can take hold.

'I'd be more than happy, you know that. I love looking after them. *Both* of them,' she adds, nodding at me. 'I've taken it on board, what you've said. I'm treating Molly the same, making a point of it.'

'I know. I've noticed. Thank you.'

I think about her offer while I'm taking the children to school, but I still feel uncomfortable about the idea of expecting Barbara to be on call permanently for me just so that I can go back to the career I used to love. I've got responsibilities; George has to come first. Accepting the occasional offer of help from Barbara is different from expecting it whenever George isn't fit for school. Especially as, much as I hate to have to think about it, that might be happening more and more frequently. No, I need to be realistic. I need a job where I can work flexibly, preferably from home. I go back to searching the Internet for vacancies as soon as I get home, but I'm beginning to think I'm going to have to head for the Job Centre, and I'm going to have to tell Ben. I can't go on like this indefinitely.

Barbara comes with me this afternoon to collect the children, so that I can have a word with Mrs Austin about George. She looks genuinely upset as I describe the bleak scenario Dr Fischer presented to us about his condition.

'I'm so sorry, Mrs Hudson,' she says, putting a comforting hand on my arm. 'I'll make sure Miss Brent knows and understands about this, for when she needs to call you if George is unwell at school.'

I thank her and go on to have a quick word with Molly's teacher too, explaining that Molly's quite worried about her brother at the moment.

'She's actually been better, in class, since I had to have a word with your husband about her,' she says after she's expressed her sympathy. 'But I'm glad I know now what's been worrying her.'

'It's not the only thing,' I admit. 'I'm afraid the atmosphere at home hasn't been good recently.'

'It must be a very stressful situation for you as a family,' she says gently. 'I do hope George's condition can be improved.'

* * *

If I Lost You 173

'She's still here,' Ben says pointedly to me when he comes home from school to find Barbara listening to the children's reading while Ebony's curled up on the sofa between them.

'Yes, and still being really helpful.'

'That's all very well but I don't want her getting the idea she can stay indefinitely.'

'I know.' I sigh. I know Molly wants her room back to herself, and I know the longer I let things drift, the harder it's going to be. 'OK, I'll talk to her. I'll take her home tomorrow.'

I wait until the children have gone into the kitchen for their after-school biscuit, before sitting down with Barbara.

'I'm sorry,' I tell her. 'But I need to take you home.'

She looks startled. 'What, now?'

'No. Tomorrow, though. Don't look at me like that – we've talked about this; you know you can't stay forever.'

'I thought you said it was helpful, me being here.'

'It is. Honestly, I'm really grateful, but we can still help each other when you're back at home, can't we, like we did before. I'll take you shopping first, get you stocked up with everything you need, then I'll take you home and make sure your flat's clean and tidy.'

'I'm not going back there,' she says.

I stare at her, confused. She's not saying she's not going back *yet* – just that she's not going back, full stop.

'What do you mean? You haven't got anywhere else to go.'

'Why can't I stay here? You've got plenty of room; I'm not putting you out. I help with the kids – I've offered to look after them while you work.'

'That's not the point. You just can't stay here, not permanently. It isn't right. I've already told you, the children want their own rooms, and we want that for them too. I'll try to see you more often, OK? I know you must get lonely, and I know you can't get out and about very easily, so I'll try to call in on you during the week as well as at weekends.'

'If you're not too busy with your adoptive parents,' she says sulkily.

'My *parents*,' I correct her, beginning to feel annoyed.

'You still think of them as your real parents, then?'

'Yes, of course I do. They brought me up. They are my parents. I was legally their child from the moment they—'

'*She* wasn't the one who gave birth to you, though, was she.'

I'm so taken aback by this, I don't know what to say for a minute. She's never talked like this before. I know it's only because she's disappointed, hurt. She doesn't want to go home, I get that, but she's not a child, she can't expect to have her own way just because she wants to.

'Don't be like that,' I say, trying to keep my patience. 'You said when we first met that you were glad my parents gave me a good childhood. You must realise I love them, that I'll always think of them as my parents. That doesn't mean I don't love you too.'

She looks back at me steadily.

'Do you? I told you to call me *Mum*, when we first met, but you never do. Why's that, then, if you say you love me?'

'What? Yes, you're my mum too, but... in a different way. I'm sorry I don't call you that, but it would be difficult. Confusing.' I pause. She's still looking disgruntled. This whole conversation has shocked me, but I don't want her going home upset. I don't want us to fall out – she's the only person who's consistently been on my side recently. 'Let's move on,' I suggest. 'But please don't expect me to stop loving my parents, visiting them, caring about them, like I care about you. That's ridiculous.'

She doesn't reply. I can't spend any longer sitting here trying to get through to her, and besides, frankly, I've got other things to worry about. She'll come round; she knows I care about her really, she's just disappointed about having to go home.

28

'I feel wheezy again, Mummy,' George says the next morning, as he comes downstairs for breakfast.

'Is he going to stay off school again?' Molly's following him down the stairs. 'It's not fair, I wish I had asthma, or whatever it is.'

'No, you don't,' I tell her. 'It's horrible for him.'

'So is Granny going to look after him?'

Ben looks at me. 'You can't go on like this,' he says quietly, seriously. 'You're either going to have to stand up to Trevor, or get a different job.'

'I know.' I feel another frisson of guilt. How can I tell him – now – that I'm actually at home all day? I should have told him from the start. 'I'm going to sort it out, Ben,' I say. 'But at least, for today, Barbara's still here.'

'I thought she was going home today.'

'She can go later. After school.'

He nods. 'Fine. But we really can't keep doing this. You need to—'

'I know. I'll talk to Trevor today,' I lie. Perhaps I can pretend the supposed talk goes so badly that I have no option but to walk out. At least then I can stop lying to him.

* * *

I search for jobs all morning, while Barbara sits with George, reading to him and helping him do a jigsaw. Every time I glance at him, I feel a wave of panic and desperation. He looks so pale and tired, so small and thin. How have Ben and I been fooling ourselves for so long that this was just asthma? It's obvious to me now that it isn't. In the afternoon he has a sleep, and I talk to Barbara about how to sign on as unemployed. I'm going to need to do it – and Ben's going to need to know. She's so sympathetic and helpful about it that I feel bad all over again about the conversation last night, bad about sending her home to her miserable little flat. But I have to stick to my guns. The kids come first.

'There's only one biscuit left in the tin,' Molly says later, when she goes to the kitchen for the usual after-school treat.

George stirs from the sofa. He's only had soup today but he perks up at the mention of biscuits.

'Well, I want one, Molly,' he says, getting to his feet.

'Shall we open another packet, Mummy?' Molly says.

'That was the last packet.'

'Who's been eating them all?' she demands. 'The tin was full yesterday.'

I feel a flush of guilt. Have Barbara and I really eaten that many biscuits – comfort food – while we've been sitting around at home all day?

'Is it Daddy?' George says, giggling. 'Does he eat all the biscuits after we've gone to bed?'

'Maybe.' I break the last Digestive and give them half each. 'There you go – that'll have to do for today.'

'Molly's half is bigger than mine,' George protests, predictably.

'No it's not,' she says with a superior air. 'Halves can't be bigger or smaller, can they, Mummy – they have to be the same size otherwise they're not halves.'

'Your half's still bigger than mine.'

'So it's not a half, it's a *piece*. Daddy says it's maths, George.'

But he ignores her and goes back into the lounge. Molly shakes her head, as if in despair.

'He needs to learn these things,' she says, 'or he won't get a good job when he's grown up, will he?'

If I Lost You

I give her a hug. 'I don't think we need to worry too much about that just yet.'

Then I turn away, because the thought that's come into my head is so awful, I actually feel sick: *If ever.*

* * *

'I'm going to take you home now, then, Barbara,' I remind her when I hear Ben's key in the door. 'But thank you, I'm so grateful again for today.'

'You're welcome,' she says, a little stiffly.

'Does Granny *have* to go home?' George says.

'Well, we all have to go home sooner or later, when we've been staying somewhere else, don't we?' I try to reason.

'Yes, George,' his sister points out. 'Like last year when we had to come home from our other grandma and grandpa in Spain, and you cried.'

'That was different. And I didn't cry, I just stopped smiling.' He looks up at me and goes on, 'I wish Granny could live with us for always.'

'*I* don't,' Molly says before I can stop her. 'Because if she did, I'd always have to have you in my bedroom with me.'

* * *

'Ben doesn't want me around, does he,' Barbara says flatly. We're on the way back to her flat after stopping off at the supermarket to get her some shopping.

'Don't be silly, of course he does. Come on, we've been through this already. I know it must be hard, going back to your flat again, but it just makes it harder, the longer you put it off.'

'You don't know, you've got no idea how hard it is. Not at all. You live in that lovely house with all those rooms, and your own garden, you don't know what it's like to live in a cold, damp flat with horrible neighbours, when I can't afford heating in the winter and my arthritis plays up something awful.'

She sounds so wounded, I actually stop feeling unjustly criticised and start wondering if I could have done any more than I already have, to help her. Should I try to help her find a better flat? Would the council take any notice if I badgered them to move her somewhere better, or get the damp sorted out? I don't know how these things work. I've never needed to help Mum and Dad with anything; they've always been so capable.

'Perhaps you need to be more specific and tell me how I can help,' I say. 'Apart from taking you shopping every week. I'm happy to clean your flat for you, for instance.'

'I'd sooner not live there.'

'Yes, well perhaps that's something else we can look into together.'

'Really?' she asks, brightening up.

'Yes. Perhaps we can compose a letter to the housing department, explaining about the damp in your flat?'

'Oh, that'd be a waste of time,' she retorts. 'I thought you were going to say I could move in with you.'

We drive the rest of the way in silence, because quite honestly I don't know what else I can say. I can understand how miserable she must feel, going back to her lonely life after staying with the family. But I can't let myself be swayed by this emotional blackmail, however fond I've become of her. I'm sure she'll settle down once she's back in her routine.

Ben's in the kitchen, cooking dinner, when I get home.

'Was she OK about going home?' he says.

'Not really. But she'll get used to it, I suppose.'

'And how did it go with Trevor today?'

I swallow. Here we go. 'I tried talking to him. But he was so unreasonable – he won't give an inch.'

'So what are you going to do? You can't keep asking Barbara to come round every time George isn't well enough for school, and your mum's too busy with your dad.'

'I know. I... told Trevor I'm leaving. In fact, I've walked out.'

I wait for the shock and condemnation, but for a moment he just keeps turning sausages under the grill. Then he nods and says, calmly, 'Good for you.'

I'm stunned. Has he actually understood what I've said?

'I'm unemployed, Ben,' I say, to underline the fact. 'I'll have no money coming in.'

If I Lost You 179

'So sign on at the Job Centre while you look for something else.'

'Barbara says I might not get any benefits right away because I've left voluntarily. But if I explain the reason, explain about George, perhaps there's a way...'

'Meanwhile start looking for other jobs.'

'I *have* been looking, Ben. There's nothing about, I keep telling you, nothing that fits around school hours. Even the work-from-home jobs are mostly full time. It's all very well for you, as a teacher. I wish I was still teaching my classes, to be honest. If anything, it's been harder to take the days off I've needed for George since I've been working at a part-time office job than it was when I was my own boss.'

'We've talked about this already,' he reminds me, sounding irritated now. 'It wouldn't be easier, not now George has... this diagnosis. You're probably going to need to be around even more for him. Working from home is the only option, and you can't exactly take yoga classes here.'

I'm grateful – and surprised – that Ben's taken my resignation so well, but still, I wish he'd at least try to understand how much happier I'd be if I could only go back to teaching my classes. It's not until the kids are in bed, and I'm sitting with my laptop in front of me yet again, looking for non-existent jobs, that something occurs to me, and I wonder why I haven't thought of it before. Couldn't I just hold classes at weekends? And perhaps I could try starting *children's* yoga classes during the school holidays. That could be popular. I stare at my screen, not seeing it, imagining myself instead advertising courses for kids, different levels for different age groups, keeping it simple, teaching them easy movements accompanied by music – kids' music for the youngest ones. It would be fun. Children are so supple, they'd find it easy, they'd enjoy it; it would be good for them too. I bet a lot of parents would sign their kids up. Then maybe I could run adult classes during the evenings? Yes! A couple of evenings a week, while Ben's at home with the children. Why have I never thought of this before? I must have been so busy, so frantically caught up on the treadmill of rushing to and from that awful, awful job, working for that awful man, that I just didn't realise there was an option almost staring me in the face.

'Ben,' I begin, my heart racing with excitement. 'I've had an idea.'

'As long as it's not for Barbara to move in with us and look after the children,' he says.

I close my eyes. It's no good, I'm not telling him. The way we are together these days, how can I suggest he covers the childcare at weekends or in the evenings? He'll just keep saying it'd be easier if I found a work-from-home job. He doesn't want me to go back to teaching, he's made that clear. Even my mum thinks I should stick with office work. Barbara's been the only one to give me any encouragement.

It's what I want, I think to myself, a little resentfully. I'm going to look into it anyway. If I can present Ben with a fait accompli, he'll have to agree. Why shouldn't I put my own wishes first for once?

29

I tell Ben I'm going to the Job Centre the next day – the lies are second nature now – but spend the whole day researching venue options for my new classes and, having found a small hall that isn't too expensive and which would work well, I decide to start promoting them on social media right away. It's the most cheerful, or perhaps I should say the least depressed, I've felt for a long time.

Over the next few days George seems to settle down a little; while he still gets very breathless with any kind of activity, the cough has eased, and he hasn't had any more night-time attacks of wheeziness. I start daring to hope that the steroid medication might be working. Dr Fischer warned us George might have side effects and he'll need regular check-ups, but the fact that he seems so obviously better is making my heart sing with relief.

Nadia calls me the next week. I nearly don't pick up the call as I've written our friendship off, but curiosity gets the better of me.

'I should probably say sorry,' she says, a little reluctantly.

'Well, OK, I suppose. And I should probably ask how things are going now for you.'

'I'm back with Ahmed. He took me back. I couldn't stand it with my parents any longer.'

I want to say that surely isn't a very good reason for going back to someone she's not happy with and raising his hopes. I imagine she'll leave again as soon as she *falls in love* with the next man. But she's not my responsibility, and I'm not giving my opinion any more.

'And how is it at work?' I ask her.

'Same as ever. But Trevor's realising, already, how much work you were doing. Until he gets someone new in, he's had to ask Ramona to do some of it, and she's so annoyed about it, she's threatening to resign now. He's stressed out of his mind. You never know, he might even beg you to come back.'

'He knows where he can go, if he does.'

We both manage a little laugh, but I don't think either of our hearts are really in it. The friendship isn't going to survive my departure from the office, but at least she had the decency – in the end – to apologise. After I've hung up, I call Barbara. She hasn't picked up the last couple of times I've tried her, and I'm not sure if she's been out – where would she go? – or is just refusing to speak to me. But this time she does answer, and she still sounds grumpy.

'I've been to see my doctor,' she says. 'Don't worry, I got the bus.'

'Well, that was silly – I'd have taken you if you'd called me; you know I'm not at work now,' I say, exasperated. Is she really going to punish me like this because I couldn't let her move in with us? Surely not. 'What did you see the doctor about?'

'My knees. The arthritis has got worse. And he said I'll probably die from pneumonia this winter if I'm still living in that flat. Still, at least you'll be rid of me then.'

'Oh, come on, please don't start being melodramatic. Of course nobody wants you to die. But you need to ask the council to find you somewhere else to live if that flat is really making you ill. I've already offered to write you a letter for them, spelling it out.'

'No, don't you worry about me,' she says. 'I know you've got enough on your plate. How's my poor little Georgie? I haven't seen him for ages.'

In fact, it's only been about a week. I start to tell her how he seems to be improving now on the medication.

'Well, that's good,' she says. 'So I suppose you won't need me any more,

If I Lost You 183

to look after him. Not till he gets ill again and you need to pretend to Ben that you've got to go to work.'

'Ben knows now. I've told him. Look, please don't be like this. I'd still like you to come round to see us,' I say. 'The kids miss you.'

'Well, I'll have to see if I can fit you in,' she says sarcastically.

I tell Ben about it this evening, but predictably, he just shakes his head.

'Is her flat *really* that bad?'

'Yes. It's cold and damp during the winter, that's what worries me. She's not in very good health, and her doctor's apparently warned her she could die if she has to live there for another winter.'

'And you believe that, do you? You're even more gullible than I thought.'

I close my eyes, sighing. Perhaps he's right. Perhaps Barbara is exaggerating, or making things up completely, to try to get me to give in and let her live with us. Perhaps I need to harden my heart a little more. However fond I've got of her, the fact remains that we've only known each other for a matter of months. Even if we did have a spare bedroom, I'm not at all sure I'd be willing to have her move in. Not yet – if ever.

* * *

By the middle of the following week, I've already got classes booked for the summer holidays, which are approaching fast. They're introductory courses, one for adults and one for children. I'm hoping that these will lead to people signing up for evening or Saturday classes in September; I've booked the hall for those already, and I've got a list of people interested in them, a few of whom were my previous students from years back. I've done all of this, but I haven't told Ben yet, and I realise that if he doesn't agree, all my plans will collapse. I veer between excitement at the thought of my new career and fear at having to cancel everything if he doesn't agree. I can't exactly force him to have the kids every Saturday morning and on two evenings every week if he's so dead set against it that he'd actually oppose me on this. And what if we don't end up staying together? I can't pretend there's no possibility, even if we are more reluctant than ever to upset the children any further.

Despite not telling Ben yet, I've been talking to Mum about it; we're phoning each other every other day now, like we used to. I like to check up on my dad, of course, and she says he's doing well. But she's struggling to come to terms with the fact that George is actually ill – that it isn't just a figment of my imagination – and I still find that quite hurtful. And it doesn't help that she's not supportive about me going back to teaching, either.

'If Ben's not behind you, supporting you with this, Jo, it's not going to work,' she says. 'I do think it's a shame that you gave up that job. I know your boss could be unreasonable, but still.'

'Unreasonable? Mum, he would have actually fired me for coming to see Dad when he had his heart attack, if I hadn't got in first and told him to stick it.'

'And now you're out of work.'

'But not for long.'

And, if anything, this conversation has made me even more determined: I'm going ahead with this, whatever happens.

* * *

George has been missing Barbara. I've told him she's been busy, and had a lot of appointments, but the truth is that I thought we should probably have a short break from her following the contretemps about taking her home.

'I'll see if she can come round next week,' I promise as I'm kissing him goodnight. He might be feeling a little better, but he still looks so small and sad, wearing the same pyjamas as last summer as he's barely grown since then. Ever since Ben brought Ebony back, George has had him sleeping on the end of his bed every night. I actually think that seeing how distraught the children were at the loss of their cat made Ben back down on the whole issue. I'm still finding it hard to forgive what he did, but I tell myself the stress of George's diagnosis must have made him lose the plot. I sometimes feel like I'm losing it myself, but I just have to go on, keeping my smile in place for George's sake. For Molly's sake, too, because I'm all too aware of how upset my precious daughter gets about things. I ask her this evening, as I do regularly now, if she's worried about anything.

If I Lost You

'I'm *trying* not to be,' she says. 'But I still don't like it when I hear you and Daddy arguing.'

'I'm sorry, sweetie. I don't like it when I hear you and George arguing, either, but it's just what we do with people at home, sometimes, isn't it.'

'I suppose. And at least Sophie likes me again now cos she says I'm not being naughty any more. I told her I wasn't being naughty, I was just being worried about things, and she was nice to me then, she said I could talk to her about stuff. She says she worries sometimes too, cos her mummy cries at home when her daddy shouts at her, and at least when you argue with Daddy he doesn't shout and make you cry, does he? So it's worse for her.'

I hug her tight and kiss her goodnight, and go back downstairs feeling sick with a kind of shame. My daughter thinks she's luckier than her friend because even if Ben and I argue a lot, he doesn't shout and make me cry. What does that say about us?

The next day, I call Barbara with the aim of asking her to come over at the weekend. I'm sitting in the garden, lifting up my face to the sunshine, feeling almost relaxed for somebody who's currently unemployed.

'Hi! How are you?' I ask cheerfully when she picks up.

'Not good. My arthritis is playing up something awful.'

'I'm sorry to hear that. Why don't I pick you up and bring you over here at the weekend? The children are missing you. So am I.'

'Don't bother. I was going to call you anyway, to let you know I've told the council I'm giving up the flat.'

'You've what?' I sit up straight. 'Are they going to rehouse you somewhere better? Have you written to them?'

'No. No point. But I've got to get out of here, I told you what my doctor said.'

'You can't just *give up* the flat; you need to wait for the council to find you somewhere else. I told you I'd help you write a letter, or Ben will.'

'I can't wait. I need to move now. I can't stand it here any longer.'

'So where are you going to live? You can't just make yourself homeless.'

'Well, that's really up to you, isn't it? But I know what you'll say – or what Ben will.'

'Look, if it's really an emergency and it's only temporary, I can talk to him, but—'

'But I know what he'll say. I know he doesn't want me around, and the trouble is, Jo, you haven't got the backbone to stand up to him, not even for me – your mother, when I might be putting my life at risk by living here. You don't care.'

I'm too stunned to respond for a moment. I actually can't believe she's talking like this. Has she suddenly gone mad, had a stroke or something? This is the same woman who was talking about us loving each other just the other week – the one person who's been on my side about everything. Until I told her she couldn't move in with us, apparently. I have to take a deep breath before I can reply.

'That's completely untrue and unfair. Of course I care about you. I'll talk to Ben tonight about putting you up temporarily, OK?'

'Oh, don't bother yourself. I've got an alternative plan. There's someone else who cares enough to help me, to let me live with her and help to look after me.'

'Who?'

'My second cousin Pat, in Liverpool. She says I can move into her spare room and pay her a bit out of my benefits for rent. She says it'll be company for her, and two can live as cheaply as one.'

'I didn't even know you had a second cousin in Liverpool.'

'You didn't ask.'

'Well, I've tried to ask you about your family – *my* family – but you only ever told me about your parents, nothing about a cousin.' She told me, early on, that her parents – my grandparents – were both alcoholics who didn't give a damn about her, so I've never wanted to hear any more about them. 'I'd have *liked* to know about your cousin. I'm related to her too, so I might have liked to meet her myself.'

'Well, if you jump on a train to Liverpool, you can. That's the only way you'll get to see *me* after this week, anyway, cos unless you can find it in your cold heart to let me move in with you, I'll be going up there and that's that.'

I feel like I've been hit over the head with something. This is beyond her being hurt about not moving in with us – it's downright spiteful. For a moment I consider cutting off the call. I should do. I should just tell her to go to Liverpool, if this is really how she feels. She won't, surely. She'll calm

If I Lost You   187

down when she realises I'm not going to be spoken to like this, treated like this, *threatened* like this. But something about the mention of the cousin has brought me up short, reminding me again that Barbara's *family*. OK, of course it's different, a world apart, from my proper family, my parents, my children – of course it can never be the same, never come near it. But I've never had actual biological relatives before. If she goes – if she cuts herself off from me – it's going to hurt. I've had too much hurt, recently. I don't want any more.

'Look, just give me a bit of time. Let me see what Ben says, and talk to the kids; perhaps we can put you up for a short time, while we try to get you rehoused.'

'I don't just want another *temporary* stay, Jo. It's disruptive, in my state of health, moving in and moving out again, feeling unwanted. I want to get myself settled somewhere permanently. Somewhere nice and warm, with my own room. I'll get that with Pat, if you can't even tell your own kids they've got to share.'

'It's difficult,' I begin, but I can hear her sighing with impatience.

'Fair enough, so if it's too difficult for you, I'll go to Liverpool. You could come with me if you wanted,' she adds. 'We could rent somewhere; we could afford it, between us – somewhere just for you and me and the kids. George would come, I bet. Not sure about Molly.'

'Now you're being ridiculous. I'm not going anywhere. I've got Ben to consider, as well as *both* my children.'

'Fine, I didn't expect you to say any different. I know you don't really give a damn what happens to me, so, well, I don't suppose I'll see you again.'

And she hangs up.

You can't just leave it like that, I think, indignantly. I try, twice, three times, to call her back, but she doesn't pick up. Well, she's blown it now. If she's really planning to go to Liverpool, she can get on with it, see if I care. I'm so shocked and cross about it, I can't even sit out here enjoying the sunshine any longer – I go indoors and work out my anger by hoovering the whole house. But I'm still feeling furious when I go to meet the children.

I find myself asking if it's me. After all, I argue with Ben, I argued with my mum, I upset Nadia, and now I seem to have fallen out, possibly terminally, with my birth mum too: the only person who's comforted me and agreed with me throughout all my problems. What have I done wrong? What did I do to deserve this?

'Are you all right, Mummy?' Molly asks anxiously as we head back to the car. 'You look cross and you're walking very fast, and George can't keep up; he can't breathe.'

'Oh, I'm sorry, darlings.' I stop and manage a smile. 'I'm all right, I was just... thinking about something.'

'You mustn't worry. That's what you tell me every day,' Molly reminds me, and I give her a hug.

But inside, I feel the anger rising up to choke me again. And I wish I didn't also feel so very, very sad.

30

After I've settled the children in bed, I ask Ben to turn off the TV so we can have a talk. He looks at me slightly warily.

'What about?'

'Well, we can't go on like this, Ben. We've both got a lot to deal with, we're both on edge about George's diagnosis, but it doesn't help the situation if we keep on arguing all the time like this. The kids are picking up on it. It's been upsetting Molly in particular. She told me that at least she's not as badly off as her friend Sophie, because when *her* parents argue, her dad shouts and makes her mum cry. I don't feel great, knowing she's bonded with her friend over how much their parents argue.'

'No,' he agrees. 'It doesn't say a lot for us, does it.'

'We need to try harder to talk things over civilly. Even if we do decide, in the end, to separate.'

'Agreed. And I'm not sure it's the right time to talk about separating. George doesn't need any disruption to his life.'

'Neither of them do.' I hesitate, and then go on, wanting to have this conversation while we're both in a more co-operative mindset. 'I need to tell you something important.'

'Go on.'

I hesitate again, and then suddenly decide that, while he's in an approachable mood, I'll tell him about the classes first, because once I start talking about Barbara his mood is probably going to change.

'I'm not going to the Job Centre. I've stopped looking at jobs. I've already made up my mind what I want to do.'

'Which is?'

'I'm going to start the yoga classes again.'

He sighs. 'I thought we'd talked about this. It won't work, Jo—'

'Yes it will, because I'm going to do children's classes, a couple of days after school, after you're home, and run some courses during the school holidays, and, if it's OK with you, I'll do some adult lessons a couple of evenings a week.'

'I don't *mind*,' he says, frowning. 'But is it really the best thing for you, or for the children? Don't you think you should be here for them as much as you can, especially now, with George's illness and Molly feeling so anxious? I still think you'd be better off working at home, while they're at school.'

I feel my mood changing rapidly.

'As I've said before, find me a job working from home, during school hours, and I'll consider it.'

'Go to the Job Centre.'

'No,' I say firmly. I've had enough of this. We're going round in circles. 'I'm not going to, Ben, because I've already booked some introductory courses for the summer holidays, and I've got the hall booked for September, with lists of people—'

'You've done all this without talking to me about it?'

'Yes. Because we haven't exactly been talking to each other, have we, not civilly, not in a way I'd have felt comfortable to have this conversation. I thought now, you might actually listen, you might support me. Do you know what? Barbara's the only person who has.' I swallow, hard, before going on, 'And that's the other thing I need to talk to you about. She's talking about moving away.'

'Oh, really?' he says. I try to ignore the hopeful tone to his voice, but it hurts.

'Yes. I've only just got used to having her in my life, so I was really shocked and upset to hear her threatening to leave London.'

If I Lost You   191

'*Threatening* to?' he says, frowning. 'That's a strange way of putting it, isn't it?'

'Well, she's apparently got a cousin in Liverpool who's offered to have her living with her. Barbara says she's already told the council she's moving out of her flat, and that the only alternative to going to Liverpool would be if she could move in with us.'

'Which is out of the question, obviously,' he says immediately.

'Yes, I know. I've told her that. But couldn't we just have her here temporarily, until the council can rehouse her? If we don't, she's definitely going, and I don't want to lose her, Ben.'

I'm so intent on pleading my case that I'm almost forgetting how angry I felt with Barbara for putting me in this position. For accusing me of not caring. I want Ben to agree to this, because I don't think it's unreasonable.

'Just a temporary stay,' I repeat, 'and I'll get onto the council myself about rehousing her.'

'You know as well as I do that she won't want to go. She *won't* go. She'll turn down whatever the council offers. She wants to move in, Jo, and I'm not having it.'

'So my opinion doesn't count?' I'm being petty now. I just want to fight my corner, even if Ben's probably right, even though Barbara told me herself she doesn't want a temporary stay.

'We agreed, Jo. We agreed it wouldn't be good for the kids, apart from anything else. Look, you can go and visit her, can't you? I could come with you, we can take the children, during the school holidays. I do understand how you feel – after all, my own parents live in Spain. And of course I miss them, but we call and videocall each other, and we visit every year. I haven't *lost* them; you won't lose Barbara. It'll be fine, we'll make it work.'

'But why can't we make it work, letting her stay here?'

There's a silence. The sympathetic expression has gone, replaced with one of exasperation.

'No,' he says firmly. 'It's just not going to happen, and that's the end of it. I'll tell her myself if you want me to, if you're too afraid of hurting her feelings, but I'm *not* giving in to an ultimatum. If she's threatening to go, let her go. She shouldn't be putting you in that position, expecting you to disregard my feelings, upset the children—'

'I know,' I interrupt. 'I don't like the way she's done this either, but you know how much I wanted a relationship with my mother. And she's been so helpful, too.'

'Your *mother* is the lovely woman who brought you up.' He's raising his voice now.

'They are both my mothers – in a different sense. And frankly, Barbara's been a lot more of a support to me than you *or* Mum have been recently. She's the only person right now who I feel has got my back.'

I'm deliberately blocking out of my head the spiteful words Barbara was using to me on the phone. I'm too upset with Ben for not even agreeing to have Barbara here temporarily to admit that I know he's probably right. I'm deliberately focusing on how helpful she's been, how she's listened to me and believed in me when neither Ben nor Mum have done. And despite my best intentions we're arguing again. We sit in silence for a few minutes, both of us breathing heavily as if we've been running.

'Look,' Ben says eventually, in a tone of exaggerated patience, 'you're taking this far too seriously. I bet the whole thing about going to Liverpool is just a threat, to try to get you to give in to her demands. She's being manipulative. She could easily call the council again and say she's changed her mind and wants to stay where she is until they can rehouse her.'

'I don't think it's just a threat,' I say wearily. 'She'll definitely go.'

I'm tired of this conversation already. Ben's trying to sound reasonable, but really he's just hoping Barbara will go. He's pretending to understand my feelings but he doesn't, he can't. It's not the same as his parents living in Spain; Barbara has threatened that I'll probably never see her again. She won't keep in touch – she'll cut me off, to spite me. A little voice inside my head is trying to tell me this is hardly the behaviour of someone who loves me – that, in fact, Ben's right, she's being manipulative. But I can't listen to that voice of reason, because I'm too upset by the thought of losing my birth mother so soon after I've found her. Instead, I've made up my mind: it's Ben that's being unreasonable.

* * *

If I Lost You   193

I wait to talk to the children until after I've picked them up from school the next day.

'Granny might have to move away,' I say, watching both their faces carefully.

'Move away?' George repeats, staring at me. 'Move away where?'

'To Liverpool. It's... a long way away.'

'Longer than where Grandma and Grandpa live?' Molly asks.

'Yes.'

'Longer than where the other Grandma and Grandpa live, in Spain? Will she have to go by plane like when we go in August?' she says, sounding genuinely interested.

'No, but it's quite a long way to drive. It'd take... most of a day to get there.'

George is just staring at me angrily. 'Why? Why does Granny have to move away?'

'Because she needs to live with somebody who can help to look after her when she's not well. She's got a cousin there who says she can live with her.'

'But she can live with us, can't she?' he says, crossly. 'I want her to live with us, Mummy. I like it when she lives here. Don't let her go there; we can look after her, can't we? I want her to live *here*.'

'I don't,' Molly says bluntly.

'Well, it isn't really up to either of you, it's for Daddy and me to decide, and we don't think it would be very nice for you two to have to share a bedroom for the whole time.'

'I don't mind.' George is starting to cry. 'Granny can have my room, she can have it for ever. I don't want her to go to Littlepool.'

'It's *Liverpool*, George,' Molly says in a superior tone. 'And I'm *not* having you in my room for ever, you keep me awake and I get tired at school.'

'All right then, I'll just sleep on the sofa,' he says, pulling a face at her. 'Mummy, tell Granny not to move to Livingpool.'

'I'm trying to persuade her, George, and I'm hoping she'll decide not to go, but at the end of the day it's her decision, OK? Now, come on, stop crying, Georgie.'

'Yes, stop being a baby, George,' Molly joins in, laughing at him, and

George immediately retaliates, giving her a push so that she almost falls off the sofa.

'That's enough, both of you. Come here.' I pull them towards me. I feel a bit like crying myself, but I've got to hold it together, pretend to be cheerful and reassuring for the children, especially for George. 'I'll make sure you can say goodbye to Granny before she goes – *if* she goes.'

If I can't do anything to stop her. But I'm not giving up trying.

* * *

'Have you told Barbara our decision yet?' Ben asks me while we're preparing dinner this evening.

Our decision? When did that happen?

'No,' I answer him. 'I haven't, because I don't want to hear her say that she's definitely going.'

'You have to call her bluff,' he insists. 'Once she knows our decision is final, she still might cave in and stay where she is. If you don't even call to tell her, she might just up and go in a fit of pique, without saying goodbye.'

I can't even argue with him now, because I know he's right. From the way she was talking on the phone, I realise she might just do that, and I can't let her. I've promised the children now.

'OK. I'll call her tonight,' I agree. I don't want to, obviously. I want to keep putting it off, hoping something will change: that Ben will back down and agree to her moving in temporarily, or that Barbara was just having a bad day yesterday and she hasn't really got any intention of leaving. To be honest, I'm still angry and upset about the way she spoke to me, the way she's threatened me. But my feelings are so confused, I can hardly bear to make the call, telling her flat-out that she's not welcome here.

As it happens, I don't have to, because almost as soon as the children are in bed this evening, she calls me.

'Well?' she says.

No *hello*, no tactful lead-in. Just the question. The demand. I feel so irritated by this – that after I've spent the best part of two days of painful soul-searching, to say nothing of arguing with Ben, upsetting my kids and having a sleepless night, she can't even address me with anything better

If I Lost You   195

than a one-word *demand* – that for a moment, I forget all my planned apologies and explanations and pleadings, and just come out with it.

'It's a *no*, Barbara. I'm sorry.'

'So Ben's got his way, as usual.'

'No. It's not like that. We've talked it over, at length, and if you must know, I've cried myself to sleep over it.'

'Your tears won't help me, though, will they. Right, well, at least I know where I stand. So I'm off to Liverpool tomorrow, then.'

'Please don't. Please let's talk some more about this.'

'Talking won't help me either, Jo. I need to be with someone who's going to care about me, care for me when I'm not well. Where I won't be in the way.'

'That's not fair. I do care about you, you know that.'

'Come with me, then, if you really care. Ben won't miss you. He's selfish. Like all men, he just wants his own way. We can stay with Pat till we find ourselves a little place to share. We won't need much. I'm renting a van and driver to take my stuff up there, and I'm going up by train. I'm going first thing in the morning, so if you want to come, you'll have to come round tonight.'

'Don't be ridiculous. I can't leave my children.'

'You can come back for them. After we've got settled.'

'It's not going to happen, Barbara. I'm not leaving them, or Ben, or my house. I'm sorry if you think I've let you down. I don't want you to go. I do care about you.'

'So you say. But not enough, it seems.'

And again, she just hangs up.

Ben comes into the kitchen to find me sitting with my head in my hands. I'm not even crying; I'm too stunned. She's actually going to do it. After everything I've done for her and everything she's done for me, she's moving away because we can't – won't – let her come and live with us. I wait for Ben to say something – to at least say he's sorry about how things have panned out – but he just stands, looking at me for a moment, before saying, half under his breath, 'All right, Jo, let's get over it. It's not the end of the world,' before he turns and walks out of the room.

And I've never felt so alone.

31

If Ben hadn't spoken to me like that – if he'd only come over to me, given me a hug and said he understood how I felt – I don't think I'd be doing what I'm doing now. Or would I? Would I still have been marching into the lounge, my tears suddenly dried, my mind set on a confrontation with him – set on giving him an ultimatum, in fact, that could change the course of our marriage, even the course of the rest of my life? I'll never know, because I'm too fired up now to consider any alternative. I stand in front of the TV, forcing him to look up at me, forcing him to take notice of me.

'You don't seem to realise,' I say, 'how serious I am about this.'

'Well, it's quickly becoming apparent how seriously you're *taking* it,' he says.

The fact that he sounds neither sympathetic nor even alarmed by my tone, but frankly just bored, makes me even more determined.

'Yes, I am taking it seriously. I'm taking your lack of understanding and support seriously, Ben, because it just proves to me that our marriage is completely on the rocks and not even worth fighting for any more.'

'You're being hysterical. I'm sorry if you think I haven't been supportive. I've tried as hard as humanly possible. But if you can't stand up to that woman's demands, if you insist on putting her before me and the children—'

If I Lost You

'If *you* can't do this one thing for me: an act of generosity—'

'No, I can't. I won't. She's not coming back to stay here temporarily, because we'll never get her to move out, and that's not happening. I've already made that clear, and that's the end of it.'

'Then I might as well go up to Liverpool with her. She's asked me to, and she seems to care about me more than you do.'

'Oh, stop being so ridiculous and dramatic. She only cares about herself.'

'I'm going, Ben. Our marriage seems to be over, my mum never seems to see my side of things, I've lost the only friend I had. I might as well go with Barbara and start afresh.'

'You won't go,' he says, laughing – actually *laughing* – at me. 'You won't leave the children.'

'Of course I won't. They'll come with me.'

He laughs again. 'Like hell they will. You don't seriously expect me to believe you'd take the kids away from their home, their school, their friends, from everything they've ever known – let alone from me. You couldn't put them through that disruption, going to God knows what situation Barbara's going up there with no idea where they might have to live, no schooling arranged, no doctor or hospital arranged for George – what? You hadn't even thought of that?' He shakes his head at me. 'That woman's robbed you of your common sense. You're not going anywhere, Jo. Or if you really think you are, you'll be leaving the kids behind.'

'Fine,' I retort. I'm so angry now I don't care what I'm saying. I just want to shock him into some kind of compassion, some kind of understanding. 'I'll leave them here for now, and come back for them as soon as I'm settled.'

'No. You. Won't.' He stares back at me. There's absolutely no affection, let alone love, left in his eyes, only contempt. 'If you leave us, you go alone, and you don't get the children, not now, not ever. You make that choice, you live with it.'

I'm not being influenced by his threats. He won't get to keep the children. I'm their mother, they'll want to come to me. I'll start again, a new life with them in Liverpool. But he's right that I need to get everything prepared for them up there first. It won't take long – finding a school, a doctor, transferring to a different consultant for George. He'll be happy about coming to live with his granny, and Molly will come round; I'll make sure Barbara always remembers to treat them both the same. I can cancel the yoga classes I've arranged down here – unavoidable circumstances, people will have to understand. It'll be easy to start again up north – Barbara will look after the kids whenever I'm teaching, and I'll be available for her whenever she's ill. We'll make it work.

I turn on my heels and go upstairs.

'You're not taking them,' he shouts, beginning to follow me. 'I'll come after you.'

'Calm down, I'm not taking them, not right now. But I'll come for them later, whatever you say.'

'I'll see you in court first.'

I don't even bother to reply. I haven't got time for any more arguments. I go into our bedroom and start packing a suitcase. I'm shaking as I do it – part of me is asking myself what the hell I think I'm doing, but I can't seem to stop. If I listen to the side of my brain that's telling me I'm acting like a madwoman – completely out of character, completely against everything I've ever thought I was capable of – then it'll be too late, and I'll always regret not going, always feel guilty about Barbara, always wish I'd made more of an effort to keep my birth mother with me. With only the minimum of clothes and hardly any other possessions thrown into the case, I leave it on the landing and tiptoe into Molly's bedroom.

The sight of her spread of beautiful dark hair across the pillow, and her hands curled beside her face in a pose that could almost have been supplication, makes me pause briefly to swallow and what? – gather strength? – before continuing to her bedside, picking up her school cardigan from the floor and hanging it calmly in her wardrobe, as if it matters. As if she's going to care, in the morning, waking up to find me gone, that I've bothered to hang her cardigan nicely.

'Bye, darling,' I whisper, kissing her cheek very gently so as not to wake her up. 'I'll be back for you very soon, I promise. I love you. I'm not leaving you.'

I head into George's room and look down on my sleeping son. Instead of feeling the anguish of imminent separation, I notice random things like

If I Lost You

199

the graze on his chin where he came off his little bike last week, the frayed edge of his pyjama sleeve that he has a habit of chewing when he's going off to sleep, the way he sleeps with one bare foot hanging out from under the duvet and the way the cat's stretched out on the end of his bed – even Ben's turned a blind eye to this now. And I find myself, incredibly, *smiling* as I cover him over and bend to give my son a parting kiss, whispering the same promise that I've made to his sister and quietly closing the door to his bedroom.

Ben's sitting in the lounge again when I go back downstairs, the TV still showing the same programme.

'For God's sake,' he says, looking up at me, seeing the suitcase. His voice sounds scratchy, now, like sandpaper on a bare wall. 'Don't, Jo. Please don't.'

'I have to. You've haven't left me any choice.' I don't feel any emotion. Why not? What's wrong with me?

'There's *always* a choice. You stay, we keep talking, we both calm down, you put our children first.'

I shake my head. 'I'm sorry. I'm going, but I'll be back for the kids – no, don't start arguing again, I'll be back for them,' I end, my voice raised now.

'You haven't even said goodbye to them? What am I supposed to say, when they wake up tomorrow and you're not here? Don't you *care*?'

'Of course I care. I'll call them. I'll explain – they'll be excited...' I stop, shake my head, because I can't go on, I'd be lying. They won't be excited, they'll be distraught, and I don't want to think about that. 'Tell them I'm just going to help Barbara move. That she needed me to go right away but I didn't want to wake them up.'

He shakes his head. 'Why should I lie to them? I should just tell them you've walked out.'

'That would be cruel,' I say softly.

'And that's not what you're being?' He raises his head, finally, meeting my eyes. His eyes are tired, and red, as if he's been rubbing them. A momentary stab of sadness pierces the muzzy protective blanket that seems to have wrapped itself around me. I don't want him to look at me like that – hurt, accusatory. I want him to understand; to see that it's because he's being unreasonable that I've got to go.

But he just gets to his feet, unsteadily, taking hold of me by the shoulders so that I flinch and try to look away.

'Your *children*, Jo!' is all he says – but it comes out as a deep groan from the depths of his being that makes me shudder in the wake of its reprimand. 'You can't leave your *children*.'

'I'm *not* leaving them,' I insist.

But his words echo in my head as I pick up my bags, as I get in my car, as I speed off towards Barbara's flat, a sense of disbelief at what I'm doing making me feel weak and sick. *Your children! Your children! Your children!*

I'm less than halfway to Barbara's when I break down in tears and pull over to the side of the road, howling with disbelief at myself – at the realisation that I've even come this far. Was I actually prepared to carry it through, taking the risk of Ben fighting me for the custody of my kids, risking having to actually give them up – for Barbara's sake? Of course not. I know, knew all along, deep inside, that I wouldn't be able to do it. Of course I can't do it. But I can't call Ben and beg his forgiveness, either, or go crawling back to him after only ten minutes, because I'm still so angry with him, so resentful about his lack of understanding.

For probably another ten minutes I sit in my car on the side of this fairly quiet road, trying to pull myself together and stop crying. I'm crying now because I realise I'm losing Barbara. She'll be leaving for Liverpool in the morning – that's what she's threatened, anyway – and I've now proved to myself that I won't be joining her. OK, I know she's being unreasonable right now – unkind, ungrateful even – but I wanted to keep her nearby, I wanted her in my life and I know there's no way of doing that permanently now.

When I eventually look out of the window to see where I am, through the darkness I notice the illuminated sign on the front of the building on the other side of the road:

Belgrave Hotel, B&B.

That's what I'll do, I decide. I'll let Ben suffer for one night. I'll think it all over more calmly if I'm on my own – then I'll call him in the morning. I'll tell the children I stayed at Barbara's for the night to help her prepare

If I Lost You 201

for her journey. It's not ideal; the atmosphere at home will still be awful, I'll still be angry with Ben – and he with me – and I don't know if we're going to be able to resolve it. And I'll still be upset and overwhelmed with guilt about Barbara but I can only hope she'll relent and let me have her address in Liverpool. Anything's got to be better than being without my children, even for a week, even for a few days.

But I still lie awake all night in the uncomfortable bed in the B&B, crying every time I think about how I kissed my babies goodbye in their beds without flinching, without feeling a single pang of guilt. I've got to live with that, now, for the rest of my life, and I can only do it by reassuring myself that I knew I would never actually go through with it. I'd hoped Ben was going to stop me, and the worst thing is, he tried, but I wouldn't let him. If I'm honest, I just wanted to hurt him. What does that say about me?

32

I'm up early in the morning, holding my phone, Ben's number in front of me, my finger hovering over the *call* button, trying to work out what to say. I know I need to apologise, but am I the only one at fault? Ben seemed so uncaring last night. I don't think he'll ever really understand how it feels to have found, after all these years, the person who gave birth to me – how much it's affected me, how emotional I've felt about having a biological mother. Can't he, for my sake, just be a bit more tolerant and under-standing?

There's a little voice of reason in the far reaches of my brain telling me that it's me that's being unreasonable, me that's not prepared to understand or accept *his* feelings – but that little voice has been drowned out by my need to be understood, my desperation to keep my birth mother close to me, and the knowledge that I'm always going to feel regret, not to mention guilt, for letting her go.

It's because of these lingering thoughts that I suddenly decide to call Barbara before I call Ben.

'Hello,' she says. There's a question hanging in the air – I can hear it in her voice, in that single word.

'I'm sorry,' I say. I brush away a tear. 'I can't come today. I tried. I've had a fight with Ben, I've even walked away from the kids. But I can't. I just can't

If I Lost You   203

leave them, even temporarily. I hope you'll be happy, I really do, but *please* let me have your address in Liverpool. Don't cut yourself off from me. I haven't done anything to deserve that.'

She waits till I've finished, till the silence hangs in the air between us.

'I'm not going today,' she says eventually.

I gasp. Has all this been for nothing? 'But you said—'

'I was, but I couldn't get the van today. It's booked for Monday.'

I don't know whether to feel relief or despair. If she'd gone today, then despite the heartache, at least I'd know it was all over, that it was too late to change my mind. Have I got to go through it all again: the indecision, the soul-searching, the last-minute pleading with Ben?

'Monday,' I say bleakly. It's Saturday today. That gives me two more days. At least I could go and see her. Perhaps Ben might even agree to her coming for a final Sunday dinner tomorrow. 'Right.'

'If you change your mind you'd better let me know,' she says, and again, the call's ended, abruptly. No goodbye, no attempt to understand how I might be feeling – how devastated I might be – no promise to send me the address. I feel a sudden spark of anger. Whatever she thinks, I *have* done my best to look after her. I've cared about her, argued with Ben and Mum over her, forgiven her for upsetting Molly, spoiling George, and even now, when she's hurt me and insulted me, I've been prepared to forgive her. Is Ben right? Has she simply been manipulating me, taking advantage of me? I can't bear the idea of having to admit it.

I shake my head, dismissing the train of my thoughts. Whatever comes next, I need to call Ben, I need to get back to the children. I feel a warm surge of relief at the thought. It's still only half past eight, but even on a Saturday, Ben will be up, because of the children. *Because of what I've done*, I correct myself, shame coming over me like a dark, heavy cloud.

But it isn't Ben who answers his phone: it's Mum.

'Oh.' I stare at my phone in confusion. I've definitely called Ben's number. 'What's happened? Why—'

'Why am I here?' she retorts – and I blink in surprise at her tone. Cold, angry. Nothing like my mum. 'Why do you think? Ben's in pieces, Jo. He called me last night, after you *ran away* – and I came straight over. He needed me to help him calm down before he had to face the children this morning. He was so distraught he didn't know how he'd cope. He doesn't want to talk to you, and I can't say I blame him.' She drops her voice to a hiss. 'What the *hell* do you think you're doing?'

'I don't know,' I admit. My voice is shaking. 'I'm at a hotel, Mum. I couldn't go, I couldn't go through with it. I came straight here. I just needed time to think.'

'So you're not on your way to Liverpool with that woman?'

'No. She hasn't even gone yet.'

There's a tut of exasperation. 'So you're still contemplating it?'

'No.' I try to make my voice sound firmer than I feel. 'No, I'm not going, I can't, I knew all along that I couldn't. I can't leave the kids, not even for a day, not ever, I was just upset with Ben.'

'That's nothing to what you've put him through,' she says crisply.

'I'm sorry, honestly, I'm really sorry, but I didn't know what to do. I can't bear the thought of losing her. He doesn't understand.' I'm crying now – yet again. Will I ever stop?

There's a silence for a couple of minutes. I'm wondering if she's hung up. Then, to my surprise, she says, far more gently, 'Tell me where you are. I'll come and meet you there.'

* * *

I wait for her in the breakfast room. I've sent the server away – I can't eat – but I've got a pot of tea and I'm sipping a cup when she arrives. She pulls out a seat at the table and accepts the offer of a cup from my pot.

'I'm sorry,' I say again. I can't meet her eyes. 'I don't know what to say. I think I might be having a breakdown or something.'

She puts a hand over mine. My tears are dripping on them.

'Dry your eyes,' she says calmly. 'Crying isn't going to help.'

I do as I'm told. I'm fifteen again, in trouble with her for staying out late at night, answering back, causing her the kind of heartache all parents go through as their kids grow up. She always understood, even when I didn't deserve understanding. She was a perfect mum.

'Is Ben going to take me back?' I ask flatly.

'Oh, of course he will. He loves you.'

'No, he doesn't. You don't realise, because we've kept it from you, but we're at the point of breaking up with each other. We've only stayed together because of the children.'

'Of course we've realised that. We're not blind, your dad and I. We know you've been arguing, but all couples argue, especially when they're under a strain, like you are with George. I'm sorry I didn't take on board how seriously ill he is. You were right, I didn't want to acknowledge it, but I understand now what you've both been going through. Ben will take you back, even if you *are* both unhappy at the moment, because he loves the children as much as you do and wants them to be happy. He's absolutely distraught, thinking you were prepared to leave them – and him.'

'I wasn't really going to. I just feel so torn. I can't bear the thought that Barbara went to the trouble of seeking me out, after all this time, and now I might never see her again.'

'Liverpool's not the other side of the world, darling,' she says reasonably.

'But it might as well be, if she refuses to give me her address there.'

'Is that what she says? Is it just a threat, to persuade you to go with her?'

'I don't think so. I don't know.'

There's a silence. Mum sips her tea, watching me over the rim, before putting her hand on mine again and saying softly, 'Either way, it's hardly *loving*, is it.'

Hardly loving. I've been thinking similar thoughts myself, haven't I? And yet, hearing it from Mum has made me suddenly aware of how true it is.

'Perhaps she doesn't really care about me at all,' I whisper, hoping Mum will contradict me. 'Perhaps all she ever really wanted was to move in with us.'

I wait for Mum to reassure me, but she doesn't. She just looks back at me, sadly, waiting for me to finally understand.

'I think I'm going to cry again,' I say.

'She doesn't deserve your tears.'

Then her tone softens as she adds, 'You've been caught up in a fantasy. We all understand, sweetheart. You just wanted a family. But, you silly, silly girl – you already have one, a wonderful family: a lovely husband, two beautiful children. And two parents who really do love you, who have always loved you, who still do, and always will.'

There are tears in her own eyes now, which she wipes away angrily, with a little half-laugh, as she adds, 'Now look what you've made me do.'

'Oh, Mum.' I don't care what any of the other hotel guests in the breakfast room might think: I get up and pull her into my arms. 'I'm so sorry, so, so, sorry. I've been a complete and utter idiot. You're right, it was all about having a birth mother, someone who knew me when I was a baby. But what does it matter? I was fine without her until she turned up. Out of the blue.'

'And now she's disappearing. Back into the blue.' She lowers her voice again, stroking my hair as she adds, 'Let her go, now, love. Come back to us.'

'I never left you,' I retort. But she's right: in a way, I did. I chose Barbara because at times I felt like Mum wasn't backing me – but in reality, Mum was just being honest with me. Even if I sometimes disagreed with her, about George's illness, and about my choice of new career, to say nothing of Barbara, I realise she only had my best interests at heart.

We order another pot of tea; apparently crying makes you thirsty. We talk a little more, going over much the same things. I think it's going to take a while before everything sinks in. The habit of believing Barbara cared about me has taken hold so quickly, but so strongly, I suppose the truth will take a lot of getting used to.

'I think I want to go home now,' I say eventually.

Mum gives me a regretful look, shaking her head.

'Sorry, Jo. Ben's not in the right frame of mind. You might have to give him a day or two. You've hurt him badly. He was beside himself when he called me.'

'Was he really? He just seemed angry with me when I left.'

'Don't be fooled. He does have a heart, you know. Let him lick his wounds for a while – that's only fair.'

'I suppose so.' I look down at the table, feeling the weight of my shame even more now. 'I'd better reserve my room here for another night, then.'

'If that's what you want. I guess it's more convenient. But I'd quite like it if you'd come home with me for the weekend. We haven't seen much of you lately.'

If I Lost You

'I'm sorry – you're right, I've been a terrible daughter.'

'I'm not saying it to make you feel even worse,' she laughs. 'I just mean it genuinely. We'd like it if you'd stay with us, at least until tomorrow. Then maybe call Ben and see how he feels. He knows I'm talking to you this morning. He knows I'm going to ask you to come back with me. He wants to devote himself to the children today.'

'Do you know what he's telling them? About where I went?'

'Exactly what you suggested he said: that you've just gone to Barbara's to help her pack, and say goodbye.' She pauses. 'George will be upset that she's leaving, won't he. But he'll be fine once he's got you back. Once things are back to normal.'

Back to normal. Suddenly, that's all I want. I sip my tea, thinking about normality, with all its worries, fears, frustrations and arguments. Wishing I'd never even met Barbara so that I wouldn't have had to come crashing down to earth like this and could have just gone on with my normal life.

'Your phone's ringing,' Mum says, jolting me back to the present. I grab it out of my bag and to my surprise – after what she's just been saying – it's Ben calling. Perhaps he's changed his mind, perhaps he wants me to go home right away.

'Hi,' I say. 'Ben, I'm so sorry about—'

'No time for that right now,' he says abruptly, making me blink in surprise. 'You need to come home – quickly. Your mum too. I need her to stay with Molly.' His voice is shaking. I'm suddenly shaking too. Something's happened. Something really bad, and it can only be... 'There's an ambulance on its way,' he says. 'It's George.'

33

Mum's already outside, heading for her car, while I still have to check out of the hotel. There's someone in the queue in front of me and I shift from foot to foot with impatience. The receptionist gives me an odd look. I must look a fright, but I can't worry about that. I'm in my car and heading home as soon as my payment's been accepted, ignoring the speed limit, screeching to a halt outside the house. The ambulance is here already, the front door's open and I charge inside, where two paramedics are bent over George. One's fastening an oxygen mask over his face, the other's inserting a line into a vein in his thin little arm.

'Your mum's here already,' Ben says without taking his eyes away from George – from his frightened, tearstained little face, blue from the lack of oxygen that's evidently now being treated. 'She's gone upstairs with Molly.'

The paramedic who's been fitting the mask straightens up and turns to look at me. 'Hi,' she says, giving me a sympathetic smile. 'You must be Mum. Try not to worry, we're doing everything we can to help George and then we'll be going to hospital with him. We understand from your husband that he has childhood interstitial—'

'Lung disease, yes,' I interrupt. 'He's only recently been diagnosed. But what's happened? What's suddenly gone wrong? He's on steroids, he's been improving.'

If I Lost You

'OK, it's probably just a temporary setback. We'll take good care of him, and one of you can come with us in the ambulance of course.'

She looks from me to Ben, and immediately he says, 'You. You should go with him, Jo. He'll want you, he's been asking for you. I'll follow in the car.'

He's been asking for me – and I wasn't here. My poor baby boy, struggling to breathe, calling for his mother while I blubbed to myself in self-indulgent self-pity in a hotel. I'll never leave his side again – or Molly's. I can hear her crying upstairs, hear Mum trying to soothe her and calm her down. She must have been so frightened by all this. I know how much she really loves her little brother, even if I do spend half my time stopping them from fighting.

'OK,' I agree with Ben. 'Thank you. I'll... just go and pack a bag for him. For me too,' I add.

There's no way I'll be leaving him there. If George has to stay in, so will I. I squeeze his hand, stroke his head, tell him I love him and that I'm coming with him, that he mustn't be frightened, he's going to be OK, before rushing upstairs to sort out the things we're going to need.

'Mummy,' Molly sobs as she sees me looking into her room. She's sitting on her bed with Mum's arms around her but she breaks free to hold out her arms to me. Her little face is red and swollen from crying. 'I don't like it – what's happening to George? He couldn't breathe *at all*; he went a really funny colour and Daddy kept giving him his inhaler but it didn't help, and he couldn't speak or even cry, it was just me and Daddy crying. Are those people making him better? Can I go back down and see him?'

'Yes. I'm just going to pack a bag for the hospital, then you can come down with me, OK?'

I know she's scared but I'm not going to prevent her from saying goodbye to her brother. Goodbyes are important, I realise now. If we don't say goodbye to people, we never know if or when we're going to see them again. I swallow back my own tears. George and Molly need me now; I've got to be their strength; I can't waste time on any more crying. When we go back downstairs, the paramedics are just about to take George to the ambulance, but they step back to let Molly go and hug him.

'Please try to get better, Georgie,' she says, her voice wobbling. 'I don't want you to be in hospital.'

He blinks at her; he's calmer now that he's taking the oxygen but I can see the fear in his eyes and my heart feels like it's going to break.

'He'll be fine, love,' says the male paramedic. 'We're going to look after him, don't you worry.'

I turn to Ben as I follow the paramedics out to the ambulance. 'I'll see you there, OK? And—'

'Don't say anything. Just go with George,' he says.

I turn to Molly. 'Grandma's going to look after you but we'll be back the moment we can, OK?' I pull her into my arms, kiss her and add, looking into her eyes, 'I promise.'

* * *

The ambulance speeds towards A&E with its siren and blue lights going, and I sit beside George, holding his hand, watching his every breath. He looks exhausted – exhausted just from breathing. Is this going to be our new normal, I wonder, dashing to hospital with our hearts in our mouths, desperate to save our son? It was bad enough having to drive him to A&E on the odd occasion that his asthma – what we then presumed to be asthma – was really bad.

Then I bring myself up short. This isn't about me, or Ben. We can't afford to feel sorry for ourselves, because if, God forbid, this *were* to be our new normal, then that's what we have to get on with. I've accused my mum of being in denial about it, but I've been almost as bad. Ben and I have to get into the mindset that this won't be easy. It might be awful. It's going to be scary, for all of us but especially for George. Whatever happens, I've promised myself now that I have to be here for him, strong for him, and so does Ben. We need to put aside our differences; we're the grown-ups, we need to face up to this, the worst challenge any parent can have, and concentrate our energy on giving George the happiest childhood we can, in case... I don't finish the sentence, not even in my head. But it's out there, and I've got to acknowledge it even while I'm determined to fight against it. To fight for George's health, whatever it takes.

If I Lost You

'I'm going to be with you the whole time,' I tell him now, stroking his hair, holding tight onto his hand. 'The doctors are going to make you better.'

Whatever it takes.

* * *

Ben arrives at the hospital fairly soon after us, making me wonder if he's jumped every red light on the way. Doctors and nurses have been coming and going, checking George's oxygen levels, his pulse, his temperature in case a virus might have caused this sudden deterioration – everyone being constantly calm and reassuring.

'They're going to take him to a ward soon,' I tell him. 'They want to monitor him overnight. And they've called for a paediatric consultant. Perhaps it'll be Dr Taylor – he knows George's case.'

'I'm sure they'll all be suitably qualified,' he says. 'We have to trust them.'

'Yes.'

George has actually fallen asleep. We sit beside him in silence for a moment, and then, suddenly, as if he can't help himself, Ben reaches out and grabs my hand.

'I don't want us to break up, Jo,' he says earnestly. 'We need each other, to get through this. Whatever happens.'

'I know. I don't want it either.' I pause. 'What did you tell the children – about where I'd gone last night?'

'I told them what you said: that you'd gone to help Barbara pack, and see her off, and say goodbye. George was upset, of course.' He turns to look at me, and there's pain in his eyes. 'I know he loved her. I'm sorry.'

'It's not your fault she's gone, Ben. You were right, and I knew it. I just didn't want to admit it.'

'But now this. Poor George. Does it mean he's getting worse already?'

'Let's hope not,' I say. 'It might just be something temporary. Dr Fischer at Great Ormond Street said he might have an exacerbation like this if he gets an infection or a virus, didn't she – and she's the expert. Perhaps he's coming down with a cold.'

I look at Ben's hand holding mine and ponder on the fact that last night I was convinced our marriage was over.

'Your mum's been brilliant,' he says after we've sat here, watching George's breathing, for a few more minutes. 'She rushed straight over when I called her, completely took over with the children – and with me, frankly – and told me things I needed to hear.'

'She told me what *I* needed to hear, too. What did she tell you?' I ask, out of curiosity.

'That I should be patient and understanding with you, because finding your birth mother has been such a huge thing for you and you were quite obviously going to be devastated by her leaving you.'

'*Leaving me,*' I repeat, blinking at the starkness of the words. 'She's not going until Monday now, Ben. Something about not being able to get a van yet. But you're right – she *is* leaving me. And I don't think she cares.'

'I'm sorry it's turned out this way for you,' he says. 'I really am.'

'But the thing is, I don't care now, either,' I reply, surprised by my own words even as I utter them. 'I can't. Everything else is too important. More important than that woman. All she wanted was to move in with us. I think it was all a charade – and I got taken in by it. I really did think she loved me. I really did think she cared more about me than my mum does.'

'Or me?'

I turn to look at him. We need to be honest with each other now if this is going to work.

'Yes. More than you, because we've been so distanced from each other, haven't we. Barbara seemed to be someone who listened to me, and understood me. I fell for it,' I add bitterly.

'It must be so disappointing for you to have to admit that,' he says.

'It is, because she gave birth to me. But really, what does that matter? As you said – as Mum reminded me too – I already have a mother. I already have so much. But if George—'

'Shh.' He puts his hand gently over my mouth. 'Don't say it.'

'We can't lose him, Ben. We have to fight for him.'

'And we will.' He looks up and adds, 'He's waking up. And here comes the doctor now. Let's see what he has to say. And let's try to stay optimistic, for George's sake.'

34

I stay in hospital with George for two nights; Ben's taken compassionate leave from school to spend as much time as possible with Molly. He brings Molly with him to visit her brother on the second day, once I've told him George is looking much better now. She looks frightened by the monitors he's connected to, but once I've explained in simple terms what they're doing, and she's realised her brother looks *normal,* as she puts it, she relaxes and sits on his bed, telling him what exciting things she's been doing at school today, and how Ben has been making her favourite dinners.

'That's not fair, I'm just getting yucky hospital dinners,' George says at once, and I feel like standing on my chair and cheering. He really is back to normal.

The doctors here have indeed consulted with Dr Fischer by phone, and George's medication has been changed. We've been quietly warned that it's possible, if this sort of exacerbation starts to happen frequently, that George might need oxygen at home, but we're not thinking about that unless – or until – it happens.

'One day at a time,' Ben says, squeezing my hand, and I nod agreement. And I suspect he's referring to our relationship as well as George's condition.

SHEILA NORTON

* * *

It's not until we're finally home from hospital, having our first meal together, that I bring up the subject of Barbara with the kids. I've barely thought about her myself since George was rushed to A&E, but we need closure, and the children need to understand.

'I'm sorry I had to rush off to help your granny the other night. And I'm sorry you haven't had a chance to say goodbye to her. I was hoping she might change her mind.'

'She hasn't, though, has she?' George says sadly. 'Daddy said she had to go because her flat was horrid.'

'Yes. I know it's sad that Granny's gone – I'm very sad too – but it'll be better for her to live with her cousin in a nice warm house. So we have to be pleased for her, and be brave about it. OK?'

George nods. 'I wish we could go to Livingpool to see her.'

'Well, maybe,' I begin, but then I stop. It's better to be honest – with myself as well as with the kids. It's not going to happen. 'But probably it'll be too difficult. Anyway there are lots of other exciting things to look forward to.'

'Like our holiday to Spain, to see our other grandma and grandpa,' Molly says helpfully.

'Exactly, Molly.'

'And like my class party,' George puts in, suddenly looking excited.

I glance at Ben. We'd decided, since there are only two days left of the term, that it would make sense to keep George at home now. But his face has lit up so much at the thought of the little party they're supposed to be having in their classroom, playing games and taking their own cakes or biscuits in to eat, that I suddenly realise we'd be doing the wrong thing. We've been so pleased to see him *back to normal*, but if we start treating him as an invalid during periods when he's managing everything OK, we're in danger of holding him back.

'Perhaps,' I say, 'you should just stay at home tomorrow, Georgie, so that I can feed you up and make sure you're completely better.'

Ben nods at me, but George is already asking if that means he'll get his favourite lunch (beans on toast), and all of us laugh – even Molly.

If I Lost You 215

'Definitely,' I promise him. 'Then I'm sure you'll be OK to go in to school on Wednesday. For your last day.'

'And the party,' he confirms happily.

'And it isn't even a whole day,' Molly reminds him. 'We finish early on the last day.'

'Good,' he says with his mouth full of mash. 'As long as I can go to the party.'

* * *

On Wednesday morning the children get ready in double-quick time and I duly drop them off at school with their party cakes. Mrs Austin looks delighted to see George back, and I tell her briefly what happened at the hospital. I've just got home and I'm sitting quietly with a cup of tea, trying to distract myself from finally having the time to think about Barbara, who I presume will now be in Liverpool, by making some lesson plans for the beginners' yoga courses I'll be starting as soon as the school holiday begins next week. Ben and I finally talked civilly about my idea for the new classes, during the hours George was asleep in the hospital, and he's finally agreed that it could work, and that he'll play his part, so I want to make sure the classes are a success. The distraction isn't working very well, though, because I'm looking at my phone, wondering, despite everything, whether I should call or message Barbara, just to wish her good luck in her new home. If she hangs up on me, at least it will finally draw a line under everything. But just as I'm about to pick up the phone, it rings. It isn't Barbara – it's Mum.

'Darling, are you busy?'

'Er, no, not specially. Why? Is anything wrong? Is Dad—'

'He's fine, we're both fine. But I'm not working today so we wondered if we could come and see you – and see the kids after school.'

'Well, yes, of course you can.' I smile happily at the thought of it. I'm so glad to have our relationship back on track. 'And the children finish early this afternoon. You can come with me to meet them.'

I get up, forgetting about the lesson preparation. It'll be about twelve-thirty by the time they arrive, so I make sandwiches, ready for lunch. Then

I remember I was planning to call Barbara, but when I try, her number seems to be out of service. I suppose she's changed it. Would she really do that just to stop me from even speaking to her ever again? Well, at least that gives me some kind of closure.

Mum and Dad arrive just as I'm putting the kettle on for tea and coffee. It's good to see them. Dad looks like he's lost weight already from the exercise regime and strict diet Mum's put him on to help keep his blood pressure down. They both tell me, while we eat our lunch, how much they're looking forward to seeing George now that he's better. When I tell them Ben's agreed to me doing the yoga classes, Mum nods.

'Well, perhaps I was wrong about that. As well as being wrong about George's condition,' she says ruefully. 'It was so dreadful seeing him the way he was on Saturday – being carried into the ambulance.'

'We've all been wrong about... different things,' I say, thinking again about Barbara. 'But Ben and I have agreed to try to move on.'

'We're glad about that,' Dad says. 'He's a good guy.'

They both come with me to collect the children from school at two o'clock. Molly comes out first, chatting happily to her friend Sophie, and squeals with excitement when she sees her grandparents waiting for her. I leave them together while I go to wait at George's classroom. I'm smiling to myself in the sunshine. I know life's going to be tough, going forward, with George's condition, but at least it looks like Ben and I are going to be working together now, instead of against each other, and my parents are supporting us too. I watch the children pour out of the classroom, all chattering to their parents about the party; it seems like George is going to be the last out – I feel a flash of anxiety.

'Is George OK?' I ask Mrs Austin. 'He hasn't been sent to the medical room or anything, has he?'

'No.' She stares at me in confusion. 'No, he's been fine today, Mrs Hudson. But I presumed you knew – perhaps there's been a misunderstanding. His granny picked him up earlier. About half an hour ago. She said you wanted him home early today, I presumed because it was his first day after his time in hospital.'

'What? Hang on, what are you saying?' I can't take it in. 'George has been picked up by his granny? She's – no! No, he *wasn't* supposed to be

If I Lost You

going with her. I didn't know anything about this.' I have to steady myself against the classroom wall; I feel like I might faint. 'She's supposed to be in Liverpool by now,' I go on, my voice beginning to break. 'She said she was going on Monday. Oh my God. She's taken him. She's waited till he was out of hospital, that's what she's done – and she's taken him with her.'

'Wait, what do you mean?' Mrs Austin says. Her face has gone pale. 'His granny's...?'

'She's *taken* him,' I repeat. I can feel hysteria building in me. But no, I can't – I can't give in, I can't collapse, I've got to act – and fast.

'Mum, Dad!' I yell across the playground. Molly, fortunately, is still too busy chatting with Sophie to notice the tone of my voice. 'Please could you take Molly home and look after her? You'll have to get a taxi, I've got to...' I run up to them, taking hold of Mum's arm, trying to tell them as fast as I possibly can what's happened.

'I'm calling the police,' Mum says immediately.

'I think Mrs Austin might be—'

'Better that I do it too. And I'm coming with you.' My dad starts arguing that he should come instead, but she overrules him. 'No. You take Molly home. I'm not having you getting stressed.'

'Tell her I've got to... I don't know, go somewhere, urgently,' I babble.

'Just go. Leave it with me,' he says. 'Just bring him back, Jo.'

And I'm legging it across the playground, out into the street. I can hear Mum, behind me, panting as she follows me, holding on to her 999 call.

'Tell them they've got to stop her,' I scream at her as we're both jumping into the car. 'They need to stop her before she takes him – oh my God, she can't take him to Liverpool, he'll be terrified, and I'll never find him, she hasn't given me an address or anything.'

I pull out into traffic while Mum's still holding onto the phone.

'I'm going to her house,' I shout. 'And if she's not there I'll go to the station.'

'Wait,' she says. 'I'm talking to the police right now, they're going to—'

But I don't wait. I can't. The image of my little boy being taken to the station, probably being promised a day out, a treat, going willingly because he trusts this woman – this wicked, deceitful woman who claimed to love him, claimed to love *me* but never did – is too much to bear. She's taken

SHEILA NORTON

him to spite me, to pay me back for not going with her, and not allowing her to live with my family. She's disrupted our lives and upset everyone and I'll never forgive her for this, ever. But there's only one thing that matters right now: I have to get my son back, and if it means chasing the train all the way to Liverpool, that's what I'm going to do.

35

We're already halfway to Barbara's flat when, after another brief conversation on her phone, Mum hangs up and tells me to pull over.

'What? Why?' I'm at traffic lights. They turn green and I shoot across the junction but Mum's yelling at me to stop and turn around.

'The police are already at Barbara's flat. She's not there. They forced entry but the place is empty. She's gone. They say they've got officers heading to the tube station now.'

I turn into a side road and screech to a halt before doing a reverse turn in somebody's driveway and heading in the opposite direction.

'We should have got a taxi. You'll never be able to park at the station,' Mum's saying anxiously.

I don't bother to reply. Quite frankly, parking's the least of my worries. I'll park on the platform if I have to.

'She might already have got the train,' Mum's going on. 'She'll be heading for Euston, for the main line to Liverpool.'

'I know. We'll go there if necessary.'

'The police might already be—'

'Well, if they're not there, we will be. I've got to get to George, Mum. He'll be scared, he'll be terrified. He'll be terrified if the police turn up before us, too – we've got to get there first.'

220   SHEILA NORTON

'Oh, be careful, Jo,' she yells as I career round a bend, narrowly missing a bollard. 'We can't have an accident.'

Thank God, the tube station's in sight. I pull up outside with a screech. There are two police cars here already, and an officer is barring the entrance.

'I'm sorry, ladies – police incident here at the moment,' he says as I try to barge past him.

'We *are* the incident,' I scream at him. 'It's my son. My son's with the woman you're looking for. I've got to get to him.'

'I've already been on a 999 call about it,' Mum confirms as the officer speaks into his walkie-talkie. '*Please* let us through – my grandson will be frightened, we need to see if he's still here.'

'Hold on, please.' He turns away from us, still talking into the device, before turning back to us and saying, 'The incident's over. The officers are about to leave – the station's reopening.'

'It can't be over,' Mum starts to protest, but I pull her away.

'It's over because they're not here. They've gone. Come on – we have to get to Euston.'

'Hold on,' shouts the policeman. 'The detective sergeant's coming to see you.'

A large, florid man is pushing open the doors of the station, striding towards us, followed by a worried-looking PC.

'Mrs Hudson?' he says. 'I'm DS Copperfield and—'

We haven't got time for niceties. 'I've got to go,' I tell him, turning to run back to my car.

'Wait! You can come with us. We'll have the blues-and-twos on, we can get across London faster. Two of my colleagues have gone ahead by tube in case that turns out to be even faster.'

'Oh, right. But my car's right outside the station. I can't leave it—'

'Not a problem. Give us your keys, we'll get it moved it to a legit space in the car park and put a "Police Aware" label on it.' He takes my keys and passes them to the constable who was on duty at the station entrance. 'Come on, let's get your son back,' he goes on, marching ahead as the PC takes my arm and leads us towards the police car.

If I Lost You

'You can tell us the full story on the way,' she says, looking at me kindly. 'Try not to worry. We'll find him, trust me.'

I don't reply. I can't. I know they're doing their best, but how can I trust them – trust them to find my little boy, when I don't even know where in the world he might have been taken?

'She could even have been lying about Liverpool,' I try to explain as we pull away from the tube station, sirens blazing. 'I don't believe a word she said, any more. She could have taken him anywhere... *anywhere.*' I drop my voice because I can hardly bear to say it. 'She might be taking him abroad.'

'An alert's gone out to ports and airports,' says DS Copperfield.

'And he's... not in good health,' I go on, blinking back tears. I can't cry. I need to focus. 'He's on medication, and he won't have it with him.'

The PC turns to give me a reassuring look.

'We'll find him,' she reiterates firmly. 'Trust me.'

But that's my problem. I trusted someone. And now I wish I'd never even set eyes on her.

We pull up outside Euston station with a screech of brakes. The front of the station is sealed off by tape in the same way that our local tube station was, but this time there's no need to explain or argue with the police officer on duty, because as soon as he sees who we're with, he lets us through, announcing into his radio device that *the mother and grandmother are here*, and we stumble down the steps and round the corner onto the platform we're being directed to by one of the officers.

There's a stationary train at the platform, with police officers swarming around it. And the destination board shows there's a Liverpool train at 2.30 p.m.

'That was ten minutes ago,' I wail. 'We've missed it. They might have been on it. We'll have to—'

'This *is* the 2.30 train,' DS Copperfield replies. 'We've had it held up for searching.'

'If she was here, planning to get on it, she'll have seen all the police officers and changed her mind – gone somewhere else instead.'

'The officers have only just got here.' He smiles at me. 'I sent instructions ahead for all the doors of the train to be locked. If she's on board, we've got her.'

'And if she's not?' I retort. 'Then we're wasting time.'

'We'll catch her. We'll find your son,' he says firmly, marching off down the platform to liaise with the other officers.

'This is so frustrating.' I want to scream. Standing here, waiting, watching the police further down the train go in and out of one carriage at a time, I can feel the minutes passing by. 'Why can't *we* check some of the carriages? We know what she looks like. What if George is in one of those carriages and he's looking out of the window, seeing us standing here doing nothing?'

'And he might *not be* in any of these carriages,' Mum says quietly.

But before either of us can say any more, we're suddenly startled by a commotion further along the platform. Two police officers are taking someone off the train in handcuffs, and she's struggling, swearing, shouting insults at them. It's Barbara. And behind her comes the female officer who came with us in the car – with her arm around my boy, my Georgie. Even from the other end of the platform, I can hear his wails of distress.

'*George!*' I yell, running full pelt the length of the platform until I'm with him, taking hold of him from the PC, pulling him into my arms and holding him so tight that he cries even harder.

'Mummy,' he sobs. 'Mummy, I want to go home. I didn't want to come here; why did Granny make me come here? I just want to go home.'

I'm crying almost as hard as he is, and behind me I can hear Mum sobbing too. The realisation that, if the police hadn't acted so quickly he'd have been on the way to Liverpool now – if that was really even where Barbara was going – is so terrifying that my whole body's shaking with relief. Whatever DS Copperfield said, I can't believe it would have been easy to find him, with no address, no surname for Barbara's second cousin and no knowing if I'd been told a complete fiction.

I can't even look at Barbara as she's being led away, but she's continuing to shout abuse – at me as well as at the police – and I close my ears to it. I'm never going to have to listen to that woman again. From now on, I don't have a birth mother; she doesn't exist; it doesn't even matter.

DS Copperfield comes back down the platform to join us.

'We'll get you home now,' he says. George is still buried in my arms, sobbing, beginning to sound breathless. I'll kill that woman, kill her with

If I Lost You 223

my bare hands, if he ends up back in hospital, if his condition gets worse because of her. 'I'm afraid we'll have to ask you a few questions. It shouldn't take long.'

'Of course.' I wipe my eyes, wipe George's face, and when I look up at the sergeant I'm sure I catch the glint of tears in his own eyes. After all, he's only human. 'Thank you,' I say softly. 'Thank you all so much. I can't even begin to say how grateful I am that you got here in time.'

'We're grateful too,' he assures me.

Mum and I take one each of George's hands as we follow the officers back up the steps and out into the fresh air. George is still crying quietly, despite all my reassurances that we're going straight home now, that every-thing's all right, that nobody's going to hurt him and I won't leave his side for a single second until we're safely indoors.

'Why was Granny being horrible?' he persists between his sobs, as we settle into the back of the police car. 'She wouldn't let go of me, she wouldn't let me come home, she said I had to go with her and you'd never find me. I didn't like it, Mummy, I wanted you.'

'I know, sweetheart, I know and I'm here now and she'll never come near you again.'

The shock of all this has been so sudden, everything has happened so fast, that I feel dizzy with it, but I know I'm going to be spending a long time now trying to reassure George, to comfort him and eventually rebuild his confidence. I'm going to have to do all of this when I should be concen-trating on caring for his lung condition, helping him to live the best life he can despite its limitations. All because of Barbara and her wicked, wicked spitefulness.

'Granny came for me in a taxi, like that other time,' George sobs. 'So I thought it was all right, I thought you knew about it, Mummy. I should have said no, shouldn't I? I should have stayed at school.'

'Georgie, it wasn't your fault, baby. Not the slightest bit. You couldn't have known she wasn't being kind and that I didn't know about it. Nor could Mrs Austin. Granny was allowed to collect you.'

I allowed it, I think to myself, regret flooding me and provoking fresh tears. I thought she loved me, thought she loved my children. How could I have been so blind?

'It wasn't your fault either, darling,' Mum whispers, pulling me close to her in the back of the police car. 'Don't start blaming yourself. There's only one person to blame for all this.'

* * *

I call Ben as we're travelling back across London. It's after school now. I assume he's at home and that Dad will have explained what's happened, because Ben picks up straight away and sounds terrible.

'I'm so sorry I couldn't call you – it all happened so fast,' I begin, but he stops me, asking with a shaking voice, 'Have you got him? Did the police catch her?'

'Yes.' Finally, I feel the beginnings of a smile – a smile of pure relief. 'It's OK, Ben. We've got him. He's safe. We're on our way home. Please give Molly a kiss for me. She must be so frightened.'

'Your dad's made up a story for her, don't worry; something about you needing to collect George from a friend's house.'

'Good thinking.' There'll be time enough for explanations later, when we're all calm. If we ever can be, ever again.

The two officers come inside with us, and a few minutes later, while Mum's making us all a cup of tea, DS Copperfield asks if it's OK to ask us some questions now.

'It's better to do this right away, if possible,' he explains. 'I know you're all still upset, but we really need as much information as you can give us, while it's all still fresh in your minds.'

'George is really tired from it all,' I say quietly. 'And he's only five.'

'I know. We won't push it, but whatever he can tell us will be really helpful.'

'Molly,' says Mum, coming in with the tea tray and catching the end of the conversation, 'why don't you come upstairs with me and show me the paintings you brought home from school?'

'Yes,' Molly agrees. She's been staring at the police officers, confused, worried by everyone's tears, and I've had to tell her I'll explain everything to her later. And, in fact, George is amazing when the questions start. His breathing seems to have settled again, and even through his tears, he's able to tell the officers exactly what happened, in his own words. I think he's so upset and cross about what Barbara's put him through, he's almost grateful for the chance to let it all out.

'But she's my *granny*,' he explodes when he's finished his story. 'Why was she horrible to me? She's usually *nice*. She frightened me; she said she was taking me a long way away and Mummy would never find me.'

He bursts into tears again and I hold him in my arms, rocking him like I did when he was a baby.

'And I'm *hungry*,' he bursts out angrily as the police officers start to take their leave – and the relief that, despite everything, he's still just a little boy who wants his dinner makes me smile and hug him.

'I'm going to get us all a takeaway,' Ben says. 'Special occasion.' He opens his laptop to the delivery menu. 'A pizza, is it, Georgie?'

* * *

Ben and I manage to hold it together throughout the eating of the pizzas, through saying our goodbyes to Mum and Dad, and getting both children settled in bed. I stay with George for longer than usual, aware that he might have trouble going to sleep, but in fact he's out like a light within minutes, exhausted from his scare and his tears. Then I sit with Molly while I give her a carefully edited version of what's happened, making it sound as if Barbara was somehow just mistaken in thinking George would like to go for a little holiday with her. Molly's not so easily fobbed off, though.

'But George says she was horrible to him,' she retorts. 'I know she was our granny, I know she was your birth mother, Mummy, but I don't actually think she was very nice at all. I'm *glad* she's gone to Liverpool and I don't ever want to see her again.'

'We won't,' I tell her firmly. I stroke Molly's hair. 'You're right, sweetheart, she wasn't very nice, in the end, but she's gone now. There's no need to worry about her any more.'

* * *

'That wicked, spiteful *cow*,' Ben mutters, when I finally collapse onto the sofa next to him. His fists are clenched as if he'd like to punch something. Some*body*. 'I'll never forgive her for this. Poor George. Is he going to be OK, do you think? Will he need... I don't know... counselling, or anything?'

'Perhaps. Let's see how he is during the summer holiday.'

'Thank God you're not working at the moment. You can spend time with him here, spoiling him, helping him recover.'

'Yes.' Thank God I'm *not* still in that awful job, scared to take time off, always afraid of putting a foot wrong. How did I stick it out for so long? 'It's going to be difficult, financially, until I can get my classes up and running, though.'

'But we'll manage,' he says, pulling me towards him, sighing. 'We've been through worse.'

'Yes.' Today we've been through the worst thing possible. At the moment I'm not sure either of us will ever be able to let go of our anger. Barbara could have got away with almost anything and, like an idiot, I'd have still forgiven her, but *she took my child*. She frightened him, she might have left him with lasting trauma. It's just... unforgiveable.

From now on, I only have one mother. My mother is the one who brought me up from the age of two, who always loved me, who never did anything to hurt me, and forgave me everything. We'll never need to think about my birth mother again. As far as my family is concerned, she no longer exists. The children have two lovely grandmas; they didn't need to have a new granny at all. And now they don't.

36

Mum and Dad come again a few days later. It's Saturday, and Mum's pretending she had nothing to do at home, but we both know they just wanted to check on us all, to see how we're coping with the shock, and I appreciate it. It's a warm, sunny day and Ben's in the garden with the children, playing football with Molly while George acts as goalie, when there's a knock on the door and it's DS Copperfield again.

'Sorry to intrude, Mrs Hudson,' he says. 'Can I come in?'

'Of course.' I watch his solemn face as he takes a seat. 'What is it? Did you have some more questions for us?'

'I've got news for you. But first, I'll just ask this: you told me Barbara King was your birth mother. How long have you actually known her for?'

'Only since March. Why?'

'And it's definite that she's your birth mother, is it?'

I stare at him, puzzled. 'Well, yes. The adoption agency put her in touch with me, so she must be.'

'She is,' Mum confirms, looking at me a little sheepishly. 'I went to the agency to check myself, and unfortunately they confirmed she's definitely your birth mother.'

'Why did you do that?' I ask her. 'You never said.'

'You'd have been annoyed,' she admitted. 'But I didn't trust her. I wanted to be sure.'

I look back at DS Copperfield. 'Why do you ask?'

'Because we've discovered she also goes by another name: Barbara Smith.'

I stare at him. All I can think of saying is, 'Smith. The most common surname.'

'Yes. Hard to trace someone with a name like that. We'd been looking for her for a while; she lived over the other side of the river at the time these crimes were committed.'

'*Crimes*?' Mum and I both say together.

'Mostly shoplifting, but she also carried a knife. She threatened shop staff with it, if she was challenged, and then made a run for it.'

'*Run*?' I exclaim. 'She can't run, she's got terrible arthritis.'

'Has she? Really?' He looks at me sympathetically, and I shake my head, bewildered, more than anything, by my own naïvety.

'So it's definitely her – the woman you've been looking for?' I ask him, bitterly. 'Well, good. Lock her up, throw away the key.'

'You have my word,' he says. 'Threatening people with a knife is a serious crime, to say nothing of child abduction. She tracked you down to this area,' he goes on, quietly. 'She won't say how, but she's admitted it. She says she wanted to find her daughter. I'd hazard a guess that she wanted to... take advantage of you in some way.'

'Oh yes. I know that now, unfortunately.' I'm still struggling to get my head around this. It's so shocking: an elderly woman like Barbara, threatening people with a knife.

'I'm sorry to bring you bad news,' DS Copperfield says. 'I realise how upsetting all of this is for you. I know she's your birth mother, but you really are better off without her. She's a nasty piece of work; manipulative. Hardly ever done any work in her life.'

'She said she used to be a nurse,' I protest, but he just shakes his head, and I feel another of my illusions falling away.

'Sorry,' he says. 'But we know her entire history. We've been after her for years. She did work as a nursing auxiliary for a few months. She'd prob-

If I Lost You 229

ably had her benefits stopped, and then gave it up as soon as she could get them started again.'

I think about the visit to the Job Centre, and nod slowly.

'I trusted her with my children,' I say quietly. 'My son – I thought she knew about his condition, knew what she was doing. And she wasn't even a nurse.'

He gets to his feet, and I show him to the door. 'We'll keep you updated, Mrs Hudson.'

'I feel such a fool,' I say quietly to Mum after he's left. 'I believed everything Barbara told me. I felt sorry for her. Now I don't know whether to believe *anything* she said at all. Was it all lies? Did she really only give me up after two years of enduring beatings from my father, or had she just had enough of looking after a toddler?'

Mum stares at me for a moment. 'Is that what she told you? You've never said.'

'I suppose we weren't talking too often, were we?' I admit. 'Especially about Barbara. I knew you disapproved. I thought you were just jealous.'

She shakes her head, sadly. 'Jo, there was no father listed on your birth certificate. I presume she didn't even know who he was. Your dad and I never met her when we adopted you. We were told she was so completely uninterested in what happened to you, right from the moment you were born, that she just abandoned you in the hospital and refused to have any contact.'

I can't think of a single word to say. I can feel my mouth opening and closing, but no words are coming out.

'You were taken straight to the foster parents I've told you about – lovely people who cared for you beautifully until we adopted you, just after your second birthday.'

'I always thought I'd just been placed with them for a little while, while the adoption was going through.'

'You misunderstood, obviously. Perhaps you were too young when we told you about the adoption.'

'No, I really appreciate how you answered all my questions, right from my childhood. I just... must have filled in the gaps, used my own imagination.' I sigh, shaking my head. 'And when I met her, I just wanted to believe her.'

Mum moves closer to me and puts an arm around me.

'All this must be so hard for you to hear, sweetheart.'

'Actually it's not, Mum.' I swallow. 'If anything, it just makes me feel better. At least I didn't have a violent father after all. I had one who didn't even know I existed.'

'You're not going to try to find *him*, are you?' she asks, looking anxious – and I look back at her, suddenly bursting out laughing. *Laughing*, after all these revelations – perhaps it's hysteria.

We're still sitting with our arms around each other when Ben, Dad and the children come back inside.

'What's happened?' Ben asks, looking at me anxiously. 'Are you OK? Who was that at the door?'

'I'll tell you later,' I promise, getting to my feet. I reach up and kiss him. 'Nothing to worry about.'

I look around the room, look at my parents – my real parents, the only ones I've got, the only ones who ever cared about me – at my husband – the husband I thought only a short while ago was soon going to be my ex – and at my kids, both of them flushed from the fresh air and sunshine, making George's colour so deceptively healthy that my heart almost bleeds for him. And I think, *No, Barbara was nothing to worry about*. Nothing to care about. I've got everyone I really care about right here, in this room. Roots, genetics, they don't really matter after all. I've been loved all my life – that's all that matters. And I'm going to spend the rest of my life giving that love back.

And if love can be enough to save my boy's life, he's going to survive. We're all going to do our absolute damnedest to make it happen.

* * *

MORE FROM SHEILA NORTON

Another book from Sheila Norton, *A Good Enough Mother*, is available to order now here:

https://mybook.to/GoodEnoughMotherBackAd

ACKNOWLEDGEMENTS

This book was a tough one to write, and more than ever I need to thank my editor, Emily Yau, for her invaluable hard work and advice. Thanks also to everyone else at Boldwood Books for all their work and their dedication to every book they produce, to copyeditor Candida Bradford for her input (and lovely comments about this book), to proofreader Helen Woodhouse for spotting everything I'd missed, and to my agent, Megan Carroll, for her support – and sympathy when necessary! Lastly, but importantly, I need to thank my friend and neighbour Melissa, a GP, for her much-needed advice with the medical theme in this story. Thank you all.

ABOUT THE AUTHOR

Sheila Norton is the author of contemporary, feel-good fiction set in Devon. In 2022 she won the RNA's Best Christmas Novel and now writes emotional women's fiction for Boldwood Books. When not working on her writing, Sheila loves exploring the contrasting countrysides of Essex and Devon.

Sign up to Sheila Norton's mailing list here for news, competitions and updates on future books.

Visit Sheila Norton's Website: www.sheilanorton.com

Follow Sheila Norton on social media:

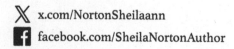

ALSO BY SHEILA NORTON

A Good Enough Mother

Not Your Child

If I Lost You

Boldwood

Boldwood Books is an award-winning fiction publishing company seeking out the best stories from around the world.

Find out more at www.boldwoodbooks.com

Join our reader community for brilliant books, competitions and offers!

Follow us
@BoldwoodBooks
@TheBoldBookClub

Sign up to our weekly deals newsletter

https://bit.ly/BoldwoodBNewsletter